Charlotte Badger

Books by the same author:

The Boy from Buninyong

Junior Fiction:

The River's Revenge
Poles Apart

Charlotte Badger – Buccaneer

Angela Badger

Indra Publishing

Indra Publishing
PO Box 7, Briar Hill, Victoria, 3088, Australia.

© Angela Badger 2002
Typeset in Palatino by Fire Ink Press.
Made and Printed in Australia by McPherson's Printing Group.

National Library of Australia Cataloguing-in-Publication data:

Badger, Angela.
Charlotte Badger – buccaneer

ISBN 0 9578735 2 2

1. Women prisoners – Fiction. 2. Mutiny – Tasmania – Fiction.
I. Title.

A823.3

To Alan, Ruth and Louise Badger, and Michelle, Kent &
Lawrence for their children David, Paul, Ann and John.
With much love.

Acknowledgments

I would like to thank the management and staff of the following institutions for their assistance.

Central Library, Sutherland, NSW; Eden Killer Whale Museum; Mitchell Library & Dixson Collection; National Maritime Museum Library; Public Records Office, London; The State Records NSW.

The following sources were referred to:

Historical Records of New South Wales; Historical Records of New Zealand; Joseph Banks *Endeavour* Journal; Rev. Knopwood's Diary 1803-1838 (First Chaplain of Van Diemen's Land); *Tasman to Marsden* 1642-1818 by McNab; *Tongans* by William Mariner, 1817; *The Twofold Bay Story* by J.A.S. McKenzie; Visiting Magistrates Minute Book of Worcester Gaol, 1797-1800; and *The Dictionary of New Zealand Biography*, History Group, New Zealand Ministry of Culture and Heritage.

Grateful thanks to Chris Arms (Archive Research Services, Hereford UK); Brian Cook (The Manuscript Appraisal Agency); Jan Cornish and her Group – Tony Hunt (Project Director, James Craig Restoration); Rosemary Howe, Tony Howe, Leone and John Jauncey, Steve Thomas, Dorothy Turnbull, Steve Wade, Nan Wright; and especially the late Dennis Thomas for his unfailing support.

Angela Badger-Thomas

CHAPTER ONE

PROCLAMATION OF PIRACY

Public Notice in the Sydney Gazette, July 18 1806

Whereas the persons undermentioned and described did, on the 16th day of June 1806, by force and arms violently and piratically take away from His Majesty's settlement of Port Dalrymple, a Colonial Brig or Vessel called the *Venus*, the property of MR.ROBERT CAMPBELL, Merchant of the Territory; the said vessel then containing certain stores the property of his Majesty; and a quantity of necessary Stores the property of the Officers of that Settlement; and sundry other property belonging to private individuals.

Benjamin Burnet Kelly, chief mate, 5 foot 7 inches pock marked. Thin visage, brown hair, auburn whiskers says he is American. Came to this Colony as mate of the *Albion* south sea whaler, Captain Bunker.

Joseph Redmonds, seaman (2nd mate). A mulatto 5 foot 6 inches stout. Broad nose, thick lips, hair tied. Holes in his ears, wears large earrings. Came in *Venus* whaler.

A Malay cook.

Thomas Ford and William Evans. Boys. Latter a native of Colony.

Richard Thompson 27. Soldier. 5 foot 8 inches. Fair, light, brown hair.

Richard Thomas Evans. Convict 5 foot 7 inches stout, brown hair, broad visage. Came out as Gunners Mate on the *Calcutta* deserted. Afterwards transported for 14 years.

John William Lancashire, convict 5 foot 4 inches sallow, brown haired, marked with pox. Emaciated. A painter by trade.

Catherine Hagerty convict middle sized fresh complexion much inclined to smile. Hoarse voice.

Charlotte Badger convict very corpulent, full face, thick lips, infant child.

This is therefore to caution all Governors and Officers in Command at any of His Majesty's Ports, and the Honourable East India Company's Magistrates or Officers in Command, at Home and Abroad, at whatever Port or Ports the said brig may be taken into, or met with at Sea, against `any frauds or deceptions that may be put in practice by the offending Parties; and to require their being taken into custody wherever found; and information rendered thereof to the Governor or Officer in Command at those settlements or to any other British Authority, that they may be brought to condign punishment.

By Command of H.E
G.Blaxall Sec
Government House, Sydney in New South Wales

Yes, that's me. Me and little Anny tagged on at the end as though we are of no import whatsoever.

Every other person on that list is dead – hanged, killed and eaten by the Maoris or just plain drowned dead. Yet we are alive and I fully intend that we go on inhabiting this world for our full span before we go to meet our Maker.

Folks may shrug their shoulders and say my story is a make-believe. A fancy dreamed up by a scheming woman. But I ask you, how could a young girl from a little country town ever have imagined such happenings? Ships, prisons, back-breaking work, black faces, white faces, heaving seas and threatening skies.

The first nineteen years of my life I'd scarce stepped outside our town of Bromsgrove. Then it was four years in Worcester Gaol, nine months sailing the high seas on the *Earl Cornwallis* and finally five years washing and rinsing, sweeping and scrubbing for a mistress who never once split her face with a smile. Against this backdrop my life seemed destined to be spent upon the treadmill of labour. I'd never expected much from the world so I'd never been very disappointed.

I'd even become used to being considered a felon. If the theft of four guineas convinced King George that I needed to spend seven years in his benighted Colony, then so be it. Two years remained of my sentence.

T'would be fair to say I'd accepted my punishment. I'd come to terms with my lot in life. Admitted I'd lost my place – me expecting little Anny sent the old beldame into such a fury she sent me back to the Factory at Parramatta; but that's life.

Even that was a blessing in disguise as I'd met Kitty. She was the truest friend anyone could wish for. Bright as a butterfly she skimmed over every hardship whereas I put my head down and beetled along with a steady will. We were as different as chalk from cheese and therein lay our pleasure in each other's company.

When the overseer at the Factory told us we were to go down to Van Diemen's Land we rejoiced that we would not be separated. A new life was opening up, in a place miles and miles away from the misery of Sydney.

How could anyone have seen that in the space of a few weeks we'd be branded pirates, fit only for the gallows?

Love was the culprit. Love stepped into our bleak lives and started the chain of events which caused all the trouble. And as always happens with love – it turned our world upside down.

But who could ever have imagined the mutiny?

We were huddled together against a bitter westerly wind waiting to go on board the *Venus*. Our Kitty, the two fellows and me with young Anny nuzzling at my breast. Our guard was no more than a lad; back home he'd still be mucking out the cowsheds.

"Yes Sir," he bent his head respectfully at the furious man standing at the top of the gangplank.

For the man standing at the top of the steps was a personage who obviously did not intend to be ignored. From the outburst of foul language scorching the air he was not very pleased with the sight that met his eyes.

A string of oaths was followed by a furious outburst which boded no good for our coming journey.

"Women! My God it's bad enough having to take prisoners on board, but women! Women and even a brat! What do they think my ship is? First I have to take the rabble from the *George*. Then these misbegotten convicts. This is a trading vessel, not a stinking transport!"

His wide shoulders were outlined against the sky. With the sun behind him I could not see his features until he strode down the steps and confronted our wretched escort. Then I wished I hadn't.

"You can take these trollops straight back to barracks my man, straight back!"

How thankful I was to hear those words for I had shuddered at first glimpse of him. Back in that cell at the barracks was just exactly where I most wanted to be. My nose was running and my chest ached from the chill that had never left me since Anny was born. In all my five years in the Colony I'd never been so eager to be under lock and key again.

The ship's captain was almost as broad as he was long with a thick bull neck and powerful shoulders, but once below the top half, his body dwindled away for he was quite short. His legs were so bandy I doubt he could've stopped a pig in the road. The huge face looming over us was devoid of any vestige of humanity. If that man had ever had a drop of the milk of human kindness then it had long ago curdled into sour whey.

"Yer name?" he demanded of the soldier.

The fellow stammered and shifted from one foot to the other struggling to get the words out.

"Speak up man! Yer name ... I can see you've got no rank ... what's yer name?"

"... Thompson, Sir ... Richard Thompson."

"Then, Thompson, you take these women straight back to where they came from."

T'was easy to see the young chap was in a real fix. He couldn't leave the four of us prisoners unattended whilst he went back to barracks for more orders and he couldn't disobey such a stern command. Luckily he was relieved of his anxiety by the arrival of one of the sergeants from the barracks who'd followed behind with a sheaf of papers under his arm.

"Captain Chace ... begging your pardon, there's matters need to be discussed in private, Sir."

So we waited while the two men went up onto the deck of the ship. For a while their heads were bent in argument.

"Phew," our soldier wiped his brow, "just in time he were."

"A dirty Proto if ever I saw one, that captain," muttered Kitty. It was unusual for her to condemn any member of the male sex in such an outright fashion. "Real dirty."

And that opinion didn't change one little bit when the sergeant hurried down the steps and went off back into town without a single word to the escort or to us. Immediately we were summoned up on deck and stood in front of the captain.

His hooded eyes peered from under low brows. His beak-like mouth was a thin line above the several chins disappearing beneath his dewlap. Captain Chace looked out at the entire world with an expression of great distaste.

"Trollops! Whores! Harlots!" Spitting out those words gave him great satisfaction, you could tell that.

Real fear snatched at me as I held Anny close. He did not miss one movement ... "and you, you great mooncalf of a woman, it'll be the worse for you if that little bastard of yours yells its head off."

I looked away. I was used to being the butt. 'Never set the pond afire with her looks,' our Ma often said. Apart from being ruddy-faced and square jawed I was sturdy and tall as well. I could give that captain a couple of inches and like most short men he'd take it badly.

Even Kitty was silent as he strode up and down in front of us yelling at the crew and giving orders for our quarters to be made ready and secure. His main complaint was that he'd been told he was taking four convicts, nothing had been said about two being women. Against usual practice he had us all put in the one cabin, all the better if we were to have only one soldier guarding us. We were soon herded down into that stuffy hole with scarce any room to shift ourselves.

"And you," he wagged his finger at Richard Thompson, "you lock 'em up and don't you leave that door. You're responsible for this rabble."

You couldn't help feeling a bit sorry for young Thompson. If the powers that be sent one soldier with four prisoners they must have been pretty sure there was no hope of escape for us. Even so it would be an onerous task watching over four people.

Not that he had much to worry about from the likes of us. Poor old Lanky was coughing his lungs out again – the strong sea air took a bit of getting used to.

"Here, take a sip of this."

I'd managed to scrounge some sugar and water back at the barracks, nearest thing to dillwater I could get for little Anny's gums.

"You're a real soft cratur youse are," Kitty shook her head, "'tis for the wee one, not the likes of him."

"Leave her be. Kind hearts is worth mor'n a sup o' that stuff," Dicky Evans sat working away with a piece of rope, knotting and tying and twisting to keep himself occupied. Having been sentenced to fourteen years for desertion from the *Calcutta* he was lucky to be alive. Most would have hanged from the yardarm but Dicky was one of those mortals who'd always come up smiling.

Fate had thrown us four together. Kitty and me had been brought down the river from the Female Factory at Parramatta whilst the fellows were collected from heaven knows where, anyhow, we'd all met up at the barracks. And here we were with no other course than to rub along as best we could.

"We'll be right now. This 'ere's a brig, the *Venus* is, and th'other that's tied up next to her's a schooner. Looks like we're sailing together but she'll most likely beat us to it. We'll be down in Van Diemen's Land in no time at all," Dicky's fingers never stopped.

"Van Diemen's Land. Sounds like a land full of demons to me."

"Listen here Charlotte," he continued. "It's only three years since the first military went there. 'Tis as new and untried as the Garden of Eden. There's no food, there's precious little shelter and precious little law either. They're starvin' down there else they'd not be sending some of our precious stores to 'em. After the floods up on the Hawkesbury there's precious little enough for all of us but what's bad here is desperate down there. They even gives the convicts guns to keep the Indians away."

"Give guns to the likes of us?"

He nodded. "They'll even give guns to that scum off the *George*."

"Them as been shipwrecked?" We'd all seen the glum bunch of fellows hanging around the deck. Word had it that their ship, the *George*, had come to grief and they were being put off somewhere for a repair.

"Lost their ship more like. Lousy bunch of sealers – what else could be expected?"

He shrugged his shoulders with the disdain a gunner of one of His Majesty's vessels would naturally feel for a fishing man.

Soon Kitty was lying with her face to the wall and her hands over her ears to shut out the chatter. She'd be asleep in two seconds. When events got too much for her she had this useful knack of dropping off in a couple of seconds flat.

From the first moment she'd laid eyes on the two fellows when we'd been put in that cell back at the barracks she'd turned her nose in the air and pulled her skirts closer round her ankles. She didn't fancy spending her waking hours crammed into the space of a cabin with such as them.

I sat on my bunk with Anny in my arms. Being such a placid baby there was little to her life other than eating and sleeping.

And so the first hours passed. Except for quick trips along the passage way to the latrines we didn't poke our noses out. We saw no one except the cook who brought along the evening meal. From the clatter and thumping above our heads it was obvious the ship was being loaded at top speed for the journey.

Once that had stopped we guessed that the vessel was in readiness for departure and when a couple of hours later the floor began to lift and fall under our feet we knew we were on our way.

Our first night aboard the *Venus* was peaceful, except for Dicky's snoring and Lanky's coughs. Fresh air would have helped a bit. We had no window to the outside world, only a vent high up which let in a few gusts.

Next morning we were taken on deck for what they were pleased to call exercise. Well, the deck was the size of a ker-chief compared with the old *Cornwallis*. What there was of it was half taken up with barrels and boxes lashed to the rails and to fixings in the planks.

Thankfully Captain Chace seemed to be occupied in the front of the ship, at least we only caught sight of him once and he completely ignored all of our party. Not so the other seamen who nodded in a friendly fashion and one fellow even brought me an apple for Anny. Can't have had any lit-tle 'uns himself or he'd have known an apple was far beyond her ability to eat.

"Take a look there!" Kitty nudged me as two men made their way along by the rails. From their easy gait and the manner in which they occasionally gave one of the seamen an order it appeared they were officers.

The taller of the two was very broad, perhaps even a trifle fleshy. I'd say he wasn't quite a white man, more sort of half and half and he looked every bit of him like a real-life pirate, the ones you hear about in tales. He had his hair tied back in a pigtail and the length of it would have done credit to a Mongol, but what made him look really dangerous were the holes in his ears and the great earrings dangling from them.

Can't say I ever saw a man with a pigtail and earrings before, seen many since of course. Kitty stared open mouthed as he walked past.

"Excuse me, may I pass?"

She leapt back. The second man was looking at her with a smile on his face.

"You were remarking upon Mr Redmonds I understand Ma'am?" His tone was half joking and half serious.

So long had passed since anyone in the outside world of authority had used such civil tones that Kitty for once was speechless.

"Come Kitty," taking her arm I began to lead her away. 'Twas a certainty the captain would have words if he saw us talking with his men.

"Come on gals. What harm is there in passing the time of day? Kelly's the name, Benjamin Burnet Kelly. Previously First Mate of that renowned vessel the *Albion*, Cap'n Eb Bunker. Now First Mate of the *Venus*." Chuckling he beckoned the pirate over, "and Joshua Redmonds our Second Mate."

Storms, tempests and sheer hard work had honed and bronzed every inch of Benjamin Kelly. From his weather-beaten face to his great seaboots he was a son of the sea. He grinned down at us with a twinkling of hazel eyes then chucked Anny under the chin until the babe gurgled with delight and put out a fat little hand to touch his auburn whiskers.

"A bonny babe ma'am and ..."

An infuriated roar came from the top deck. Gripping the rail with one hand Captain Chace was shaking his fist at us all.

"Leave them strumpets be. Give 'em a wide berth or I'll put 'em ashore before they start causing trouble."

But Kelly only laughed. Admittedly he and Redmonds moved away but they weren't in any way cowed by the man.

As events turned out I don't think there was a man alive who could scare Ben Kelly. He swung away with the carefree roll of a free spirit who has spent more than half his days at sea.

"He's from the ould country. I swear he's from Cork!" Kitty whispered to me as we went below.

"Not on your life. He's American, that's what he is. One of the sailors on the *Cornwallis* came from America. Some of them just talk a bit like the Irish."

"Well, whether he's from the ould country or the new, he's a broth of a boy," the words were soft spoken and she smiled a secret little smile to herself as we went back to our poky quarters.

CHAPTER TWO

Letter from Captain Bunker to Governor King written on the Ship Albion, at sea, 5th October 1803.

I am happy to inform His Excellency that I have bin at Vandaman Land, and landid the stock and stowers on acc't of Government.

We had 12 days' passige, with 3 days that we ly in Oyster Bay, with light airs from the Sd. We obtained 3 sperm whales in sight of Oyster Bay. His Excellency mention'd of landing the stock at Relph's Bay, but Mr.Bowen and myself thought it most prudent to run up within 3 miles of Resdon Cove, and with lashing 2 of my whaleboats side to side we got them on shore very well. Capt.Cotoyes arrived 5 days before me.

I am happy to inform His Excellency that the Derwent River is one of the handsomest rivers I ever saw. There is not one rocky point all the way up the river, and every bay affords a fine run of excellent water. One that I saw runs with fourse sufishent to turn a mill. I'm inform'd by Captain Cotoyes that Relph's Bay is shoal. My short stay would not admit time to sound it. We lost one small cow on the passige, but I believe she was hurt cuming on board. We had a gail of wind the 2'd night after our departure from Port Jackson, from the N.E., and a bad sea, so I hove the ship too on acc't of the stock. I hope Mrs.King and the little gairl is well. Governor Bowen sends Mrs.King a p'r black swans, which he bages her exceptance.

I have, etc., E.Bunker

p.s. I thank your Excellency to let me have 150 ackeres of land more at the Hawksbary River, as I have only tackin 50 at Vandaman Land – E.B.

I send your Excellency a p'r of swans, which I bage his
exceptance.

"There she goes," Dicky was pointing out to sea. "Said she'd
show us a clean pair of heels and so she has." The schooner
was just a white dot disappearing ahead of us.

A spanking breeze had seen us well away from land and
then, in the tricksy manner the elements have when dealing
with us mortals, it dropped entirely and we were left wal-
lowing in light airs while the other vessel left us far behind.

Not that this worried Captain Chace. He'd only been on
deck occasionally to begin with, and it was clear now that he
stayed in his cabin with a bottle at his elbow for most of the
day and night.

Keeping our wits about us wasn't easy in those cramped
quarters. Nothing to do and nothing to look at for hour upon
hour. A torture at times, as poor Anny was beginning to feel
her gums now her milk teeth were preparing to cut through.
She grizzled and complained as, to add to her distress, her
poor little belly was swollen up and her messes were green
and vile smelling leading to a nasty red rash upon her bottom. Added to that, with Lanky's constant coughing and
spitting, the air was foul and the tempers of us prisoners
came nigh to breaking point more often than not.

"Phew!" Thompson pinched his nose with his finger
and thumb as he held the door open for the cook to bring
in our meal.

The ship's cook came from some islands north of this continent, at least that's what Dicky Evans said and he knew
just about everything about the sea and those who sailed on
her. He didn't turn out a bad meal either, a bit on the humdrum side with salt beef every day but that was not to be
sniffed at.

Even that cook, who must have smelt some strange
smells in his life, looked a bit sick when he poked his head

round the door. He held his breath as he put down the bowl of broth and then hurried back a second time with the bread.

Most of the crew would not have seen prisoners on board before. The *Venus* was a coastal trader. No doubt they were curious about us, especially us women and the baby. Looking back I feel certain that the cook must have described our cramped conditions to his fellows.

Mayhap the stink escaped from the cabin each time the door was opened. Whatever it was the whole ship's company became aware of our misery – except Captain Chace of course who by all accounts lay on his bunk day and night not caring one whit what happened. Neither did he need to in fact as his two mates looked after the vessel.

On the second night out from Port Jackson Anny was screaming her head off and for the life of me I couldn't comfort the child. She needed walking up and down to rock her off but four paces each way saw me to the back and front of our quarters. Lanky had his head buried in his blanket trying to contain a spasm of coughs which was shaking the very life out of him whilst the other two were hunched up miserably on opposite sides. Kitty still did not deign to talk to Dicky. Even his usual good nature was strained to the limit as he sat there with his hands over his ears trying to shut out Anny's wails.

Thompson opened the door and poked his head round. "Mr Mate says as how you could come on deck for a while."

Snatching up Anny's shawl, I'd tucked it round her and scrambled out of that door before anyone could change their minds.

Oh what joy! Fresh air poured down the companionway.

The sight which greeted us on deck was completely different from that of the daytime. Then the place was always busy, a sailor's work seemed to take up every daylight hour. There'd be men working on the rigging, someone around with a paint pot and usually several cleaning up their hunting gear in case a chance arose of killing a few seals on the journey. I'd seen this every time we'd come up for our meagre spells of exercise.

Night time was quite different. No to-ing and fro-ing, everyone stood about chatting. Chilly as it was the crew were nearly all on deck. Their quarters must have been as cramped as our own. A dozen or more men were gathered around a brazier filled with glowing wood which stood on a slab of stone.

"Over here Missus ... over here wi' the bairn." Obviously to these men toiling away on the sea, we were just ordinary people. Most likely 'twas just a passing thought but a kindly one.

"I'll walk her up and down Sir," I nodded my head, "she's restless, she'll settle soon." And I was right because with the comfortable rhythm of my movement and the fresh air of the sea she was asleep in no time at all.

What a relief! My breasts ached with the milk she was refusing due to her teething, but I dared not hope it would dry up. That milk was her very lifeblood you might say. If that went, there was nothing for the poor little mite. But even that nagging ache was bearable now we were out of our stinking hole for a short while.

Up and down I kept walking. My throat was still sore and my nose runny as ever but the salt air was sharp and fresh. Every step was a pleasure, every movement a comfort after the constraint of that miserable chicken coop of a cabin. As I turned at the end of each stretch I looked at the group gathered round the brazier. There was the cook, two young lads no more than fifteen I reckoned, that second mate fellow with the earrings and a couple of other seamen. Our small number kept slightly to ourselves with Thompson never taking his eye off us but the sailors certainly did not appear to shun us. One man had even fetched a jar of something for Lanky to sip.

Left to ourselves ordinary folk like us aren't that bad. It's them who's at the top who make all the trouble, set the cruel rules and regulations and punish with such pleasure.

That night, when we laid ourselves down to sleep, we were all the more content for our spell above deck.

Next day the wind still refused to blow from any one direction for any length of time more than an hour or so. The breeze was only very gentle, no more than a few wafts, so we slopped to and fro in the heavy sea and seemed to be biding our time before the real journey could begin.

The third night out we were again allowed up on the deck. I'd secretly feared on the previous night that it was merely a chance that someone had happened to remember us, stuck below like that. But obviously there was some consideration behind the action and we were being treated almost like members of the crew. After all, like it or not, we were shipmates, though I'd not expect such thinking from those above us.

First of all I'd wondered a bit if those sailors had hoped to make free with us women.

"Watch yer step Kitty!" For Kitty had an eye for the men.

I'd met Kitty when I'd been in the Factory for nigh on a month. Cold, miserable and not long up after being brought to bed with Anny I was so low I could only sit and weep.

"Cheer up, you can't sit there all day with a face as long as a Lurgan spade."

The eyes which had looked into mine sparkled with the joy of life, an unusual sight in that depressing place. I must have muttered something back because she pulled her skirts closer and sat down beside me.

"With a beautiful babe like this one – surely you could give the world a smile?"

Those laughing eyes crinkled at the corners as she ran a finger over Anny's soft hair and let the baby grasp her thumb. "What's there to smile about, you tell me." My nose was running and my throat had been sore for days on end.

"Not a lot, I grant you, but there's still a-plenty. The sun's shining, you can see it through that window up there. The accursed rain's stopped, we've got food in our bellies ... there's plenty."

Utter misery sparked by the weariness of having to face a new life yet again overwhelmed me and the tears slid down my cheeks. As the woman bent closer and patted me on the arm they only fell thicker and faster until I pushed Anny into her arms and buried my face in my skirts.

I don't think she said a word, I wouldn't have heard anyhow as my whole body was heaving with distress. She just took the baby from me and sat there, and someone even being there was the most important part of it. I needed someone in that huge uncaring world to receive the full force of my wretchedness, to be witness to my utter desolation.

That was the beginning of one of the best friendships of my life, though at the time I was in no fit state to befriend anyone and she was just the spectator to my grief.

Kitty Hagerty kept at my side from that time onwards. Perhaps my misery was so pathetic she could not abandon me, perhaps it was the baby or the fact that the other women were generally unsavoury creatures with whom she did not choose to mix. Whatever it was she was always close at hand and whenever my bitterness burst out she'd listen patiently and not tell me to hold my tongue. 'Bless us, there goes yer Ma again, wailin' like a banshee!' She'd rub her cheek against Anny's fluffy head and settle down beside me.

As I got to know her better I realised that the mere fact she listened was rather strange as she was not at all a patient person. She was a quicksilver character who skimmed through life in the same carefree way a water boatman flits across the surface of a pond. Even now she vowed she should be living in the fine brick home of her officer lover if his wife had not come out on the *Buffalo* and turned his love nest upside down.

I remember smiling for the first time in many a week as she acted out the haughty wife stalking into the bedroom and not even noticing Kitty tucked up in the blankets behind her man.

"She sat down on the bed to pull off her hose and flopped straight on top of me!" Kitty laughed, "just like this!"

Leaping up she pulled her skirts around herself and stared with popping eyes at the imaginary bed ... 'get that woman out of here. Keep your whores below stairs like any decent man ...' mimicking the woman's English accent she had to hold her sides as she roared with laughter at the memory.

Looking at the crowd who spent their days in the Factory it was plain that Kitty was a racehorse amongst carthorses. Slender and shapely she moved about with a spring in her step. Her red gold hair twined itself into ringlets and kiss curls wherever it managed to escape from beneath her cap, her grey eyes were as quick to light up with laughter as to cloud over with disapproval if she felt in any way thwarted.

Kitty Hagerty was the wayward daughter of a respectable draper's family from Dublin, brought up in modest comfort. She'd run away with a soldier to England but had been deserted and briefly entered the employ of a fishmonger in Billingsgate. She had been used to having her own way in life and taking exactly what she wanted, it was purloining a fine silk dress which did not belong to her that landed her in prison in the first place. But whereas I still blamed myself for my own condition, Kitty merely accepted hers as one of those temporary downfalls which happened along the path of life.

Pert, quick and lively. The loveliest thing about her, the memory that'll live with me forever was her beautiful voice. By some strange chance it was pitched lower than usual and had such a beguiling husky tone that I could listen to her talking for hours.

Many a time she'd come looking for me, eyes alight with the latest bit of gossip, "Let me tell you Charlotte, me dear darlin' little Charlotte ..." and I'd sit there like a rabbit caught in the eye of a fox. She could charm the birds off the trees with that voice, and she was fully aware of it too. By the time the tale was finished you knew the magic lay in the telling just as much as the tale ... though in fact you didn't really 'know' anything because you'd given yourself over to the sheer pleasure of listening and she could have told you anything ... the moon was made of cheese or that the streets of Sydney were paved with gold and you'd have believed her.

So when I told her to watch her step she just laughed at me as usual.

"Oh you're such a stick-in-the-mud country wife Charlotte! You sound just like me ould mama."

I'd been a bit wary like of those sailors, but beyond the chance saucy remark nothing was said that could give offence. Seemed to me they just liked the freedom as much as we did. The pirate-looking fellow, Redmonds, had a small guitar and strummed away by the warm embers without taking much notice of anyone else. Sometimes one of the others would catch at the tune and hum away and the two young lads on one occasion even danced a hornpipe, accompanied by much clapping and encouragement.

Our group still kept to ourselves because I'm sure we felt, without putting it into words, that we'd never forgive ourselves if we lost our little bit of freedom by putting a foot wrong and making a nuisance.

Then one night when our Kitty couldn't help taking up the refrain of Redmond's guitar we began to be really included.

He'd sat there humming softly to himself as his fingers plucked at the strings. I could tell Kitty loved the music from the way her body swayed ever so slightly and her toes tapped to the occasional jig.

"There was a little drummer boy who loved a one-eyed cook,
With a hey and a ho and a hey nonny no!"

She sang the words half to herself as he picked out the tune. Her husky voice blended like cream into the darkness of the night.

He nodded, "Keep it up girl, keep it up."

Encouraged by his words she followed with the next verse and when she came to the refrain the two boys joined in with great gusto.

"With one eye up the chimney and the other in the pot,
With a hey and a ho and a hey nonny no!"

Soon the entire group around the brazier were singing their hearts out. Some of the verses would make you blush, except it was too dark to see anything of the sort.

But it wasn't too dark for me to see what was happening. Standing back against the rail nursing the baby I became aware of another figure in the shadows.

It was Kelly, the mate. I did not need to look at his face to know he was gazing intently at that laughing girl with the golden hair gleaming in the firelight. Kitty was transformed from a convict woman in a drab dress to a young woman singing by the light of the moon.

There's times when you stand at a crossroads in life. When events can go one way or another. Like the moment when I'd stood with those four guineas gleaming in the candlelight.

Those four golden guineas which sent me to the far ends of the earth.

If I'd put them back I'd still be at home, fetching the cow in from the watermeadow, stirring the dandelions for the wine. Instead I'd tucked them down inside my bodice. I'd taken the wrong step on the wrong path and there was never going to be another chance of going back to our cottage with the apple trees blooming in the springtime and the larks singing overhead.

Perhaps I should have leapt forward and grabbed Kitty from the magic circle of enchantment. Rescued her from that outpouring of laughter, that heady release from the bonds of our everyday existence. Perhaps I could have saved her from all that was to come.

Perchance I could have broken the spell. Tossed back to the moonlight the magic it so cunningly offered.

"Mighty fine, mighty fine!" Kelly strode up to the group and, as he smiled at us all, I knew we were lost to the sorcery of love. His eyes blazed with that fire which knows only one way of being quenched.

The witchery I'd witnessed had taken hold of him.

Anny whimpering in my arms brought me to my senses, but I was too late to put matters right. I'd let the moment pass, it was too late to turn back the harbingers of what was to come.

Kelly was chatting in a most casual way with all the men around the brazier and merely nodded his head respectfully at Kitty as she retreated into the shadows. Perhaps I'd imagined it all?

From that night onwards Kelly always joined our circle on the deck and, as well as the music, we had words. Songs and stories are a powerful mixture for those starved of anything except orders and commands and reprimands.

Benjamin Burnet Kelly had left Nantucket twenty years ago when he was a smooth faced lad. The whaling ships could be away for up to four years at a time depending upon the success of their voyage. He was more a man of the sea than of any particular part of the world, being equally at home in Sydney Town, the Bay of Islands or any one of the ports of the Pacific Ocean. Latterly mate of the *Albion*, an English whaler out of London, he vowed he knew the great Pacific Ocean like the back of his hand.

"Mind you, 'tis the master makes the ship. You can have the smartest vessel in the world and come to grief with a yellow bellied captain. When you've made westing round the Horn with a man like Eb Bunker then you'd never want to serve with another. A regular giant of a man, I've seen him standing by the helmsman for nigh on twenty-four hours. Icicles hanging from his beard, eyes red from peering into snowstorm after snowstorm. Tough as hickory one moment, then I've seen him carry an injured cabin boy down below gentle as a mother with her babe the next."

Kelly would refill his pipe and lean back against the rails. No one uttered a sound and I'd hush young Anny so as not to miss one word. If Kitty's voice was golden then his speech was pure silver.

When he spoke of the ships which sailed these waters I saw in my mind's eye the filling canvas, the long white wakes spreading out upon the ocean and the dolphins frolicking in the waves as clouds of flying fish swooped onto the decks. And as he recounted their names – *The Estramina, Brothers, Tellicherry, Aurora, Sophia, Ceres, Lady Nelson* and all the other noble ships – they became real beings. Beautiful, free spirits circling the globe with the ease of great seabirds. My pulse quickened and I yearned to be away on the high seas sailing on for ever and ever beneath those billowing sails.

The wizardry of his words conjured up such pictures you could hear the wing beat of the huge albatross hovering above the main mast. You almost choked on the stench of the whale oil. I wasn't the only one to hang on his every utterance. When the stories flagged for a moment or Redmonds ceased strumming, one or other of the men around the brazier would give a sly prod … "What about that chap paid us a hundred guineas for two hours with a whale? Remember him Ben?"

"And what can you mean by that?" Goggle-eyed, Kitty could not contain her curiosity as she settled herself on an upturned box and prepared to listen. "A huge creature like that could kill a man."

"The whale was well and truly dead, Ma'am."

I couldn't help smiling at Kitty's flushed face. She was very partial to being called 'Ma'am'.

"There's an old belief that the oil of the whale's a powerful cure for the rheumaticks."

"Go on, go on," the chorus came, Kitty's was not the only voice raised in anticipation. Night after night the stories rolled out like a magic carpet which carried us all away to the realms of make believe.

"Well there was this ship's chandler from High Street, so twisted up with aches and pains he could barely hobble down to the quay. One day when me and Cap'n Bunker was in his shop looking over some cable he muttered something about life not being worth living any longer. It was then the cap'n spoke up 'You know what they say in the Islands?' Well, I'd not heard it up till that time either and the old man certainly hadn't. 'That a couple of hours inside the belly of a whale newly killed will bring out all yer pain for life.'

'I'll try it … I'll try it,' that chandler nearly jumped over his counter in spite of them rusted up joints.

'It'll cost … you'll have to come aboard with us … you'll …'

'I'll pay, just let me try, I'll pay.'

"Too right you will I thought, ships' chandlers are thieving bastards …" at this Kelly bobbed his head towards us women, "beggin' yer pardon ladies … but we ain't used to female company here."

This time he caught Kitty's eyes and laughed. I held Anny a trifle closer for I sensed there might well be trouble ahead.

"… well the season was under way so we set off with this old fellow aboard and his hundred guineas in the captain's writing case. He paid alright. Didn't take us long to sight a good sperm whale … sixty barrels the captain reckoned … a good price he'd get and add to that the bit extra from the old chap. Took five hours to bring that creature to the ship's side and the lads went overboard with their knives, cut into him and lashed the carcass up against the side of the ship. Then they sliced a hole in the side of him and the steam fairly rushed out. They shoved the old man into the cavity with his head sticking out for air. We left him in there two hours cosy and snug and when he came out he was dripping with oil. Came out like a two year old …"

"Sure and did it do the job? Did it cure the screws?" Kitty was perched right on edge of the box in her excitement.

"Never knew Ma'am. Old chap got knocked down the very next day we got back to Sydney – bowled over by a dray in High Street he was. Eb Bunker reckoned he died happy though."

Laughter rippled round the group and Kelly grinned to himself at the memory.

"And what's Van Diemen's Land like?" It was I who was so bold as to ask the question because they were all in a chatty mood and it's then the truth tumbles out. We'd only heard Dicky's tales up to now and I was very curious about this land we were approaching. After all it was going to be our home for many years to come.

"Van Diemen's Land!" snorted Kelly "'tis an island, but nothin' like most islands hereabouts, nothin' like them islands out in the great ocean. The islands of the Pacific are a heaven on earth. Places like Otaheite and the Friendly Islands where it's warm and beautiful, where the local folk greet you on the sandy beaches and take you into their villages. No! Van Diemen's Land's more like the back of the backside of beyond, if you'll excuse me ladies. The Indians can be fierce, real fierce, nothin' like the tribes around the Harbour. There's no food, that's why we're going there. After those terrible flood's on the Hawkesbury the whole Colony's half starving, but down in Port Dalrymple they're nigh to death and must have vittles. I've heard tell that no crops have taken, they can't get the seed to grow, there's nought to eat 'cept kangaroo."

"Are there many more the like of us, prisoners, down there?"

"A number Ma'am, but I've heard tell as how the Indians are so savage and the food so scarce that they give the convicts guns just the same as the soldiers so they can defend the settlement and bring in game from the bush. You could say it's the very edge of the world for us humankind and it's more a matter of just keeping alive."

So Dicky had told no lies.

"'Tis a fact that the natives who live on islands seem fiercer than those who live on mainlands," Kelly mused. "Some are real savage. Look at the natives in Feejee, real warlike folk, gobble you up as soon as look at you. Then there's the Fuegans down near Cape Horn, they ain't folk you'd want to fall in with. In winter when the weather's bitter and there's no food they have to choose between eating their dogs or the old women of the tribe. Mostly they don't want to lose the dogs because they can hunt the sea otters so they cooks up the old women. And the old women knowing what's in store often head for the hills as soon as winter starts to bite."

Nothing was said for quite a few moments.

"Well I ain't saying the natives of Van Diemen's Land are anything like that," Kelly went on, "but they're very fierce and seeing as how there are so few white folk down there 'tis every man for himself."

I nudged Kitty. "Reckon we're jumping straight out the frying pan into the fire?"

Frying pans and fires! Seemed I was destined for them even from the first. Though in truth those first years back home in Bromsgrove had been peaceful enough.

Our cottage, where generations of Badgers had lived, was right on the outskirts of town and you could say we were a well set up family.

Father had his nailing machine out the back, 'twas said there were over nine hundred nailers working at their trade in the surrounding countryside.

We had our Daisy and her calf in the field down the end, not our own field but we were allowed to use it for a few shillings a year. Ma did fine sewing and mending for them up at the manor. With no lad in the family and on account of me being the strongest of us two girls I looked after the garden, dug the whole length each year, planted and weeded it too. Our Lizzy was like Ma, she was dainty and clever with her fingers, she could sew a fine seam. Ma kept her indoors mending and sewing and cooking for she intended there'd be a place for her working for the gentry.

You could say we'd a good life, nought to complain of. But nothing stays the same. It's funny how things stick in your memory, to me it all started when our parson preached his Michaelmas sermon.

'The winds of change are coming ... maybe it'll begin with a slight rustle of the leaves, maybe we'll have a storm or two but God in his wisdom is watching and we'll find peace in his eternal harbour ...'

I've never been very sure about God but there was no denying the old parson was telling the truth about the changes coming, for within a twelvemonth our Father made half his usual number of nails. Some folks had set up a place outside Worcester where all the men worked together and the price of nails plummetted like a stone to the bottom of the well.

"Don't fret. I'll be up at the big house next spring! Won't be much but it'll help." Lizzy had just turned fifteen on the day our mother took her along to speak to the housekeeper up at the manor. Her cheeks were pink with excitement when she told me this. Dear Lizzy, in spite of all Ma's cossetting she never gave herself airs. If she could help me in the backyard she'd slip out and do a bit of weeding or search for blackberries in the field.

So it happened that year whilst I was, as usual, fetching the cow in for milking, feeding the pig and scraping out the chicken house, our Lizzy was listening to her orders for the day, mending the linen and helping the nurserymaid.

But that wasn't all our Lizzy was doing and once or twice on her days off she'd bring back one of the young footmen from the manor.

Anyone connected with the gentry in any way wore a

halo of perfection in our Ma's eyes. Perhaps she was thinking of the day when maybe the footman would work his way up and perhaps even be a butler? Who knows, but Ma smiled on him whenever he came, pressed him to another glass of dandelion wine, urged him to come again whenever he was free.

How could Ma be so blind? Will Gossage was quick and smart and knew how to charm the ladies. His eyes had that same dark gleam of an earwig's body, his mouth was as soft and pink as a baby rat. He smiled too much, he flashed his eyes around too much and when he got the chance he rubbed up against our Lizzy too much.

The second winter Lizzy spent up at the manor was one of the worst we'd ever known in that part of the county. Every rut in the lane was frozen hard as iron. First it iced over then melted a mite and got a bit treacherous, then it froze again till you could scarcely walk a couple of paces without slipping and sliding. I stuffed every crack in the cow's shed with wisps of straw for the wind howled through the smallest gap and even the piss in our pots beneath our beds was solid by morning. Icicles hung like daggers from the roof and birds fell out of the trees stone dead.

For nearly two months our Lizzy never came home but when she did even our Ma was shocked by her appearance.

"You never! You foolish girl … What'll we do, what'll we do?"

"Will says he'll stand by me."

"Stand by you! What does that mean? What can he offer you?"

"The master says he'll let Will have one of the cottages … We'll have a roof over our heads."

A roof over her head and a baby in her belly.

A baby. Perhaps I was a sour old maid already, nineteen and never been spoken for, but I reckoned babies were very much mixed blessings. When all the old aunties and grannies and neighbours crowded round a cradle cooing and making a fuss I always stood back. Babies brought hard work, poverty and years and years of care ... that's if they didn't half kill their poor mothers when they came into the world.

But it wasn't only that coming baby which heralded the worst year I can ever remember. Father's nailing came to an end. Redditch way they'd set up another place like the one near Worcester where the men all worked together, they'd no place for him. No money came in for us at all, then the cow died despite all the care I'd given her.

For several weeks we just existed in the kitchen. Even the firewood was running low and the larder was so bare a mouse would have starved. So I was lucky, or thought I was, when old Benjamin Wright who had the next cottage to us nearly out of sight up the lane, asked if I could go and do for him. He was nearing eighty and he told our Ma he couldn't manage the yard and the house was in a muck.

Would that I'd never set foot in the old devil's house. He was right, it was filthy with dust so thick you could write your name on all the tables and chairs and dressers if you'd been so inclined. The mice in his larder would never have starved as there was half eaten meat, plates with egg dried hard and brittle yellow, bits of bread, bones and a mess which must have been collecting since before Christmas. It took me half a day just to get the kitchen clean and the old man grumbling all the time that I wasn't working hard enough.

"You ain't seen to that calf o' mine yet," he never ceased grumbling as I went out and took several armfuls of hay from the barn down to the cowshed. Poor little creature, thin and half frozen to death, it's trough chilled to ice and shut away by bars so it could not reach the cow's udders.

The greedy old devil had taken all the milk and given it to fatten the pig. One thing he could manage was the milking but I made sure I got a pail from him and took it out to the calf.

"You'll ruin me you stupid girl. Look that there pig's worth more money than that calf."

"He's starvin' to death." The little creature had his nose nearly drowned in the bucket of milk as it sucked and slathered away.

"Gimme the pail!" He tried to snatch it up but I was a match for his spindly old arms.

I gave him a hefty sideways shove with my shoulder and he had to grab the rails.

"You clumsy great baggage," he yelled as he rubbed his elbow. "You'll pay for this ... wastin' good milk on a runt like that! Mark my words you'll pay for this!"

Silly old fool, he'd have been better inside sitting by the fire and leaving the work to me like I was paid for.

But was I? At the end of the first week I expected my wages and nothing was said at all.

"Better not rouse him up," Ma said when I told her. "Everyone knows he's got plenty of money about him but he's so old he's possibly forgetful like. He'll pay you next week."

But even then no money was forthcoming.

The thaw finally came and Lizzy arrived with that Gossage. If we'd hoped she might have some money on her then we were sadly disappointed for the boot was quite on the other foot and as she drew me aside she could scarcely meet my eyes.

"I'm that cold ... look at my fingers, all chilblains ... I need my dress back, my only warm one, the red one with the white buttons ... I must have it."

For she had pawned her only winter dress to give the money to Will Gossage. A debt it was, he told her, but she was soon to find out that his debts were always the same – always on some wager with the horses.

As I sloshed my way through the melting snow to the old man's cottage I was puffed up and furious with rage. Why did women always have to beg and borrow and take the burden from the men? Beg, borrow ... and steal. But I had no thought of that as I banged on the kitchen door and let myself in.

The old man was sitting by the fire with his pipe in his mouth and his cat purring on his lap.

"Mr Wright," I said, " With respect I've worked for you for fourteen days and I'd like my wages, Sir."

He looked up all slylike. "You Badgers is always the same ... shifty I'd call you."

"What do you mean shifty?"

"Leaving jobs half done. The cow ain't bin milked today, there's me washin' up in the sink and where's a clean shirt I ask you?"

I could have said that the milking was his job usually, the sink had just one bowl in it and the old fool looked cleaner than I'd seen him in ages, but something told me nothing would be gained by a back answer. He was just trying to get the better of me.

"Then I an't comin' again, you can get someone else to empty yer slops and muck out the shed," I turned to go, "I can do that work at home where I'd get nothing either."

"Wait ... wait on young miss ... don't take it too much to heart ... you'll be paid alright, you'll be paid."

I hesitated. Would that I'd walked right out there and then but there's some moments when you hesitate and just hold back. It's as if time stands still and you are at that cross-roads, you can take the right road or the wrong.

At that moment something really evil slipped into my life and it was the ruin of me. "I need half a crown right now. My sister's got to get her dress out of pawn."

"Your young Lizzy, the one 'as got herself into trouble ... the pretty one eh?" He guffawed but I took no notice.

"I want that money now."

He shuffled over to the dresser and opened the bottom cupboard drawer. The leather bag he brought out was fat and heavy. He tipped it up on the table and before my eyes a fortune in gold and silver poured out on the table.

The old fellow was in his dotage, like a child he ran his fingers through all that wealth and the only tooth in his head gleamed yellow and sharp as he grinned at me.

"Half a crown you say ... wait while I get some paper and I'll make a note of it. Set it against your wages when I pays you."

I couldn't take my eyes off that pile of money. It could buy us so much. We needed flour and tea, Ma's shoes were beyond mending, Father wanted seed for the spring and some hooks for the fishing, not to mention a sack of coal which might warm the place up and stop us all coughing.

"Drat it!" I heard him mutter, the stairs creaked as he climbed up to his room in search of a piece of paper.

Like a flash my hand came out and I slipped four guineas down inside my bodice. Beads of moisture broke out on my brow and I brushed them away.

I was sweating like a pig ... scared the old man would notice I took a handkerchief which lay carelessly behind his chair and mopped my brow.

"Got it ... got it. Now I'll want you to sign when I've written," I could hear him at the bottom of the stairs with his piece of paper.

My back was turned to him so I stuffed the silk kerchief deep down inside my bodice. I signed the paper and took the half crown from him.

CHAPTER THREE

Visiting Magistrates Minute Book – Worcester Gaol
January 31st 1799

The Gaoler having reported to us that there are nine women confined in the county gaol, seven of whom are under sentence of transportation two committed to take their trials for housebreaking but there being but two womens cells in said Gaol, in consequence of which seven of the Women are obliged to sleep in the Dry room which is attended with much inconvenience the Gaoler having recommended the following women being part of the above number under sentence for transportation as being very orderly and quiet in behaviour – ordered that Martha Evans, Sarah Letard, Charlotte Badger and Sarah Baylis be removed into the custody of the County Bridewell. (Bridewell being a secluded part of the main gaol)

Visiting Magistrates Minute Book – Worcester Gaol
February 8th 1800

Charlotte Badger, convict, has only one shift which is in a bad condition – order that she may immediately be supplied with a new shift.

The wind picked up and sent us scudding southwards. Perhaps the livening of the breezes stirred something in Captain Chace because next morning, for the first time, I saw him up on deck.

Since that occasion when we'd been allowed out for the night we'd also been given the chance to come up more often during the daytime. Perhaps it was because the crew felt they had the measure of us prisoners and realised we had no intention of escape – certainly no ability to do so – that the added privilege was allowed. Anyhow nowadays the cabin door was frequently left ajar. Thompson as often as not was gossiping with the lads on deck and a blind eye was turned when we made our way up into the fresh air whenever we felt like it.

As bad luck would have it I was going up on deck one morning with Anny in my arms when I heard the boards creaking at the approach of someone of considerable weight.

Coming face to face with the captain was a difficult moment. He stared at me as though looking at a slug crawling across a cabbage leaf.

"Kelly!" he roared. "What's this woman doing here? Where's that bloody soldier?"

I kept my mouth shut, nothing I could say would have helped.

"Kelly!" He leapt along the deck and unluckily for us prisoners found Kelly talking to Kitty by one of the hatches.

You did not need to be a sage to work out how things were going in that direction. The two were standing, not too close but not too far apart either, by the rail of the ship. Kelly's head was bent towards her as he explained something. A faint smile played about Kitty's lips as she listened earnestly.

"Kelly!" he bellowed for the third time and the mate at last became aware of his master.

"Sir?" Turning to face Chace he must have seen, just as I saw from much closer by, the furious face of the man. Every one of his many chins shook with rage whilst his visage was twisted with frustration.

"Where's the guard? Why are these women roaming around as if they own the place? What has been happening? My oath …" and here he launched into a string of filth which any decent woman would never have heard and I only knew from my years of confinement with some of the dregs. "My oath … I take to my sick bed for a couple of days and what happens – trollops parade the deck! Harlots flaunting themselves and …"

There was no need to listen to that! Turning I hurried

back down to the cabin where Lanky was dozing after a bad night of coughing. Shortly afterwards Kitty and Dick were escorted back by Thompson.

That was the end of our freedom. We were returned to the confines of the cabin and our cramped conditions seemed all the more cruel because we'd enjoyed that lack of restraint for a while. Now the stink was worse than ever as Chace ordered we could no longer leave the cabin to go to the latrine but must manage with a bucket in the corner.

On one occasion when Kitty and myself were on deck for our twice-daily guarded exercise spell we were surprised by the sudden appearance of Kelly. His honest face was creased with concern as he asked about our conditions.

"Sure we miss the company of an evenin' ladies. And how's the wee princess?" His workworn hands tousled Annys faint fluff. "The lads reckon it ain't the same now ... nothin' like the same." His words were for both of us but his eyes were for Kitty alone.

Our days and nights became unbearably tedious. We were back with the constant nagging noises of coughing and a crying baby, the lack of exercise and the sheer boredom of each other's company. As I counted up the days we'd been travelling and put them against the time we were meant to take reaching our destination I wondered if we'd even be speaking to each other when we eventually arrived.

Imagine our surprise when next day Thompson put his head round the door and grinned at us, "Goin' ashore ... get ready, goin' ashore."

Dicky Evans jumped up and stared at the soldier. "Ashore? We can't be down at Port Dalrymple yet? Not with scarce no wind!"

"Cap'n says he's putting youse ashore for a spell, he's work to do."

Dicky sat on the edge of the bunk muttering his thoughts aloud. "Ain't no towns along the way ... ain't nothin' ... never heard of nothin' along the coast hereabouts."

Neither had I. I did have a very vague idea of how the Colony looked from being a trifle curious. Way back, one of the sailors on the *Cornwallis* had shown me a rough drawing of what our new home would look like. As far as I could recall it was all wilderness along the coast, just forest and mountains for hundreds of miles to the south and then this Van Diemen's Land right down at the end.

"There ain't nothin' like a town nor nothin' like that. Nothin' where a ship like the *Calcutta* would have called in," Dicky muttered to himself, "but there's little places, my reckoning is he's wanting rid of us for a spell, he's got somethin' up his sleeve the old bugger. Like as not he's looking to be off sealing."

Captain Chace certainly did have something up his sleeve. The sealers' ship, the *George*, had gone ashore in these parts. He intended helping them with the repairs needed and then joining forces with them for a bit of sealing. Having such experienced hunters sailing with him would be a feather in his cap.

Greedy for every spare penny, he'd do well with a few hundred sealskins to sell back in Sydney.

Added to that he'd be shot of us prisoners for a spell. I had remembered the look on his face when he saw Kelly talking to Kitty and I fancy he took a deal of pleasure at the thought of separating them.

"Twofold Bay they calls it."

We'd been ordered on deck and Thompson stood behind us, his musket by his side, staring out at the wild expanse of country with as much dread as we ourselves felt.

Without doubt it was one of the most beautiful places on earth, at least those parts of the earth I'd seen and by now that amounted to a tidy bit compared with the folk back home in Bromsgrove.

The sea rolled in along shores of a golden sand so neat and regular you'd be forgiven for thinking Nature placed them there to stop the forest from fraying at the edges. Green trees, yellow sand, white surf and blue seas. An untouched paradise lay before us with sea eagles spiralling in the air currents overhead and flocks of gulls dipping and wheeling in the sunlight.

"I don't like it!" Kelly's words were carried in the breeze as he stood close to the captain and stared out at the peaceful landscape.

"What don't you like Mr Mate?" A sly note had crept into the captain's voice, he was relishing every moment. You could tell the mate wasn't happy to see our party put ashore.

"Usually there's plenty of Indians around. Where are their canoes? I can't even see the smoke from one of their fires."

"You should rejoice, Sir that they're not waiting for us. Fearsome savages they can be – why 'tis said up in those hills they eat human flesh!" Chace threw his head back and laughed, not before I noticed he had glanced in our direction to see the effect of his words.

"Bin here several times with Eb Bunker. When the *Albion* came in they'd always crowd down to the water's edge – where are they?" Kelly was scanning the shoreline with a puzzled frown on his face.

Chace shrugged his shoulders. "Lower the boats."

The sealers left in the first boat laden with tools and materials to patch up their wrecked ship. Our little group stood back and waited while hasty preparations were made for setting us ashore.

Kelly could not conceal his concern as he watched the men toss tents, provisions and a few arms over the side into one of the boats. "If you're only sending the two lads and that half witted soldier with 'em then that's not enough to guard four prisoners against attack."

Again Chace shrugged his shoulders. "Last year we anchored in the Bay and camped here for nigh on a fortnight ... plenty of shade and a stream nearby ... there was no trouble then ... ask Redmonds!"

"I wouldn't rely on Redmonds for the time of day, Sir! Why the man's drunk as a skunk half his waking hours."

"Get those women ashore!" Chace thundered out his command and turned on his heel taking no further notice of the mate.

The two boats made several journeys ferrying us and necessary stores to the strand. On the first trip the tents had been shipped with several boxes of provisions and whilst the sailors struggled with the canvas and drove the pegs into the ground, Kelly supervised the storage of supplies. His unease had conveyed itself to the other men and as they worked they frequently glanced over their shoulders towards the forest bordering the grassy area where we were to be camped.

He'd chosen a place where there were no large trees as it was common knowledge that in this country one of the many dangers of the bush was from falling timber. Suddenly, on a clear day when there might be no hint of wind, one of the huge limbs would fall from a tree – 'widdermakers' they were called from the fact that men were frequently crushed.

T'was a common complaint of folk in Sydney town that much of the timber in this new country wasn't fit for a carpenter to use. Nothing like the oak, elm or beech of the old country. The trees which grew in such abundance here were lofty and magnificent but at the same time lacking the robust nature of our old friends.

Some of the trees around Bromsgrove were several hundred years old and never shed a limb. Here you could count the years of a tree's life by their tens as they grew so swiftly with no winters to hold them back. The timber of the Colony was tall and magnificent. Still, handsome is as handsome does. Whether it was from the swift growth or the poor soil or the shocking hot summers and all the teeming ants no one seemed to hazard a guess, but these giants of the forest were often stricken with hidden rot and decay.

A tidy little camp soon met our eyes, two tents on either side of a very small tree which was convenient for hanging out anything needed to dry and air. Our bedding was brought out and a few blankets draped from the branches.

A trifle exposed we'd be, being set back about fifteen yards from the cliff edge, with a similar distance on the other side between the tents and the forest. But obviously Kelly knew what he was about and one of the seamen who'd been here before assured us there was a stream nearby in the forest.

"Whalers call in here quite often … over on that other headland there's a hut, can you see it?"

"Holy Mother of God why can't we stop in the hut then?" Kitty was bold enough to ask. "Surely to goodness 'twould be better than living under canvas?"

"Keep away from there. If a ship comes in that's where the men'll be – they're a rough lot."

"Seems this is rather an unfriendly place, between the cannibals and the whalers," I couldn't help sounding a trifle flippant. Certainly little thought had been given for our safety.

"The whaling men come in for fresh water very occasionally. If you keep to yourselves you'll have no trouble. And as for the Taua, well they live their life as their tribe has lived for thousands of years – they exist in the bush but their real luxury is to catch a whale."

"Catch a whale!" I couldn't help but exclaim because once in the distance we'd seen a whale and it's calf disporting themselves upon the surface of the ocean. "Why a whale would be twice, three times, even half a dozen times the length of any Indian's canoe!"

"Ah … but the Taua have their own methods … they've been catching whales since the dawn of time and they don't even leave the land to do it."

"Away wi'you," Kitty laughed, her voice low and inviting, "'tis another of yer yarns, you'll be telling us next that there's mermaids combing their tresses out on them rocks and King Neptune's waitin' to greet us!"

Kelly smiled at her upturned face then he turned away abruptly and pointed out to the empty sea. "You may not see anything but let me tell you that out in that Bay are the killer whales."

What a place! Were they really going to leave us here with savages in the forest and animals worse than sharks in the Bay?

He continued, "The natives know them as Beowas and because they are striped black and white they believe they are the souls of their own warriors who have died in battle. For the natives smear themselves with white clay at their corroborees and the stripes are just the same.

"The killer whales herd sperm whales, seals and other sea creatures into shallow water and attack them. Twofold Bay is a wonderful hunting ground for them and many a whale who comes into the sheltered water here is hounded to its death by these relentless creatures who hunt in packs.

"Right back at the dawn of time the Taua began calling those killer whales in. Perhaps it started with some lucky natives finding a dead sperm whale washed in and whilst they were cutting it up discovering that the killers merely wanted to feed off it's great tongue. Anyhow those early natives found that by tossing them this delicacy of theirs they could call the creatures in.

"They'd stand on the cliffs, rattle their spears and sing out at the waters of the Bay so the killers knew their human allies were waiting to help. The Beowas in turn learnt that by chasing their prey towards the waiting Taua they were assured of a feast and all the best bits of the victim. The alliance between man and beast began and has continued to this day."

"Sure and you've a silver tongue in that head of yours me fine lad," dreamily Kitty stared out across the peaceful water of the Bay. A gentle smile touched her lips as Kelly moved closer to her side and stood looking out at the horizon.

They did not even touch each other; there was no need. Some farewells don't need words.

"C'mon lads. Look lively. Stow them boxes," Redmonds started to harass the two boys. He was eager to be off and away to the sealing grounds.

The sealing men returned disgruntled. They'd found the *George* but she'd been burnt down to the waterline so there was no chance of salvage. Chace ordered them back on board the *Venus* as such experienced men would be more than welcome over the next few weeks.

"Well, won't see them again for a while," Dicky Evans shook his head as he watched the sails of the *Venus* becoming smaller and smaller.

Once the *Venus* sailed out of Twofold Bay we truly settled ourselves down. Left to Thompson's notions, us women had a tent all to ourselves. I fancy this was because Anny was still suffering with her gums and the nights were very noisy. Certainly, as we arranged the bags and bundles round the sides of the tent and set down a candle on one of the boxes in the middle the place began to look quite like a home.

The other tent was larger and no doubt the men were also occupied setting the inside to rights. Even so their space was more limited and before long a shout of rage came from it's direction.

"Stupid clod! Ain't you got no more sense than that?" One of the lads had brought a pail of water inside and someone had tripped over it.

Thompson kicked the flap back and threw the bucket after the swiftly retreating boy. "Bloody numskull! Get it filled up again – and leave it out where it should be, under the tree!"

We thought no more about it as young Billy scuttled off into the forest. The men's grumbles went on for a while as between them they hung up several blankets to dry and mopped down the mess with old sacks.

Then, high pitched and piercing, there came a most dreadful scream from the darkness of the trees.

Thompson grabbed his musket and raced to the edge of the clearing. Kitty clutched my arm and with the men peering from the scant shelter of their tent we all stared at the cavernous greenery where Billy had disappeared carrying the bucket.

"Billy!" Everyone shouted together, "Billy!"

Give him his due our Dicky was no coward. Grabbing a mallet he started off into the shadows.

"Stop! What you think you're doin' ... you'll be ..." but Thompson never finished.

"Then gimme one of them guns," Dicky yelled at him, "get one of them guns. I'll wait, you follow me."

"You wait here wi'us. You wait." Thompson was never one to seek any strife.

Kitty screamed and grabbed me, "Holy Mother of God 'tis our last hour ... 'tis our last."

Her continued moans did nothing to stem the panic which was rising in me.

By now the *Venus* was far out to sea and I remembered what had been said about Van Diemen's Land; it being so wild and such a wicked place they even gave the convicts guns to carry. Well it looked as if it was just the same here and there was only seven of us to fight off any horde of savages that might descend.

At that moment Billy's white face loomed out of the dark background of forest.

"Billy! Billy!" Young Tommy leapt across the clearing, "what they done to you mate? What they done?"

The poor lad still clasped the bucket but the other hand clutched at his shoulder. Blood poured through and stained his shirt bright red.

Dicky and Thompson heaved him up and carried him into their tent.

We hurried over. By then the men had stripped his shirt from him.

The wound was not deep but the shock had set the poor

lad in such a dither I wondered he'd ever be in his right mind again. Face was white as new driven snow. Skin chilly as ice to touch. Then the shivers set in. His whole body began to shake and quiver quite uncontrollably.

Poor lad, not much more than a nipper really. Brought to the Colony as a babe in arms and as the whole of New South Wales was only seventeen years old he'd not have seen much of the ways of the world.

Don't suppose he'd had an easy young life but to be speared in the shoulder was a terrible shock for a young lad. Most likely his only experience of brutality would have been a few cuts with the strap from his old man or a punch in the jaw from his mates.

All that night we sat huddled inside the men's tent fully expecting a shower of spears to fall upon us.

Thompson had given in to commonsense and allowed Dicky a musket so the two men took it in turns keeping guard.

I swear Anny knew what was afoot as she never let out one squeal the whole eight hours.

Next morning dawned with a fair breeze coming from the east. We were chilled to the bone and I was so thirsty I could have drunk up the whole ocean, if it had been sweet water instead of salt. Making all that milk for the baby took every scrap of moisture from my own body. As she sucked so I dried up inside till I fairly withered away.

"We've got to have water ..." I approached Thompson but he merely shook his head.

I slipped out and round the seaward side of the canvas for a call of nature.

How sinister the forest looked. Mile upon mile it stretched away until swallowed up by a great line of mountains with puffs of cloud floating along the bases. How many natives lived in those hills and how many were hidden in the forest? My skin fairly crept at the thought of them. There could be a hundred eyes peering from the thickets watching our every move, biding their time.

Back with the others we started the day in fear, just as we'd spent the night before in nigh terror. But as the sun rose higher in the sky the needs of our bodies became so urgent that fear almost took second place.

"Not a drop ... not a drop ... so there's no use whingin'," Thompson grumbled at us in turn as everyone fruitlessly looked in all the jars, bowls and buckets which had come ashore. You could tell he was completely at a loss. He had no idea what his next step should be and I swear he took more comfort from the sight of old Dicky, prisoner though he might be, with a musket in his hand than he took from the sight of his own free men. Young Billy was still lying there shocked and half senseless whilst Tommy, the other lad said nothing and sat staring into space like a stunned rabbit.

"What'd you see Billy?" he kept asking his friend, "Was there many of 'em?"

Time and again Billy shook his head and always mumbled the same reply, "Nothin' ... saw nothin' "

"That'd be the Indians alright," Dicky kept nodding his head, "follow you all silent like in the bushes, come up quite close and you'd never know they was there, not a single sound would you hear. I've heard the soldiers say you can't even find their villages and give 'em a taste of their own medicine because they don't have settled homes like nearly everyone else in the world has. They just keep movin' from place to place from one year's end to the other."

"But from what I ever did see, they ain't what you call cruel. Not for no reason they ain't cruel." Thompson shook his head. "I heard tell how the governor once ordered some of our regiment to be flogged for making off with the Indians' fishing gear. Well, those there Indians wept and begged for the men to be let off. To them we were real vicious."

"Well, summat's up with 'em. They ain't too pleased with us right now. I'd say they've got their dander up and we'd best take heed," Dicky muttered.

I shivered even though my throat was burning with

thirst. My tongue felt so huge it seemed to fill my mouth and my empty breasts sagged. Not a single drink in a whole half day and as we sat and endured the long hours of inactivity I wanted to scream with the mixture of fear and boredom.

By mid-afternoon tempers were frayed all round. Kitty in her usual fashion of being able to distance herself from the surroundings was the only one managing with our enforced imprisonment. Curled up, she lay fast asleep in a corner of the tent.

The two boys stayed huddled and watchful in the opposite corner, Thompson was now nodding off over his firearm – worn out from the hours of tension. Only Dicky was managing, he sat back with his gun and watched the line of forest like a hawk.

"What are they like with women?" I asked Thompson, because I was dry as a bone and the baby had grizzled for the last two hours after sucking at my breast and turning her head away in disgust.

"What you mean?"

"Would they have it in for a woman?"

He thought for a moment before he replied, "Can't say I've ever heard. I know this, the men's the warriors and the hunters, the women go out digging for roots and the like. Don't think they take much notice of 'em, women ain't up to much in their ways … not from the sound of it."

"Strange when you think of it," perhaps I was getting light headed as my thoughts kept rambling around.

"What's strange?"

"Well here we are. Out in the back of beyond. They've not come at us again. Strange to think we're here and we don't know a thing about them."

"Why should we?" Thompson muttered, "Why should savages like them have aught to do with us?"

"Well we're on their land an't we? Without a 'by your leave' we're here and yet we don't know a thing about them."

"You're woolgathering woman. For heaven's sake hold

your tongue and stop thinking about things that's beyond you."

That made my mind up.

He was the kind of man who couldn't even begin to think of things outside his daily life. Left to our so-called guardian we were going to sit there till we were parched to death.

Slinging Anny round my neck in her shawl I tied it tight so I had both hands free. Then I picked up the bucket and went to the flap of the tent.

"Don't you be a fool, Charlotte," Dicky jumped up to bar my way. "Give old Thommo here a break and time to pick his spirits up and us men'll go and get the water."

"And have a spear in your guts for your pains?"

"Then I'm comin' with you."

"Use that loaf of yours, Dicky, they could do for us in a trice. This way at least there's a chance. A mere woman and a babe! Let me pass."

Pushing him aside I left the tent and stood for a few moments looking at that dark forest.

A canopy of dense leaves cast black shadows on all sides, no birds sang and the only movement was the occasional flicker of a falling leaf spiralling to earth.

How many eyes were watching from the shadows? How many spears were poised in readiness?

CHAPTER FOUR

On 12 February 1806 the sealing sloop *'George'* which had
a bad reputation with the natives, having over the years
become involved in several encounters with them, drifted
onto rocks in Twofold Bay and was badly holed.
A small boat was dispatched to Sydney for assistance, but
before this could reach them, the remaining crew members clashed with the Aborigines, killing several, their
bodies being hung in trees by the sealers as a warning ...

The Twofold Bay Story, J.A.S.McKenzie, 1991

Those first few minutes standing there were the longest ones
of my whole life. They could well have been my very last.

Thick bush and vines concealed the trunks of the forest
trees. Not until I'd plucked up enough courage to leave the
clearing could I even see the path leading ahead.

I took a few steps and then stood stock still. My heart
thumped like a drum. My ears resounded with a terrible
high pitched pounding. Panic? Sheer fear? Whenever something truly unacceptable was happening my senses shielded
themselves thus. When the hounds from the hunt ripped
our old cat to pieces. When Father brought in his mate to
help kill the pig and I could only think of the days when that
fat piglet romped on the grass as Lizzy wound daisy chains
around his ears.

Those were the times when my ears resounded to the
thudding of my heart.

Thump! Thump! Thump! Dizziness surged through me.
I put out a hand to steady myself against the nearest tree
trunk.

What a time to feel faint! Then I realised I'd been holding
my breath ever since those first few steps into the gloomy
woodlands. What a fool. No wonder my limbs were unsteady.

I gulped down a couple of lungfuls and my heartbeat slowed at once.

If they were going to throw those spears they'd have done it by now. Such reasoning was commonsense but it didn't stop the prickle of fear raising every single one of the hairs on the nape of my neck.

Determined not to look back over my shoulder I hurried along, head down and muttering a few words to Anny from time to time. This was more to calm my own fears than anything else because she was fast asleep.

All at once the path widened to a worn stretch of earth where patches of reeds were clumped around a pond fed by a tiny stream. Fresh water! It was all I could do not to throw myself upon the ground and lap it up like a dog, but something told me to act seemly. For all I knew this was a hallowed place for such as them. 'Twas said they held the land, the sea and the animals in great reverence and all things of nature were of real import in their lives.

Even so I cupped my hands and had a draught of that water, the most welcome taste in many a day. Filling the bucket I sped back, still keeping my head down and looking neither to left nor to right for fear of what I might see.

After that first fearful journey to the stream it became my sole task to bring the water back. We all agreed it was far too risky for anyone else to attempt it, another might in some way be unacceptable. Perhaps a woman with a child was so lacking in any threat we would not be harmed.

Several times a day I made my way to the pool, always with Anny tucked in her shawl upon my back. Never once did a soul stir in the bushes.

Whether those natives remained in the forest watching us for the next two weeks or whether they'd in fact all gone off hunting remained a puzzle for us, but at least we survived. Many a time, as I made my way up and down the path weighed down with buckets in each hand and Anny hanging there like a lucky talisman, I cursed that Captain Chace for caring so little for our safety All the same it was a healthy task and my sore throat and runny nose were a thing of the past.

I'll give Kitty her due – her spirits bucked up and she took on every task she could shoulder, she never let me do a thing. "You're our lifeline, our Charlotte. You're a brave girl. Here let me take Anny." She washed the baby and settled her down for me, she tended the fire and made the damper, she chopped up our dried beef and doled out the sugar and the dried grapes for us all to eat.

Young Billy's wound was still open and it was my opinion that the spear which went into him might very well have been dipped in poison. One day it seemed to almost close over and then next day the skin all round would be red raw again and weeping with the infection.

All the while Lanky never got rid of his cough but he'd sit there, staring out to sea watching the porpoises tumbling around in the bay. He never complained, never fussed.

On the other hand Dicky felt uneasy in the fresh air with the tent flapping all the while. Half his life having been spent between decks had accustomed him to overcrowding and confinement. He'd have felt safer in a pox ridden room with the vapours of the open drains drifting up and the pure finders scouring the streets for the dogs' dung.

We were an unlikely bunch of humanity forced to endure each other's company for the next two weeks. Seven people and one baby sharing the same tent, all living with that unspoken fear.

Would the natives attack? Their absence could be explained if they'd all gone off hunting up in the hills, but what if they came back and resented us still being on their land?

"Some cap'ns never get back." Dicky grinned as he saw our worried faces. "'Tis well known along this coast. They put folks ashore to lighten the ship and they goes off huntin' seals. Mebbe they go to the bottom in a storm, mebbe they just don't bother. I've heard tell of ships coming across deserted islands where poor souls have had to shelter in the rocks and live off shellfish for years on end."

"Can't keep me sides from splittin'. Sure you're a grand feller to have around for a laugh!"

"Laughing! 'Tis the truth Miss Kitty, nothin' but the truth."

"And what would you be knowin' about the truth me fine fellow?" There'd always been a bit of feeling between those two. It went right back to the day we were put in the cell next to them back at the barracks and Kitty'd realised she'd be in the company of a common sailor man when she'd got it firmly in her mind that she would be finding another officer to warm her bed.

A curious expression flitted across his face. Half annoyance, half regret mixed with something else – something like indignation.

"I'm no stranger to the truth. I was a good lad brought up to fear God and shun the devil."

"Go on wi' yer. I was only havin' a laugh." She'd seen that look too. Dicky was never a serious fellow but a nerve had been touched.

"Takin' some nails along to my master I was. Me old man'd just signed the papers and I'd bin with Mr Miles the carpenter for little more'n a month when they took me."

"The press gang?" Thompson asked.

Dicky nodded. "Never bin further'n Portsmouth in me whole life. I'd seen them ships and wondered about the great world out there but I was a happy lad and there was no hankerin' …" he shook his head sadly.

"But couldn't yer old man get you off?"

"He never even knew." Such pain crossed Dicky's face we all looked away. "My old man'll have thought I'd run off. You don't know the half of it. They never calls by and knocks on yer family's door and says, "Please Sir, can we have yer lad for His Majesty's Navy?"

We were silent, what could we say?

"Them gangs lurk in the streets at night mostly. I was late.

The master was working into the small hours on a longboat down at the sea wall and I'd bin sent back to bring them extra nails. 'You keep to the street lad ... stay where there's folks about. Don't you go taking no short cuts.'

"But when you're only fourteen years old you always know better. You want to get places faster and you ain't takin' heed of no greybeards.

"'Grab'im me lads!'

"They sprung out of the shadows.

"Six of 'em with boots that kicked and great hams of fists which fastened on like they'd got me in a vice.

"Next thing I woke up with a splitting head and the ground heaving beneath me. We were at sea!

"And what would they be thinking back home? For all my master and the old man knew I'd just run off. They always reckoned I was one for me own way, didn't take kindly to being ordered about."

Again he shook his head. "As if I'd ever leave me old mother and sisters and all of 'em like that. Now they'll never know will they?" He looked up as though asking us a question but there was silence still.

"They'll never know I've felt the lash, bin buggered more times'n I'd care to recall an' slept beside me gun day and night all for His Majesty."

"They says the gun crews have the worst of it," Thompson shook his head.

"Skilly, biscuits and salt pork was our rations ... and the grog. Them gun-ports were kept closed tight as a duck's arse 'cept during drill or action so 'twas always deep gloom with the stink of candles and oil. The deck's so low any man taller'n a dwarf were bent double from dawn to dusk. Nothin' but drill, drill and more drill and if you stepped out of line 'twas a floggin'. Can't even recall the number of years I spent in a gunport. Two ships o'the line I served in. And when we went into action all you could think of was being blown to kingdom come. Shittin' yerself with fear."

"But you made a break for it?" Thompson nudged him along.

"Thought I'd got an easy berth at last. New ship, the *Calcutta*." He shook his head as his thoughts became too painful.

"Storeship, brand spanking new, reckoned I'd found me feet. Ship's may be new, but them captains stick with their old ways. Mean as buggery. 'Twas then I lost any hope I'd had left. Could see my life stretching ahead till the day of Judgement ... not worth living. So I made a break for it."

"But you was caught?"

"Two hundred lashes. And they told me I was lucky not to be hangin' from the yardarm ... and all for takin' a short cut through the backstreets o' me own hometown."

Everyone started to talk at once. Where had the *Calcutta* sailed? Where did he make his break?

"All I'm sayin' is 'tis best to expect nothin' of life. Those in high places don't give a tinker's cuss and them in between like that there Chace don't care neither way. One moment they're creepin' up the arse of some bigwig, all mealy mouthed. Next minute they're dishin' it out to us as is below them. Never trust 'em I say."

"Lookee! Look out there!" On the fifteenth day we laid eyes on the *Venus* again.

By the time the boats ground onto the strand we were all gathered at the water's edge ... in fact we'd waded into the surf in our excitement.

"You're safe!" Kelly stared at Kitty as though he could eat her.

Time stood still. It might well have been that this was the first time since he left his home in Nantucket that Kelly had cared so much for another human being. They say that you've found true love when you care about another more than yourself.

He could not touch her. Instead he held out both hands.

Those two just stood there. Their bodies separate but their eyes as one.

From the gabble of conversation as the men came up to the camp and helped us collect our belongings together it soon became apparent that we had indeed been very fortunate to escape with our lives.

"Them mongrels," Cook muttered to us, "them wicked mongrels off the *George*." The reason for the Indians' anger had become apparent to them all once the *Venus* was out at sea.

Drinking too hard and too long one of the sealers had boasted of stringing up six of the natives from the trees at Twofold Bay.

When they'd called in at the bay for wooding and watering those months ago, the *George* had slipped her cable and been washed up onto the rocks. As soon as the natives appeared the seamen had foolishly tried to press them into helping refloat the vessel. The Indians are people of the forest and the seashore, not labourers of any kind and a dispute arose when half a dozen were taken by force. Those ignorant whalers in their fury hanged six of the Indians before leaving in their boat. They left their bodies dangling in the wind just to warn the rest of the tribe what could happen.

No wonder we'd had such a fierce reception.

I shuddered. How fortunate we had been. Perhaps the sight of a lone woman with a baby had tipped the balance after all? Otherwise we might be laying out there, our bones picked white by the seabirds and the great lizards.

As we sailed out of Twofold Bay my whole being rejoiced at just being alive. The possibility of death had been a constant companion for so long. Living with fear has a powerful way of concentrating your thoughts and, not for the first time, I felt like falling on my knees and giving thanks. But thanks to whom? I never mentioned this because Kitty had her rosary and the others said their prayers at times, but for myself I could not believe in a truly holy being, there seemed to be more of a force which levelled out the good from the bad, the decent from the perverse. How could any thinking god put innocent folk through some of the misery I'd seen. No, it was Nature which ruled and if you respected her laws then you wouldn't go too far wrong ... keep to the rules and things'll work out.

But that night the rules were put aside and we were all tipped over into chaos.

Captain Chace had muttered something to himself when he saw us coming over the side, his piggy eyes glinted with annoyance. No doubt he'd fully intended that the enforced separation of Kelly and Kitty would finish any association between the crew and us convicts. He could not have been more wrong for all of us were greeted more like heroes and you'd have been hard put to tell the prisoners from the seamen.

Over and over again Dicky Evans told the tale of Billy's encounter. Each time he embroidered it a bit more. He made us sound as though we'd been at death's door through terror of the savages and lack of water. Everyone stared goggle-eyed as he told them how 'our Charlotte, with her babe in a shawl went off into the wilderness'. He got every last bit of excitement out of that event. Thompson was a trifle sheepish when it became apparent he'd never once ventured into the forest, but everyone agreed that a woman and a baby might well be better received than a soldier or sailors.

Cook now proved himself a deft hand with the few balms and dressings he could find. In and out the galley with bowls of water he soaked off the makeshift rags we'd used for stemming the flow of blood and dressed young Billy's wound for him.

Catching sight of the gathering of crew and convicts later that day incensed Chace once more. "Below with 'em. Put 'em aft." Bottle of rum in his hand he retired to his cabin.

Our confinement in our own poky cabin did not last long. Unseen hands cracked the door open and left it invitingly ajar. When Dicky peered out later in the evening Thompson was not on duty. "Stir yer stumps Lanky ... come on," both men hurried out.

"C'mon you old sobersides. What you waitin' for?"

"Go easy," I had my hand on Kitty's elbow.

"What's up Charlotte? What's ailin' yer?"

"That man ... he's right bad. 'Sides which they're drinking hard up there. We don't want to walk into trouble."

"Trouble!" Her eyes shone with excitement, "Haven't you said we've done nought but labour these five years, this is the first bit of pleasure I've had and I'm not turning me back on ..."

"Careful," I warned.

"Careful!" she was impatient to be up on deck. "You and your curtain lectures ... just like home it is listening to youse. Was it being careful that got you young Anny?"

"No call for dirty talk."

"Well then I'd say 'tis no time for the pot calling the kettle black neither." She flounced out of the cabin leaving me holding Anny close and tight.

I'd never spoken about Anny to anyone. Well, truth to tell I'd never been one for the lads. Not that I hadn't looked at them but 'tis only human nature they went for the pretty ones and I'd never lay claim to that.

Seemed to me that lads brought more trouble than pleasure. Not the lads themselves, but the babies. 'Twas on account of my dear Lizzy getting herself in the family way that I stole those four guineas. On the *Cornwallis* two young girls died in childbirth. No, I wanted no chances like that to befall me and I'd kept myself to myself, thank you very much.

I'd been twenty-two when the old *Earl Cornwallis* came through the Heads. For all those four years in goal and five years in this benighted New South Wales I'd kept to myself. With my nose to the grindstone for most of that time and precious little inclination to make my life more difficult it seemed the natural way of things.

Anny's father was a soldier. Didn't even know his name! First and last time I'd ever gone with a man and look what happened.

He'd come to the house searching for some fellow who'd taken rations from the store and made off with them. He was such a handsome young fellow. Not too tall but every inch of him well covered and his uniform red and his boots gleaming in the evening sun.

He didn't put himself forward. He was lonely, you could tell that and on his way next day up to Coal River to guard all them wild Irish. I think he was a bit scared to tell the truth and just welcomed having someone to chat with, for my missus was away from home.

Well, one thing led to another. I'd never been down that path before but it was obvious he had.

I still can't really believe I was so easy.

So very strange it was when you come to think of it after all my fears and turning my back on men.

Perhaps it was meant to be. He was kind and gentle and when he laid a hand on my shoulder then put his arm around me all I could think of was that I was entering a haven. I knew it wouldn't be for long but suddenly the warmth and the closeness made up for so much.

"Charlotte! You comin'?" Kitty's voice cut through my reverie.

"I'll be up. Wait on," I dragged myself back to the present. I didn't often think of that young fellow. I'd almost forgotten if his hair was brown or black or whether he'd bothered to take his boots off. I just knew he'd been kind and he'd made me feel so good – and he'd given me Anny.

"C'mon. Hurry up! Thommo and the lads're all here!"

They were all up there on deck, just as they'd been on those first days at sea. It was just like rejoining your own family again.

Redmonds sat as usual with his guitar and the boys were squatting on the deck with Billy all bandaged up and flushed with the excitement of telling of his ordeal over and over again. Tobacco smoke filled the air and they'd already had enough tots of rum to grease their tongues and get them chattering.

"Cap'n ain't the happiest, keep the noise down," Redmonds warned.

"What's up with the ould divil this time?" Kitty's face bloomed in the twilight.

"Fed up to the back teeth – scarce picked up a dozen seals," one of the seaman told us. "Had us searching in them islands to the north, them ones we passed on the way down."

"He'll find plenty when he gets down south … and he won't even need to put the boats out. The women'll do it for him." Kelly smiled at Kitty and I swear it was no accident that he was sitting right next to her, and somehow in the darkness I could sense his arm was about her waist.

"Women go sealing!" The disbelief in her voice was leavened by that particular depth and softness which was hers alone.

"Not sealing. 'Tis called beguiling down there."

"Away with you. Beguiling means making up to something, making a kind of fuss. You'll not catch a seal that way I'll be bound."

"And there you're wrong Ma'am," he turned to look her full in the face, their eyes dark pools in the moonlight.

"Go on … 'tis another of your tall stories."

"Mebbe some would say so, but they'd be wrong and there's many a sealer'll tell you how it comes about. It's the singing that does it."

"What would singing do for catching a seal?" she jibed gently and their bodies moved closer.

"The native women are very clever … and very strong too. They dive in amongst the seals and swim with them. Imagine swimming in those icy waters. Well, they spend a fair while cavorting with the pack of seals and when the animals lumber ashore, great clumsy things that they are, the women slide along the sand with them and when the creatures roll over and take their ease the women sing to them. That is the beguiling. The native women sing and 'tis well known that the seal loves the sound of the wind and the waves and the call of the birds. So he nods off to sleep as though he were listening to a lullaby ..."

Transfixed I listened to that storyteller's voice, there was magic in his tongue. I could see so clearly the fat, sleepy seal and the black woman lying by its side. The seal would be dreaming of shoals of mullet and perch and plump sea trout, and all the while death was creeping across the sand. As the woman sang, the man with his club drew closer and closer.

"... and as the great creature twitched for a moment and snuffled down even deeper into the depths of sleep then that club would crash down. Thump! Thump! No more was needed, his head was split in two."

I should have sensed then the peril we were in. But like the snoring seal, I clutched the moment, the pleasure of the company, the mug of rum which was pushed into my hand, the rippling chords of Redmond's guitar. It was all so easy, so pleasureful ... and so dangerous.

"Kelly!" Roaring out of the darkness from above our heads came the pent up rage and fury of the master. "Kelly! Get those sluts below."

The sheer unfairness welled up inside me. Perhaps it was the strong liquor, for nothing had passed my lips in that direction for many a month. Perhaps it was just the fact that we'd been facing death for nearly two weeks and to feel you are alive again is a heady potion. Up till then I'd cast my eyes down and taken no notice of the captain ... but not this time.

"Sir!" I stood up and stared into the darkness above my head where I knew him to be. "I'm no slut!"

The roar of rage which rolled out across the deck brought everyone to their feet, Redmonds dropped the guitar and Kitty without thinking grabbed Kelly's arm.

"And that other one," he spluttered as he stumped down

the steps to where we all stood, "that skinny looking trollop ... the Irish whore, take her below while I attend to this slut." He repeated the word with all the arrogance of someone who means to rub your nose in it.

So I repeated what I'd said, tit for tat, "I'm no slut."

He grabbed my wrist. To my surprise his touch was warm and soft and unmanly. "You, Redmonds, fetch the rope."

"Sir!" Kelly's voice was hard and urgent. "Send the women below, let them go back to their cabin."

"Since when did I take orders from my mate, Mr Kelly?" The man's voice had lost its hard edge. Now it was as soft as his touch, but that very softness spoke of something sick and cruel concealed from view.

"Make the woman beg your pardon, Sir. T'was not said with evil intent, a woman could well be expected to defend her reputation."

"Yes, yes," a muttering came from the crew.

To my surprise, Thompson spoke up, "Charlotte never meant no harm!"

"Ha!" muttered the man, "Charlotte is it now? Charlotte the harlot," and he sniggered.

I was on treacherous ground. Instinct told me there was that in Captain Chace which was cruel and twisted. With his pudgy warm hands, his gimlet eyes and hissing voice, he was not a real man at all. The sight of our robust little circle and the strong emotions running between Kelly and Kitty must have inflamed him beyond bearing. He was the kind of man who would always be on the outside looking in.

"Well you heard what Mr Mate said. I'm waiting."

Not a sound could be heard on deck except the slap of the waves against the ship's sides.

All eyes were fixed on me. Kitty's lips were moving as she felt for her beads. Dicky and Thommo stood side by side, concern writ large upon their features. From the edge of the circle I could just make out the lads and Cook. Everyone was looking at me.

And this handful of people were my friends. For the first time in all my time in the Colony I'd found friendship.

I couldn't back down and beg this creature's pardon in front of my friends.

I may have looked just a sullen, dull-witted creature but my thoughts were flying hither and thither and I was thinking hard. I was at one of those crossroads again. One of those moments when one word would send me off in another fateful direction.

I said nothing.

"Lash that slut, that great puddin' of a woman to the mast ... no wait ... first take off her bodice."

A wave of sickness swept over me as someone dragged the top from my shoulders and my back was exposed. All I could think of was, thank heavens Anny's down below with Lanky, for the sick man was sleeping in the cabin with the child.

The captain's hands shoved me across the deck and someone, I don't know who, threw some rope around my waist and wound it round my hips and pulled it tight.

I could see nothing as my face was jammed against the wood of the mast but I sensed them all standing there in the moonlight. All I could hear were the curses and heavy breathing of the captain as he unbuttoned his jacket and threw it on the deck.

"The whip, hand me the whip you fool!"

"Charlotte!" Kitty screamed as they bundled her away along the deck. "Charlotte!"

"You'll have your turn young madam, no need to get impatient," the captain's voice now had a positively silky tone. I shut my eyes tight as I tensed myself for what was to come.

The first cut of the whip was the worst. I bit hard into my lips and vowed not one sound would escape me.

There was a commotion on deck. I heard a scuffling and the captain swearing loudly at someone to 'back off' or it would be the worse for them. After that the blows came fierce and strong and with all my might and main I just kept my teeth ground into my lips and emptied my mind of every single thought. I stood there like a block of wood and – funny the trivial things that come to mind – I wondered if my skirts were much stained with blood.

Then I remember nothing. I still can't recall the bonds being released but I know the hands which grasped me were not the captain's slimy paws, someone had hold of me with hard workworn hands quite gentle for the strength in them, and a voice muttered, "Keep up girl, keep up … you'll be alright … keep up girl."

Next thing I was lying face down on the bunk and Lanky's horrified voice was close by.

"The filthy buggers. The filthy beasts." Nigh choking with rage his fingers smoothed back my torn bodice and dabbed at the cuts of the whip with a bit of cloth. "Get some more water, Thommo, there's a good lad."

I must have passed out again for next thing I recall was the sound of someone being tended in the other bunk. Kitty was back. The thought of dear, jaunty, ever good-humoured little Kitty in that state was too much. I could not lift my head from the bedding.

CHAPTER FIVE

Governor King to Viscount Castlereagh – 27th July 1806

Item 22. Being disappointed in the Opportunity, I had promised myself of sending these dispatches by a British subject going by an American Ship, I have deferred closing this dispatch until this date, which has imposed on me the painful necessity of informing Your Lordship, that Being anxious to send to Port Dalrymple and Hobart Town a Supply of Salt Provisions and as much Grain before the Winter set in as the Deluge enabled me to spare, I availed myself of a Vessel belonging to Mr.Campbell going to Port Dalrymple and Hobart Town and of a private Colonial Schooner, the latter of which I had hired for the purpose of taking Supplies. They sailed from hence 29th April, and after some delay from contrary Winds both arrived at Port Dalrymple. But I am sorry to add that the Venus belonging to Mr.Campbell which had the most considerable Supplies was taken away by a disaffected part of the Crew and a Convict a few hours after her Arrival at the Entrance of the port. Where the Master had in the most imprudent and unjustifiable Manner left her to go 10 miles to wait on the Lieut:Governor.

There was a strange smell in the cabin. First I moved one shoulder, then the other. Every muscle creaked within me as I stretched out that arm and sniffed the air again.

The strange smell was drying blood.

"Didn't want to add to yer pain," Lanky muttered. Down on his haunches he was peering at me with concern all over his face, in his hand was a damp cloth stained with blood.

"Seems best to leave it to get scabby like, best way to heal."

Kind old fellow, putting out his hand he patted me on the

wrist, "the bairn's alright, and that Kelly's sent down this."
He pushed a mug towards me.

My stomach turned over as I smelt the rum. Only too
vividly it brought back the scene on deck the night before.

"Take it away."

"You need something girl, you need something for the
shock."

"The shock's over. Anyhow, this kind of shock isn't put
right by a tot of rum."

The physical pain that your own humankind can inflict
gives you such a turn, such a jolt to your whole spirit that
nothing would put that right for a long time … if ever. It's
difficult to explain how you feel. It's like being brought up
sharp against a brick wall after walking along in peace and
tranquillity. You always knew there were such things as flog-
gings and beatings and those terrible things others could
inflict, but they'd not touched you until that very moment.
My feelings had nothing to do with the actual pain – it was
the violation. To have been at that man's mercy was the rub
and what had happened to me was just the same as a rape.

And what of Kitty? She was a slight little thing compared
with me – how had she stood up to it?

As if he knew what I was thinking Lanky moved across to
her. She lay burrowed in the blanket like a wounded animal.

"Kitty!" I muttered as Lanky stroked the tumbled cover.
"Kitty, 'tis alright now, we're back in our cabin."

"Go 'way." The heap under the blanket moved and kicked
out furiously.

"Give over Kitty, give over."

It took us half the morning to get her to put her head out.
Grief filmed over her eyes and a bitter twist hovered round
the corners of her mouth. We did not say a word to each
other; I sat and fed Anny while she slumped in the corner,
completely lacking any will to move.

The two fellows were kindness itself. For once Dicky
stopped talking about himself and even took the baby from

me to bring up her wind. Lanky was racked by another fit of coughing and could only shake his head in sympathy with us between the bouts.

Thompson put his head round the door half way through the morning. "Exercise time the captain says. You ain't been above for yer spell yet." He shouted these commands into the cabin for all to hear, then crept in with his finger to his lips whispering to us. "The lads is takin' this pretty bad. Mr Kelly and the captain's had a big set-to. Floggin' women ain't done, not often nohow, not regulations. Best come up now."

So Chace had not finished yet. He intended to parade us in front of the rest of them in our degraded, dishevelled condition.

I couldn't get Kitty to shift first of all. She was buried once again beneath the coverings. Looking at the cuts on her shoulders I guessed we'd both endured the same amount of punishment. My own back was stiff and stung from the wounds inflicted, but I was strong and that would have helped withstand the whip.

Her skin was paler and softer and her shoulders had a more dainty set about them.

"No," she muttered, "I'm not comin'."

"He'll make it worse for us, that he'll do. He's a wicked man and that's the start and finish of it. We've got to get to the end of the journey. No good makin' matters worse."

Thompson shouted from the doorway, "Cap'n says right now, youse to be on deck quick sharp."

Half cajoling, half dragging her I managed to reach the steps then Thompson came and gave a few shoves to start her on her way up to the deck.

Chace stood with his legs straddled wide, his fat face larded over with triumph. In his hands were several sheets of paper. There was no sign of the whip and the rest of the crew appeared to be going about their business as usual, but from the covert glances in our direction it was obvious they were all consumed by curiosity.

"Stand over there!"

I grabbed at Kitty's hand and made sure we walked backwards. I did not want to give him the satisfaction of seeing our wounds. The crowd of faces was a blur. All that stuck in my mind, and I'll never forget till my dying day was Ben Kelly's agony. Etched in misery his suffering was reflected in his eyes as he stared at Kitty.

"Back over there," Chace drew himself away as though to be near us was nothing but contamination. "You may be pleased to hear my report upon the whole disgraceful business. Your new masters'll know how to deal with such as you ... they're fully aquainted with the habits of harlots."

I remained silent. No point putting myself in line for another beating, but I could feel a tremor surge through Kitty as her hand clenched itself into a ball.

"Nothing to say?"

I looked into those hooded eyes. They held the ultimate thrill of inflicting pain upon others. Plain for all to see was that dangerous sensation of power which possessed him. That need of his to watch the suffering of others before he could himself feel pleasure. A shameful, twisted emotion.

"Answer me! Can't you understand what I'm saying?" Now he was shouting and I could tell by the sharp edge to his voice that he was speaking from a part of his inner self where vice ruled and the grasp he had over us could make him quite deadly.

There was no knowing what excesses his evil nature might drive him to. We were in the palm of his hand and commonsense bade me tread warily.

So I replied. More to calm him down than anything. "Yes Sir," and then I looked away.

His voice came again, "I'll read out the charge ..." there was a rustle of paper. You could have heard a pin drop on that deck.

Insofar as being master of this ship, the *Venus*, property of Robert Campbell, merchant of Sydney, I was ordered to take on board four prisoners bound for the settlement of Port Dalrymple.

In the course of our journey I observed their behaviour to be insolent and out of order on many occasions but I tolerated their presence as being on the high seas no other course was open to me. It was only when I found the women had ingratiated themselves with members of my crew and importuned those in charge to allow them certain liberties that I realised the full extent of the insubordination they were causing amongst my crew.

Upon the night of 14th June the two women, Charlotte Badger and Catherine Hagerty instigated a drunken orgy ...

But he did not finish. Snatching her hand from mine, Kitty leapt at him. His eyes must have been upon the words for he never saw her coming. She grabbed the paper from him.

Kitty flew to the side of the ship ripping it into shreds as she ran. For one second she was poised at the rail.

"You filthy old man!" She threw the scraps of paper to the four winds.

Stunned, we all stared at them both.

No more was this the captain of a ship taunting a convict.

We were seeing a twisted bitter man faced with a furious woman. For a fleeting moment their positions in life did not matter a jot.

Chace roared across the deck. He pounced on her like a cat leaping on a mouse. Digging his fingers into her shoulder he positively hurled her back at the mast. "Bind her ... bind her ..."

Not a sailor moved.

Thompson teetered as if he could not put one foot in front of the other and his thoughts were in just the same predicament.

"Kelly! Redmonds! Fetch the rope."

Still no one moved.

Chace spat with rage as he looked from face to face. Only sullen looks met him.

"The whip, fetch the whip from my cabin. Fetch it boy!" He yelled at Billy but the boy stayed rooted to the spot.

Everyone on that deck was frozen to the core. No one knew what to do. Kitty clasped the mast and buried her head in her arms.

The two mates stood side by side, their faces quite expressionless. Not a sailor shifted.

The silence was broken by Kelly. His face was a mask but a muscle twitched in his cheek as he tore his eyes away from Kitty. "Sir! This is a matter for the authorities. For us, being a trading vessel and not a navy ship, the captain hasn't such powers over the passengers."

"Passengers! You call this rubbish from the gaols passengers?"

Kelly gulped back whatever reply was on the tip of his tongue.

For a moment there was silence as the two men faced each other.

Then the honey slowly crept into Kelly's voice. I daresay he knew it was the only way to save Kitty from another thrashing. "Sir, you don't want no trouble down there at Port Dalrymple."

Still not one single man moved upon that deck.

Faced with dumb defiance Chace stood stock still. A livid flush spread across his visage, his chins drooped as his hands fell to his side.

"You Kelly, you'll pay for this. Do you refuse to follow my orders?"

Put in such a position what could Kelly do? Again he manhandled the words as best he could. "For the good of the ship Sir, for your wellbeing I'd caution against any ..."

"Mutiny!" Chace hissed the dreaded word.

"No Sir! Not mutiny. I'm speaking for the welfare of our vessel and all who sail in her. As these lads'll vouch, I've preached no sedition."

For quite a while that fat, ugly man stood motionless upon the deck.

Perhaps he was searching for any shred of dignity which would allow him to walk away from the situation that had developed. Perhaps he was grovelling around in the deepest parts of his mind for a chance to pay the mate back. Whatever it was that occupied him so intently he finally grunted to himself, swung on his heel and made for the steps to his quarters.

Pausing, he looked back over his shoulder. "Under lock and key with 'em. Two days before we reach port and they are not to be allowed outside their door."

When we were locked up again I had a good look at Kitty for the first time. If the beating had been bad for me, it had been a catastrophe for her. I'll wager her parents had never ever laid a hand on her. She'd always brimmed with that happy confidence of someone who's been loved and cossetted by a good family.

For me, well it had been dreadful and truly a violation, but I could not say it was an unprecedented event. I'd never forgotten the clank of the buckle on our old man's belt, too well I remembered the stinging upon my buttocks. Bad as a thrashing was, it was like all things, if you've had it once then next time it's not as terrible.

But for Kitty this was not the case at all. Such violence truly entered into her soul.

"To hell with the old divil, to hell ..." she screamed as I tried to calm her.

Then she reached up to the shelf above her bunk and pulled out her rosary. Instead of her usual reverent handling of the beads, this time she wrenched it out full length with such force it might well have snapped.

"No! No!" I tried to snatch it from her.

"To hell with it!" She threw it straight into the slop pail.

Those beads sank amongst the piss and the filth from our bowels.

I've never really believed in any god. Can't get along with the rantings of the Papists any more than the sermons from the old parson back at St Johns, but I was filled with mortal dread. I'd have reached down amongst all that swilling muck and pulled it out if I'd truly thought that would help. But it wouldn't. That act had been done by a believer and any action by such as me would have been worthless.

"Kitty!" I couldn't hardly believe what she'd done, "that's a blasphemy! You could go to hell for that."

"I've been in hell. I know what hell's like!" She screamed at me. "What could be more of hell than what happened last night. I'm finished, I'm finished. Where was the Holy Mother of God when she was needed?"

The men said nothing. Well men aren't given to pondering on those sort of matters are they?

"But dreadful things happen all the time Kitty. God's never taken much notice. You can only expect real justice in the next world."

I added that bit to comfort her, because even if I had my doubts about that next world, t'wasn't right for folks to turn their backs on their beliefs, not on account of a foul creature like that captain.

She snapped her mouth tight shut and stared ahead as though none of us existed. Even when Anny whimpered she made no move in the baby's direction and usually she'd be the first to pick up the child. The men glanced at me and shrugged.

"She'll come round," Lanky whispered, "I've been beat red raw before this. You ain't thinkin' right for quite a while after that."

Being beaten is very different for women than men. It was no good trying to explain this but I could understand so well how she was suffering. I felt the same and it was only because we all had to soldier on that I was not dwelling on it in a likewise fashion.

She was still sitting upright and silent when there was a

firm knock at the door. We all pulled ourselves up sharp, was it another order? Sitting there in the gloom, not even a candle, we'd been mulling over what would be waiting for us at Port Dalrymple.

"Kitty!" It was Kelly who stood in the doorway, he held out a hand to her and beckoned. "A word ... a word."

Like a white ghost she got up stiffly and followed him into the passageway.

We never knew what was said out there, but when she came back, instead of sitting bolt upright staring into space as she'd been doing, she lay down and went to sleep. A long sleep which must have done much to wash away those terrible thoughts. But she did not attempt to retrieve her rosary for all that.

Over the next forty-eight hours we were not allowed on the deck even once. We remained, crammed in that place with the foul stink of the bucket and food shoved through the door at mealtimes. There was nothing whatever to look at and the boredom allowed us plenty of time to consider what might await us.

"They'll put us straightway in gaol I reckon," Lanky looked on the black side.

"Not a bit of it," Dicky always had a more cheerful solution to any problem. "For one thing, there ain't nothin' like a gaol down there ... maybe a bit of a cell in a barracks but that'd be all. They're that short of labour they'll never shut us up."

"Mutiny he said it was ... well there could be real trouble there."

"Said in the heat of the moment Lanky. He can't afford to lose any of his crew, can he? Wants to go off sealin'. He needs every hand he can muster. Particularly Ben Kelly, he'd be lost without him. He won't be botherin' any more, mark my words."

But when we finally arrived at our destination, as the

anchor disappeared beneath the waters of the Tamar, it did not seem to me that the captain had forgotten all about it.

He ordered we were brought up and I could tell he was savouring every bit of our miserable condition as we stood in our ragged clothes with a steady drizzle soaking us.

"Take a first look at your new home ladies!" Each word oozed sarcasm. "There's savages there as'll eat the heart out of any as tries to escape and run into those forests. And look at the forests," his face lit up as he gestured towards the land, "miles and miles of trees, rocks and vines as would tangle you up in a trice. And there's tigers there, wild cats that can tear a mortal to pieces. From one side of that island to the other there's nought but cannibals and beasts."

I couldn't keep my eyes from the dark terrain. Certainly there was no sign even of a hut or a camp.

At least when we'd arrived at Port Jackson there was something of a settlement. The further we got from Sydney the more desolate the country became. Twofold Bay had been bad enough. Could this be even worse?

"And the sea ... why the sea's full of sharks round here, great fat brutes just waiting for a feed. Not that anyone'd be stupid enough to try and get away by sea, because where is there to go? Ain't nothin' beyond this, just empty ocean and mist and snow and ice right down to the South Pole."

He stood there in his jacket with braid decorating the lapels, all decked out like some popinjay. He almost looked like an officer on the *Earl*, for all his vessel was nought but a little trading ship. You could tell he was all puffed up with anticipation at what might be our fate and the gleam in his eyes as he gave the orders to Kelly, boded no good.

"You're in charge Kelly while I speak to the authorities. Redmonds is second in command. Get them prisoners back below. "

The two men glanced at each other. It seemed to me that something was amiss for Kelly opened his mouth to say something then thought better of it.

The boat was lowered and three or four seamen disappeared over the side. Chace took one long look at us and followed them.

"Why didn't you or I go with the old bastard?" Redmonds scratched his head in puzzlement. "He always takes one of us when he goes ashore. 'Tis common practice."

"I'd say he'll be making some kind of report if I read him a-right. He knows we're safe stuck out here. If one of us were there we'd be asked questions, we could speak up. This way gives him a free hand, he can tell them whatever he wants."

"Mutiny! That's what he said a few days ago. What if he accuses us of mutiny!" Redmonds' voice cut through the damp air.

At this everyone rushed to the rails as if they could read their captain's intentions from the set of his thick shoulders disappearing into the distance.

Kitty moved gingerly along the deck and stood beside Kelly.

"Mutiny? Don't they hang a man for that?"

No one answered.

"Get the prisoners below," Redmonds snapped at Thompson but Kitty moved to one side.

"And you're all going to sit here and wait for him to come back with soldiers and the like? Meek as lambs you'll wait till they take you off. Do you want to be strung up?" Kitty's face was suddenly alight with passion.

Everyone had heard her words. Already a muttering had started amongst the seamen. Kelly said nothing and Redmonds appeared to dither for a moment or two.

This was a new Kitty. Just as full of spirit as my dear old friend always had been, just as full of life, but now she was also afire with a new purpose.

That beating had knocked the stuffing out of her for a bit but it had forced her to look at the reality which was before us all and she recoiled from the terrible possibilities.

Could the charge of mutiny be laid?

Gone were her fanciful dreams of finding an officer and living a life of luxury. Instead she had found the real chance of a future. Kelly was there, a flesh and blood man who'd share his life with her.

"How can we risk it?" She spoke aloud for all to hear but her words were for him alone. How could they throw away that wonderful chance of love?

It was impossible to take such a risk, to even countenance that the tall, strong man at her side might be reduced to a body at the end of a rope.

The choice was clear to me. We could bow our heads and go on submitting to the brutish life before us, sink further down and give up any free will of our own ... or ...

"I'm no party to mutiny, never would be," Redmonds muttered to Kelly, but the first mate made no reply.

Until Kitty spoke up I'd never thought about such a possibility as Chace going to the officers and laying a charge against his own seamen. I'd guessed he'd accuse Thompson since he was a soldier. He'd give a bad report on us prisoners but we'd already been punished and the worst we could expect was being put back in the cells. But accusing his own men!

Now a nasty niggling doubt came into my mind. Kelly could face the ultimate penalty, probably several of the others too if Chace cited their refusal to flog Kitty.

We could be charged with inciting the crew to disobey orders or something similar. If Dicky had fourteen years for desertion then we might expect at least that for our part in the matter. Fourteen years would see us to the end of our lives as like as not. For me they'd certainly take Anny from me.

Briefly I contemplated all that could happen if that vicious man came back with the soldiers.

Kelly stood up and faced the men. "It could be the drop for some of us."

All eyes were upon him, only Redmonds shuffled around trying to ignore the situation.

Our little group of convicts was silent, Thompson was pop-eyed with dismay, he did not know where his loyalties should lie. Being the only soldier on the ship put him in a very exposed position, but like he always did, he just sat on the fence and waited. Dicky and Lanky said nothing either, for all the way men hold the floor whenever they can, when it comes to the point they often leave the real decisions to the women.

"Cat got yer tongues?" Kitty jeered at the men and stepped forward.

"Speakin' for meself I'm in no hurry to go ashore in this godforsaken hole."

She did not exactly proclaim her meaning, more left it open. "What's your view Charlotte? Back to our old grind, eh?"

Now everyone was looking at me. It was like when we'd been back at Twofold Bay, everyone was waiting for someone else to make the first move.

"What had you in mind?" I asked Kelly. The same thoughts had been going through everyone's head. Everything was happening so suddenly we hadn't thought out what might lie ahead.

"These are mighty unfriendly waters," was all he said.

"There's the great Southern Ocean all the way down to the Pole and precious few places for shelter."

"Up north there's the islands," the second mate muttered. "There's the Bay."

Redmonds snorted but before he could speak Kelly went on. "We keep away from the shores of New South Wales, that's for sure, but we can make for New Zealand and the Bay. Once he puts us in with them bastards in Port Dalrymple then word'll go up to the Governor on the next ship to Sydney and every man and his dog'll be looking for us. There'll be a proclamation. Everyone'll be keepin' a weather eye open for the *Venus*. T'will be mutiny then they'll add piracy too."

"We really are between the ould divil and the deep blue sea," Kitty whispered loud enough for those near us to hear.

Her eyes sparkled as she reached out and took Kelly's hand. "Which is it to be?"

For a moment he hesitated. He peered at the shoreline where the boat had disappeared into the river mouth, then he turned and looked at the limitless ocean before us with banks of thick grey cloud filling the sky. Far away a school of porpoises leapt through the waves.

"The deep blue sea!"

CHAPTER SIX

The Diary of Rev.Robert Knopwood, First Chaplain of Van Diemen's Land. Wednesday 6th August 1806.

Weather very wet. By Lt.Symonds we had information that the VENUS brig commanded by Mr.Chace was taken by prisoners at Pt.Dalrymple and ran away with. She had property to a very large amount, 10,000 pounds both for Pt.Dalrymple and this colony. For me there was 30 gls. of spirits and a barrel of porter.

For a full minute not a soul moved on that deck. We all knew we'd taken a fateful step.

"We'll be alright ... have no fear," Kelly beamed at Kitty and she threw her arms around his neck. The two of them clung together for just a brief moment as though they were the only two people in the whole wide world.

Cook's face split in a great grin. His teeth, which would have done credit to a horse, gleamed in his coffee-coloured face. The boys threw a couple of friendly punches at each other. Lanky even stopped coughing for a couple of minutes as he beamed around at us all and Dicky Evans slapped me on the shoulder.

"What's to lose girl eh? If they ever catches up with us now we'll soon be none the wiser. Short life and a merry one eh?"

For me I could not share in that particular sentiment for I had Anny in my arms and it was her future which mattered far more than my own. But we were all together in this any-how. I had no choice in the matter, and secretly I was relieved for it seemed likely that life in that Van Diemen's Land would have been a brutish business.

Redmonds, alone amongst the others, still appeared to waver as Kelly shouted orders to get ready to hoist the sails. Several times he went to the rails and stared towards land.

"Anyone not with us can go ashore. We'll lower the boat at once." Kelly was watching him closely. Several of the seamen had kept apart from the rest of us. With the sealing men from the *George* they'd formed themselves into a little group.

"We ain't part o' none o' this," one of the sealers spoke up. "Get that there boat out."

"If you ain't with us, then you're agin us. Best be gone," and Kelly turned to give the boys their orders.

"Slacken off that line lads. You give 'em a hand Thommo."

From now on it was obvious that Thompson was no longer a soldier. He was one of us.

Everyone watched in silence.

"There's still time Mr Mate," the spokesman shook his head as he gave the second mate a solemn look, "the lads'll speak up for yer."

Redmonds watched in silence as the last one clambered overboard and took up the oars.

"Comin'?" one of them yelled to him, "'Tis a hanging matter, make no mistake Josh."

"Don't listen to 'em. We'll never want … we'll never want for nothin'," one of our lads called out to Redmonds. "There's stores here as'll last us for years … and the grog! Barrels of it, barrels and barrels of grog!"

I truly think it was the thought of all those spirits and wine and porter in the hold which tipped the balance for Josh Redmonds.

"Away wi'ye. Gimme regards to the cap'n," he guffawed as he turned his back on the rowing boat.

Already our two lads were putting their backs to the windlass to haul up the anchor while Kelly stood ready at the helm.

The wind was very light, no more than a breeze. The drizzle had eased off till it was merely a mist. The sky was grey, the land was grey and the sea was so dull you'd be hard put to it to see where the shore began and the waves left off.

What if they could not get the sails to fill? I peered across the water.

What if we wallowed about like the old *Earl Cornwallis* had slopped to and fro in the doldrums? In my mind's eye I could see boatloads of redcoats with their muskets at the ready flying towards us from the river's mouth.

"Hurry! Hurry!" Muttering under my breath I stared up at the flapping canvas and slack ropes and willed the wind to rise and speed us on our way.

The drizzle turned to rain. More like the rain we had in the old country when clouds shrouded the Lickey Hills and puddles spread across the lane for days on end. In my five years in the Colony I'd become used to the violent changes of New South Wales – the baking heat of the sun when even little beetles rolled over and fried to death inside their armour, then the fierce storms and spears of rain lashing down upon dry cracked earth.

It appeared that this Van Diemen's Land had weather closer to Bromsgrove than that of the mainland.

I'll swear my heart stood still as we waited upon the deck. Thommo and Cook were putting their backs to the windlass now and had sent the two boys aloft. Kelly never moved from the helm. All stared at the grey sky and I don't doubt many a silent prayer was offered up and many a curse muttered under the breath.

"That's a puff I'll be bound," Dicky grinned beside me. "Yes ... yes ... here she comes."

A sudden swirl of mist cut the land off from the sea. It was as though a curtain had been drawn across the shoreline.

"Where?" For nowhere was there any sign of a breeze.

"Cat's paws on the water ... see," he pointed to the surface of the sea which had been smooth as glass. Now it was spattered with ripples. "She'll pick up now ... you see."

First of all the canvas slowly lifted and almost sighed from lack of purpose as it flopped back empty and slack. Then the *Venus* shuddered and shifted.

A faint movement of the water lifted the prow.

The rain had stopped. The mist swirled away and that Demon's Land lay clear, black and sinister before us.

But at least here, out on the water, there was movement in the air and that movement could only mean the wind had begun to pick up.

Suddenly the vessel lurched. With a crack one of the sails billowed out from the masthead.

"Cat the anchor!" Kelly bellowed at the men.

A cheer came up from everyone on deck as the ship shuddered for one moment then lurched forward.

We were away.

We'd taken the first step on that journey which would lead us to waters scarcely known about. We had a tidy little ship, plenty of provisions and we had each other.

What we did not have was a master. And that problem dogged the *Venus* from the moment she sailed away from Port Dalrymple to the very end of her voyage.

Kelly being first mate took charge but Joseph Redmonds was reckoned to be a pilot as well as second mate and kept trying to claim superior status. Dicky reckoned Redmonds only knew the harbour of Port Jackson and maybe Botany Bay. He liked a sly dig at the second mate. Fairly soon it became obvious that in fact Kelly was the more familiar of the two with the waters around New Holland, so most of the navigating fell to him.

The real trouble was the difference in their natures. That was the rock on which we all eventually foundered.

Kelly at heart was a law abiding man and it had been the sight of us women being beaten which had tipped the balance for him. What had started off as an attraction towards Kitty had grown into something deeper and much more lasting.

He'd reached that age when a man suddenly hankers after hearth and home. Ben Kelly had run away to sea at twelve years old but he'd come from solid stock and now he was assailed by the same yearnings as any mortal who's getting on in years – to settle down. To smell the bread a-baking and dandle a child upon his knee.

Redmonds was a completely different kettle of fish. A man of mixed race who'd had to fight his way up from whatever gutter spawned him. You could tell he was dazzled at the riches we had come by.

First move he made was to go round all the barrels and bales and boxes lashed on deck and let himself down into the hold to look over the stores. He didn't have Kelly's forthright character, he was fidgety and propped up his lack of confidence with the bottle.

An argument soon developed as to what was to be our course. Needless to say it was vital to keep away from other vessels, as news of the taking of the ship would spread along the seaboard in a trice.

"Mutiny! They'll have the navy out." Kelly was sitting in Chace's cabin. We all crowded around but it was too small for everyone. I was just inside the door.

"Don't forget the piracy too," Redmonds growled and from my position I could see the nervous twitch upon his face. "Mutiny and piracy ... 't'ain't a pretty picture eh? Well, with a fair wind we can leave off huggin' the shore and head out to sea."

"Where to?" Dicky Evans piped up, "Where do we go?"

"Go? Where should we go?" the second mate's eyes gleamed with greed. "We'll stop at sea. There's rich pickin's to be had ... plenty o' ships like the *Venus* heading out. We'll never lack."

"No!" Kelly spoke out and shook his head firmly. "We'll never make a new life if we go about it like that. Outright piracy ain't the way to go."

"We got muskets. Why there's even a cannon down below. Headed for Launceston that cannon was, to keep the French at bay. We can make good use of it."

"We'd be on the run from year's beginning to year's end," Kelly shook his head.

"Do you want to be put ashore in Sydney Town then? Take a stroll down High Street? Drop in and ask the Governor's advice?" Redmonds sneered.

Kelly ignored him. "The Bay of Island's the place to head for, like I said."

"Bloody Hell! Live amongst a crowd of savages? Have you lost yer senses man?"

"No, I've come to them, that's what," Kelly muttered.

The taking of the *Venus* had been done on the spur of the moment and since then it was obvious he'd been giving the future a lot more thought. "Haven't you considered what's going to happen to us all? We'll be hounded and harried across the seven seas by ships of the Navy. Never a safe harbour, never a moment when we ain't keepin' our eyes peeled. If it ain't our own ships it'll be the Hollanders or the Frenchies or the Spanish. Everyone'll have heard about the *Venus*. We'll be fair game for anything that sails the seas. No, I say we make for the Bay of Islands, the Maoris rule there."

"Savages!" muttered Redmonds.

"I've been there three times, all the whalers call in. Always plenty of craft at the Bay. There's Maori villages where you aren't wanted, I'll give you that. But there's many a chieftain's *pah* where any whaler's welcomed. Remember how much we have on board. We can set ourselves up good and proper, plenty of goods to trade."

"For what?" Redmonds lips still curled.

"For time, that's what. What we need's an American ship, get back home again. None of my folk'd hand us over to the British. No love lost there."

"And while you're waiting for this ship to arrive? What of that?"

"We'd be welcome amongst many a tribe there. We've plenty to offer. Like I said, I've been there before, two years ago I spent nigh on a month in a Maori village there. They treated us like kings. Looked after me and the crew like their own they did. Took us hunting, took us searching for the timber we needed for repairs. And this time there's a lot to offer, plenty to trade ... barrels of pork, all that cloth, there's spades and shovels. Plenty of stuff."

"And the grog," Redmonds chuckled as the thought suddenly struck him. "You can get anything with the grog, food, shelter, women ... and more women!"

I couldn't help smiling to myself, as Redmonds was sorely disappointed in us two women. Kitty had moved into the captain's cabin with Kelly and I stopped firmly with Lanky and Dicky. I'm sure he'd thought I'd jump at the chance to find myself a man but I wasn't prepared to tie myself to any fellow who chanced along. Certainly not one with earrings and a great mop of hair tied back. No thank you, I'd stop on my own for the time being.

Kelly's eyes narrowed as he looked at the second mate. "Watch out for the grog. It's been the downfall of many a ship's company."

"And who give you the right to take command?" Redmond towered over Kelly who was sitting in the master's chair.

"First mate of the *Albion,* First mate of the *Venus* ... I think that gives me the right, Josh."

Joseph Redmonds had come from some place north of New Holland. Been born and raised in a port on one of the larger islands. Partly because of his many years in small vessels plying their trade in the Pacific, he considered he had a knack with charts and navigating. But if it came to the skills needed to run a ship and make the real decisions, then it seemed Kelly was our leader and should remain so.

So by popular assent we all took our orders from Ben Kelly, and a fair hand he made of being ship's captain. Soon we'd settled into a routine which rarely varied from day to day unless the lookout chanced to see a sail upon the horizon. In that case extra canvas would be hoisted and we'd scud off in the opposite direction.

Four seamen had gone ashore with Chace and four more

had chosen to follow him with the men from the *George*. Being short-handed, Kelly ordered Thommo to work with the lads and Cook on deck. Dicky Evans spent most of his time aloft, on account of him being a seagoing man by trade. Kitty and I spent time in the galley now that Cook was busy. Between us we cared for young Anny and saw to the needs of Lanky who was steadily losing the little strength he'd had.

Under Kelly's command the *Venus* was a tight little ship and run just as well or even better than when Chace had been in charge. The daily routines went as smooth as silk and if he'd ever felt a bit worried about how things might turn out, well any fears melted away as his confidence grew, a confidence fed and nurtured by Kitty, who rarely left his side.

Kitty was fair dizzy with love. Every daylight moment her eyes followed him. When darkness fell and we all gathered together for our meal she sat by his side and when they went off to their cabin for the night, they moved off, arms entwined as one person.

And for his part, such tenderness showed in his face whenever he looked at her that my heart could not but rejoice. They were made for each other.

"We're going to Nantucket. Ben's family have lived there from way back." Kitty told me more than once. On the first occasion she mentioned that town I quizzed her about the place, but it soon became obvious she knew little more than I did. "Well Ben says 'tis a grand town."

"Where is it then?"

"'Tis way over the sea, he says Nantucket's an island, thirty miles out from shore."

"Another Van Diemen's Land!" Didn't sound very nice, scoffing like that, but I felt the nearest thing to envy when I listened to all that talk.

"Not on your life. There's families living there as have been there for generations and generations ... like that Captain Bunker's, that captain Ben's always talking about. There's grand houses up on the hill and there's whaling ships lined up down at the quay." Her eyes sparkled as she saw this wonderful haven in her mind's eye.

"And how are you going to get all that way across the ocean?"

"There's many a ship that'd be eager to have him on board. We'll have no problems when we get to the Bay. Mark my words if he says so then it's right. And Charlotte, he'll speak up for you, we'll take you with us. You'll soon find a decent husband, never you fear."

I listened to this with very mixed feelings. "And what about the others? What about the boys and Thommo and Lanky and the rest?"

"They'll find a berth easy, Ben says so. Plenty of whalers call in there, they'll find work in no time at all."

"And don't you think folk'll start asking questions when they see the *Venus,* someone could send word back to Sydney, eh? People know more of what happens in lonely places than under their noses in a city street. It get's noticed all the easier."

"Oh you! You're such an old sobersides. Always looking at the things which could go wrong. Think of what's right. Think of all the wonderful things we're going to have in our lives … just think."

"We've got to be very careful. There'll be no mercy for us if they catch up with us." All the time I was thinking of Anny. Could she be left without anyone to care for her, would she end up in the Orphan Asylum?

"There you go again, always lookin' on the black side, fussing about what could go wrong. We're away, we're free, nothing can stop us now."

"Like poor Mary Bryant I suppose?"

"And who might she be?"

"T'was on everyone's lips. T'was the talk of the Colony. She was a Devon girl who met her man on the First Fleet."

"Goodness that's years and years ago."

"Not so long … fifteen years if that. And look what happened to her."

"Can't say I know."

"Mary and Will Bryant were nigh starvin' to death. They stole the Governor's fishing boat and made for islands many, many miles away. Eight of them with Mary's two babes. Well they reached this island, 'twas a miracle the distance they travelled. They pretended they were shipwrecked folk and treated right royally. But that Will liked the bottle. In his cups he boasted of their escape. Some were hanged, some died in prison. She'd already lost one little one, the other died on the journey back to London."

"They were quite prepared to hang her, make no mistake about it. But some rich, clever lawyer heard about her plight. He must have been good at heart because he defended her and it was said she got off. And good luck to her, she must have endured such misery in losing her husband and both poor babes 'tis a wonder she still had her wits about her."

"Difference with us we've got Ben. He's not going to be tricked into opening his mouth at the wrong time, he's a ..."

"But the same can't be said for Josh Redmonds can it? Give him a rum and a few willing ears and he'd start bragging and scupper the lot of us."

"Well it'll not be like that will it? Ben says where we're goin' there'll be precious few other white people ... some of course because that's where the whalers come in, but we'll be amongst the Maoris and he says they're a fine race. Honourable and very proud people. Once you're a friend of theirs you'll be alright and he's got friends amongst the Maoris."

We all looked up to Ben and it was as well he took the reins firmly in his hands because Redmonds would soon have led us all to disaster. For one thing, he was determined to find women. Familiar with every low tavern and brothel from Calcutta to Sydney, he was not viewing a life without the ladies with much pleasure. Several times he urged we went ashore. North of Twofold Bay were several settlements where natives and a handful of whites lived; he knew he'd find what he wanted there.

"With all we've got aboard, why, there'll be women all round for you. They'll be scratchin' each other's eyes out to get to you lads." He was always harping on the subject to the other men.

Whether it was to drown his sorrows or just from natural inclination, he took to the drink something terrible and in that respect Ben had little power over him. No longer did he strum happily on the guitar and sit on deck of an evening, instead he retired all by himself to his cabin where he'd lined the walls with bottles and barrels and could swig himself away into oblivion.

There was a faint undercurrent of sympathy for his views since several of the others had a hankering to go ashore as we sailed back up north.

Thommo in particular was not a seagoing man and I suspect, being a soldier, he feared more than the others the perils of the sea and also the retribution which would be laid at his doorstep if the *Venus* was taken. Perhaps he'd hoped to get away from the ship if we touched land, get himself back to the militiary – he could always deny any part in the mutiny, make it seem he was forced to join in. In his usual dithering way I could see he'd make up any tale to suit the circumstance.

Resolutely Ben Kelly ignored their backsliding opinions and set a course for this Bay of Islands he reckoned on being such a haven for us.

I listened to all the talk; the plans, the wild hopes, the craven backsliding. They'd all such different aims and our future seemed to be cloudy in the extreme. I feared much for what might happen, not for myself but for Anny. She was plumping out and was a most beautiful baby, happy at the breast, content as she lay kicking on a blanket, completely unaware of the peril surrounding her life. Too easily I could see how her innocent world might be shattered. If anything happened to me, what of her? Who would give another thought for a convict woman's child? Would she end up homeless like the gaunt, wary children of the streets or in the bleak Asylum. I lay awake through the devil's dancing hours night after night worrying about the future.

"Sure and she'll be alright, look at the child! Look at the little poppet, with eyes like that she'll come to no harm." Kitty was in that blissful state when the world outside hardly mattered at all. Her whole future was bound up in Ben Kelly. Once or twice I had a dig at her, reminded her of those officers she'd always hankered after.

"Think of all those uniforms Kit … and here you are with a pirate!"

"You wait till I'm a fine lady sitting in me parlour in Nantucket! Then you'll be proud to come calling for afternoon tea."

Kitty was wholly absorbed with the amazing twist her life had taken. Her eyes scarcely left Kelly's person. She had made the captain's cabin into a cosy little home for them both. Rummaging amongst the stores on board she found some damask, a luxury much prized from Chinee and obviously once destined for an officer's home. Soon damask draped the bed and stiff white linen covered the table. Fine china also appeared out of the hold and teacups as fine as eggshells graced the shelves.

Obviously Kitty came from a genteel home and doubtless when in service her standards never dropped. "A man needs a comfortable place to lay his head," and she made sure the pillows were of the finest down and the bunk had real linen sheets on it.

Even if those settlers down in Port Dalrymple were living on the edge of civilisation it seems they still yearned for the finer things in life. The hold was full of the little luxuries they'd ordered.

If Kitty was consumed with the need to conjure up such refinement, then Kelly was not backward in following suit. This sudden gentility must have struck a distant chord from the past. After a life of hardship where most likely the only hearth he sat beside was in a tavern or a bawdy house the sheer comfort of sharing his life with Kitty warmed his heart.

Perhaps it brought back the memory of that home he'd left. The love of a mother and who knows, maybe sisters, aunts and cousins. That gentler side to existence which had been denied him by his calling.

Whatever it was, he revelled in these new-found comforts of home. Like two doves in springtime billing and cooing in the apple tree back home the pair of them glowed with love.

Words don't matter when love takes charge. Love neither needs explanation nor brooks criticism. They'd stroll the deck together, sit and gaze upon the sea and just marvel in each other's company. In Kitty's eyes Ben Kelly was all she'd ever need in a man – steady and yet with a nature that could flare into passion. Kitty was the spark which kindled that flame. First had come the flicker, then came the fire, then the blinding conflagration consumed them both and being so close I basked in the reflected glory.

Surprised and amazed, I learnt so much for I'd never been close to two such as them before. To me love was most times a humdrum affair such as I'd seen in the farmyard. At its best the day to day existence of Ma and Father, at worst the snarls and snaps of mismatched folks who fought all day and lay in misery most nights.

Love had been a matter of necessity and habit.

Most times, not always. Admitted there'd been those few hours with that soldier. But I'd never fooled myself it was love. I hadn't shed a tear when he left. I'd not really felt for him, I just wanted to enjoy him.

Somewhere there was someone, I was quite sure of that. Someone who could make the world turn upside down just for me. But where? And when would I ever meet him?

At least I'd recognise love now when it finally came my way.

Kitty and Kelly had found love. They had the great oneness of their bodies but they also had the sharing of their souls.

CHAPTER SEVEN

Letter from Captain Matthew Flinders to Governor King, Sydney, 9th September, 1803.

Sir,

I have to inform you of my arrival here yesterday in a six-oared cutter, belonging to His Majesty's armed vessel Porpoise, commanded by Lieut.Fowler, which ship I am sorry to state to your Excellency I left on shore upon a coral reef, without any prospect of her being saved ... being 729 miles from this port.

The ship Cato, which was in company is entirely lost upon the same reef and broken to pieces without anything having been saved from her, but the crew, with the exception of three, are, with the whole of the officers, crew and passengers of the Porpoise, upon a small sand-bank near the wrecks, with sufficient provisions and water saved from the Porpoise to subsist the whole, amounting to eighty men, for three months ...

After the above statement it is unnecessary for me to make application to your Excellency to furnish me with the means of relieving the crews of the two ships from the precarious situation in which they are placed ...

I have &c

Mattw.Flinders

"Ship ahoy!"

"Tumble up lads! Tumble up! All hands ahoy!" Kelly's voice roared out in answer to Dicky's warning.

"Sail to starboard! Sail to starboard!"

"Holy Mother of God. 'Tis like every banshee in Cork was screechin' at us."

Dicky's dreaded call shattered the calm scene on deck. The lads had been below, Kitty and I were sunning ourselves in the last rays of the afternoon sun with the baby lying on her blanket between us. Thommo was cleaning the barrel of his musket and Lanky sat, head in his huge hands, letting the sun warm up his back.

On our feet in a trice, we raced to the rail.

Sure enough, far away against the horizon was the shape of a large sail and even as we all strained our eyes it loomed a trifle closer.

From the grim expression which settled on Ben Kelly's features as he gripped the glass, he had little doubt of the vessel's intention. "She's a navy ship! She's seen us alright. She's after us!"

Even I could see the predicament facing us. Ben had told us we'd be heading in an easterly direction fairly soon. That was where the Bay of Islands lay. This vessel was approaching exactly from that direction.

Fortunately on this particular day there was a fair breeze blowing. Kelly bellowed to the lads to let out more canvas. He changed course to the north so we were running parallel to the coast but the navy ship closed on us minute by minute.

"Why don't we go out to sea? We'd stand more chance," muttered Thommo as he stood near us and watched fearfully whilst the other ship relentlessly gained on us.

"We'd be run down before we'd put any distance between us," Cook shook his head knowingly, "them islands dead ahead, that's where Ben's makin' for."

Islands! You couldn't really call them that. They were just a scattering of large rocks where seals lay sunning themselves. What protection could those barren outcrops yield?

"Cook!" Kelly yelled, "you're leadsman. Take the lead."

Swinging the lead was the last thing anyone had bothered about, seeing as how we'd been well out to sea not so long ago. But Cook was nimble enough and soon was hanging over the bows. "By the mark ten ... by the mark eight ..."

As the bow of the *Venus* creamed through the waves his singsong voice led us into sanctuary.

The minutes passed by with agonising slowness as we edged closer and closer to the land.

Kelly made straight for the scattered group and had put the huge rocks between us and our pursuer within the hour. The larger vessel was unable to follow us into the shallow water in the lee of the land. Instead she backed off a way and rode the waves like a cat waiting for a mouse to come out of its hole.

Redmonds swayed along the deck, very much the worse for wear.

"Wassup? Wassup?"

"Obviously you are mister. Just up eh? Well get below again. We've trouble enough!"

"By the mark six!"

"Mighty fine. Mighty fine ... look lively lads. Tend them lines."

By the time he gave the order to drop anchor and lower sail the *Venus* had almost come to a standstill anyhow.

Within a couple of minutes the ship was quite motionless.

"And do we just sit here and wait for them to come and get us?" Kitty couldn't take her eyes from the huge vessel waiting out in the open sea.

"Look at the sun!" Kelly took her arm and swivelled her round so she was facing inland.

We all blinked as we tried to focus after staring out for so long at the gunmetal sea.

The sun was a great golden ball hanging just above a distant mountain.

"We wait till the moon's risen. 'Tis not full moon but it'll be enough to light the way. All we need is to see any rocks. Once we're out at sea again we'll be shot of them scoundrels."

There's precious little dusk in New Holland. In the old country trees and fields gradually disappear into the gloom, and darkness falls as gently as a cloak being drawn across the land. Here it's one minute with the countryside bathed in glaring light and the next darkness.

Hearts in mouths every one one of us watched the darkness fall. Even Redmonds had sluiced himself down and if it wasn't for the stink of rum you'd not know he'd been drunk as a lord.

How slowly, oh how very slowly that great orange globe descended towards earth. By contrast, once it had touched the horizon the black line of hills appeared to swallow it. Gulp, gulp, gulp and the sun was gone. Suddenly all that remained was the half light reflected down from the sky.

Then all was darkness.

A loud snuffling was to hand, probably a sea elephant or maybe seals making their way to new resting places. Then the faintest glimmer shot through the darkness. The ship was still waiting, her lights pinpointed her position.

A commotion came from across the silent waters as our pursuer let down his anchor.

"Ah … got you mister," Kelly chortled to himself.

"Seems more like he's got us," Kitty shook her head.

"Not on your sweet life. Didn't you hear that? He's dropped his anchor and he's sitting it out. He thinks we're bottled up but we ain't. Not nohow."

As we waited in silence the night became even more dark and dense.

"Black as the inside of a black cat's ear on a dark night … that's for us!" Kelly muttered "Douse them lights!" Our only two lanterns were promptly turned out.

Once the wicks had been turned down the darkness was complete. It took a few moments for our eyes to become accustomed to the jet black night.

And so we sat half the night out as that navy ship kept her vigil and we waited for the moonlight to guide us.

Finally, when the pale light was enough to light the way, Kelly made a move.

Nimble as a cat that could see in the darkness he moved about the deck giving orders to the men.

"No shoutin' or yellin'. Remember sounds travel across

water just like we're in the next room. We're slipping out of here real sneaky. Stand by!"

Sail fluttered aloft, then it billowed out.

"Two men to the windlass now. Anchor up but no shoutin' or yellin'."

After a few moments he spoke again.

"Swing the lead true! You give it to us good Cooky," and the *Venus* began to move ahead.

He called quietly up to the boys in the shrouds and they had the *Venus* shifting within minutes.

"By the lead six ... by the lead seven ..."

Ever so slowly we edged around one of the bigger rocky outcrops.

For nigh on ten minutes we continued and always it was seven fathoms deep.

Now the biggest islet was firmly between us and our pursuer. No glimmer was visible from her deck.

"By the lead eight ... by the lead ten ..."

"Damn my whistle we're through. Break out that top gallant my bonny boys. We'll show 'em a clean pair of heels."

Whoever was on watch aboard that ship didn't have a chance. Our little *Venus* slipped out from behind those rocks and we were out in deep water within ten minutes. The last we saw of our pursuer was her lights placidly glowing in the darkness as she lay at anchor waiting to pounce at dawn.

By the time the moon sailed out from the clouds we were on a completely deserted ocean.

"I'd sure like to see that captain's face at first light. My oath I'd give a year's pay for it!"

"No you wouldn't Ben. We're away and lucky to have our lives," Kitty shook her head.

All had gone so well till we came across that ship but now fate began to toss a few challenges and the wind got up as we prepared to make our way across to New Zealand.

"No point battling these headwinds, we'll make for the

Reef," Kelly and Redmonds were having one of their rare discussions.

"Could do wi' some shore leave!" Redmonds jumped at any chance to indulge himself.

"You watch yerself Josh ... uncharted waters and unknown folk!"

"Lead me to 'em. Ain't no change out of what we got here!"

I knew he was getting at me ... no bedwarming from me so he'd look elsewhere.

Well!

When we reached the Reef there followed a time of the most serene sailing I'd ever imagined.

The coast up and down to that Demon's Land had been beautiful with the sandy shores and brilliant greeny-blue forests stretching away to dark hills in the distance, but the scene which now lay before us day after day was almost beyond describing. Turquoise waters, fish leaping from the depths, little islands fringed with yellow sand and far away mountains on the mainland.

The only other craft ever seen were native canoes and they were all so absorbed in their own business no notice was taken of the *Venus*.

Sometimes Kelly would order the anchor to be dropped if we were close to a particularly pleasant lagoon. Redmonds had his wish and got ashore but whether he found women I neither knew nor cared. I fancy it would have been no, for the natives appeared to melt into the surrounding bush and just disappear when we landed. No doubt they'd had enough of marauding ship's crews.

We replenished our water, the lads swam and fished, and many a night we dined on lobsters broiled over wood ashes under the starry skies. I'd dabble my fingers in the sea as we rowed ashore and marvel at the stream of brilliance from the phosphor of the deep. My wrists and fingertips were on fire and as I lifted them out and watched the water fall back I'd muse upon the wondrous nature of this life I was living. Were these the same droplets that had washed against the great hull of the old *Earl*?

"You're nought but a country wife!" Kitty spent her time collecting shells whilst I searched amongst the undergrowth looking for likely looking leaves.

"You can't live on salt pork and biscuits alone. You need some greens inside you."

She laughed at me. "You be careful, our Charlotte. How'd you know them plants is fit to eat? Sure we'll be leavin' our bones here. How'd you know we'll not wake up dead tomorrow morning, our guts shrivelled away wi' the poison?"

"Because I know, that's why." And in a strange way I did. If you're brought up in the country there are hidden signs you look for from the time you take your first steps. The purple of the deadly nightshade bodes no good, the red of the toadstool shouts at you to keep away and the sinister dark green of the yew speaks of death to man or beast. All the world over the plants have their language and it's plain to be read.

"Just like you know when the dandelion's just right for the wine."

"Dandelion wine! A rare drop I don't doubt!" scoffed Kitty.

"The flowers have to be picked on a sunny day," she didn't worry me with her clever remarks, for just a moment I was back home, thousands of miles from all the worry of our present situation.

"Our Ma would watch the sky carefully for fear they'd run to seed before the sun came out. To pick in the damp was asking for trouble. Only the best were picked, far from the lane where the dust of the cart wheels spoiled them. When she gave the word we'd hurry out and scour every corner.

"Back in the kitchen we spilled those dandelions out on

the table and picked the yellow heads from the green round them. The flowers were put in a bucket and boiling water poured over them. Then they were left in the corner of Daisy's shed because the smell was something powerful.

"Each day the bucket was stirred. Finally the liquid was strained off, the brown remains of the flowers thrown on the rubbish heap and honey stirred into the liquid. Ma would then tip it all into the old crock in the kitchen, as now was the time for a slice of toast covered in yeast to be floated on top, and everyone knows yeast won't work in the cold.

"Each day Lizzie and I would lift the muslin cover to look at the seething mass. After the first wild frothing it worked itself out and finally died down. Then the wine was strained and corked, and within six months the first bottle could be opened."

Tears filled my eyes. For a moment I was sitting in the inglenook back home sipping that golden fluid.

"Don't seem too exciting to me!"

How could I tell a city girl who knew of nought but streets and shops how wondrous was the russet sheen on the horse chestnut, how dainty were the catkins fluttering in the wind.

I couldn't even begin to explain how my life had been ruled by the coming and going of the seasons.

Spring brought the soft yellow of the buttercup and the first lambs skipping upon the hills. When childhood had passed and I was grown broad and strong I was expected to turn the soil down each side of the vegetable patch with fork and spade then sieve out all the little lumps of earth and stones leaving it soft and smooth for the seeds. Carrots, onions, parsley and little tiny cabbages had to be planted out.

On the fair breezes of summer came the white butter-flies to eat everything I'd planted, so it meant many hours toiling in the sunshine with water in a pot picking off the caterpillars. Whilst at night I'd be out looking for slugs and scrunching snailshells underfoot. As the weather warmed up drifts of daisies and cow parsley patchworked the fields and whenever there was a spare moment I'd be down in the watermeadow and along the paths searching out where the dandelions were clustered so we knew where to come when it was wine making time.

Hard on the heels of summer came autumn. Autumn was a season which never seemed to end, it was hard work from start to finish. The apples had to be gathered in and carefully laid out in the loft so they weren't touching each other. There were crabapples to pick and jam to make, blackberries to gather in, boil up and turn into bramble jelly. Then there were mushrooms to search for, nuts to gather and occasionally, if Father had been lucky, a pheasant to pluck. The garden needed clearing of all the old plants and fallen leaves then dug over so that the frosts of winter could break the topsoil into smaller and smaller grains until, when the frost finally finished, it looked as though it had been passed through a cheesecloth.

Ah winter. That was a time when for a short while I could rest, there was little to do when the ground froze to iron and the snow banked up along the lane. I'd go up into the loft and look over the apples. Any that seemed as though they'd be on their way out had to be brought down and cut into rings then threaded onto lengths of string and hung up like giant necklaces to dry until they were needed. There was the net to mend that we put over the fruit to keep off the blackbirds, there was a pillow or two to stuff if we'd got enough feathers from the chickens ... and there was that wonderful feeling when you'd finished your work and the wind howled round the chimney while Jack Frost drew patterns on the window, that feeling that you could nod off next to the fire as there wasn't a task waiting to be done for once.

Yes, I was a country wife but that was most likely what had saved me and Anny for when you're in tune with the world around you then you can't come to much harm.

As we moved very slowly between the islands and Reef

I could have wished our journey would never end for the peace of nature seeped into my very bones.

"Can't we get a move on?" Josh Redmonds was impatient, particularly as Ben flatly refused to sail during the hours of darkness.

"I ain't familiar with these waters, I need to see what's up."

"We could shift ourselves faster than this!"

"And end up like the *Porpoise?*"

"That was on the outer Reef."

"Even so, 'tis not worth taking chances. Captain Flinders and his men got back for help to Port Jackson in just over a fortnight. Imagine, nearly eight hundred miles in that time."

But time never hung heavily. How could it in such beautiful surroundings? Once again we dropped into that cheery habit of gathering together on the deck of a night.

Up till then we'd just accepted we were heading for this Bay of Islands but in that first flurry of making off with the *Venus* nothing had been explained about the place. Most of us were hard put to even visualise where it might be, although we'd all heard of the existence of the country called New Zealand which had two islands.

"The Bay's right up in the north but 'tis the far side from the way we'll approach, on the eastern coast of the North Island," Kelly explained to us all. "I called in three times when I was mate of the *Albion*. Came in with Eb Bunker – fine ship, even finer master. I'd not want to serve any other captain and I'd still be with him but he took a fancy to come ashore ... had some crazy idea of becoming a farmer! Only lasted a year and he's back at sea but by then I'd had to find another ship. I came out from London on the *Albion* in '99 with him and it only took three months and fifteen days, that was the shortest passage ever at the time, no idea if it's been improved on since. Mind you, now he's back he'll be looking to bettering his time again.

"Eb Bunker's first ship was the *William & Ann*, came out

in '91 and '92, he'd no luck with her. But when he took over the *Albion* 'twas different altogether. I'd trust my very life to Eb, mebbe both of us hailing from Nantucket's the reason. The young lads in Nantucket cut their teeth on Nantucket Bar. Soon as he could manage an oar he'd never left the sea. There's nothing he doesn't know about the sea and its ways. Three times I've doubled Cape Horn with him."

"What's 'doubling'? " one of the boys wanted to know.

"Making it round a point or a cape. There's westing when you go from east to west and likewise easting when you leave the Pacific and come round into the Atlantic. If a ship's not lucky in the Atlantic then they make westing round the Horn and carry on the hunt for whales in the Pacific. Sometimes you're that fortunate you can have four thousand barrels or more in nine months, I've seen the ocean black with their great bodies ... sometimes if you're not lucky it takes up to nearly four years. Then you're back round the Horn west to east. I've never had it so bad that way, but coming out when you leave the Atlantic and enter the Pacific you can feel hell is at your feet."

Perhaps it was the Celtic ancestry shared by Kelly and Kitty or perhaps it was just that elusive chemistry which can work on the deck of a ship just as well as in a parlour. Whatever it was, when Kelly spun his yarns they fired Kitty's imagination and as he looked round the rapt faces of his audience it was upon her that his glance lingered.

Closing her eyes she was snared in that web of enchantment. Every word, every phrase increased the magic of the tale for Kelly knew how to use the language of epic and fable. When he spoke of the ships that sailed the oceans around Australia they billowed along the silken threads of that web with the same sureness of the old Vikings and Norsemen circling the Northern seas.

"The last time I sailed with Eb Bunker we left the Falklands with a full south-westerly blowing. That storm blew for four weeks, sending the ship on her beam ends time and again as she battled seas like mountains. Everything which could shift was secured and the hatches were hammered and wedged in place. As we reached the Horn the wind fell and a dismal fog enveloped us where the warm waters of the Atlantic meet the icy wastes of the Antarctic. After several days of this the storm returned in full force. Soon we forgot what it was like to feel any warmth, for no fires were allowed on board. Soaked to the skin day and night we finally reached the southern tip of the continent where there was nothing but low barren hills. At fifty-five degrees south the world's girt by a furious, screeching girdle of winds as thunderous waves from the lower Pacific crash into the great swells of the Atlantic.

"It was our bad luck to have this south-westerly still blowing. It took seven full days to claw our way one hundred and twenty miles to the west but then a fearsome tempest arose and Ed Bunker had no help for it but to turn tail and run. In three hours she'd lost all the distance she'd made in that week.

"Then he was faced with a decision that only he could make, him alone. Whether to try again or keep going across the ocean to the Cape of Good Hope? That's a terrible long way round to the Pacific.

"I'll always remember him as I stood at his elbow, a giant of a man fully six inches taller than myself, ice coated his jacket and his eyebrows were white with frost. He said not a word as he stood sensing every movement in that ship, he knew exactly where each blast of wind would fill a sail or what sheet needed tightening or making free.

"I guessed his main fear was how thick the ice might form upon the vessel, whether she'd become unstable and heel over. The only words he uttered were to the helmsman, his concentration on the task in hand was complete.

"I was impatient, I should have kept my mouth shut but the tension was so great I asked, 'to the Cape, Sir?'

"And he laughed … many a captain would have felled me to the deck for the brass of it. "No Mr Mate, I ain't accustomed to going back on my word, nor turning back from the Horn. We'll head for the Straits."

"There are two routes around the Horn, one round the furthest tip and one many miles to the north when you pass through the Straits of Magellan with the mainland of South America on your starboard, and the Tierra del Fuego to port.

"Roaring out above the wind he never stopped giving orders for the sails to be trimmed again and yet again as the vessel ploughed her way up through the choppy Atlantic waves till she reached the Magellan Passage.

"The Straits of Magellan are three hundred and thirty miles long. They're the wickedest stretch of water in the world and I reckon the bottom's white with the bones of drowned sailors.

"Rounding Cape Espiritu Santu you enter what appears to be a wide bay which suddenly narrows, in fact that is the first of two narrows. Both are scoured with currents of up to thirteen knots. On either side steep cliffs tower over the poor, solitary ship. Their precipices are streaked with snow and swept by violent winds. Once past these hazards the sailing seems straightforward for a while and you could be forgiven for thinking the worst is over even though the tides are enormous and run at forty feet in height.

"But with the Straits, the worst is to come and as mile succeeds mile it becomes more and more perilous. Back and forth you tack between a myriad of barren, windswept islands where the slightest mistake could send you to the bottom or leave you marooned for a slow death in that desolate place. Peaks and snowy slopes surround you; one mountain is over seven thousand feet high with three glaciers descending from its summit.

"There is no crueller stretch of water in the world and there are many wrecks to prove it; on all sides are submerged shoals and rocks with treacherous currents snatching at your vessel. So it's with relief that you reach Desolation Island and know you are near the end of your journey." Here Kelly paused for a while …

"But this can be the most perilous time of all. This is when the true mettle of a ship's master is tested for he has to balance the danger of the great rollers of the Pacific he's about to enter against the rock strewn haven he is leaving. He has to pick wind and sea and current and decide exactly when to enter that tumultuous ocean – for the Four Evangelists wait for him. Four rocky outcrops which have sent many an exhausted ship and crew to the bottom.

"At the time I'm talking about we'd already been several weeks making our passage and yet all could be lost with one false move.

"'We'll stick our noses out, if 'tis too fierce we come back and anchor in the lee of old Desolation,' Eb balanced the risks with the ease of a mummer at the fair juggling balls.

"The south-westerly still blew ferociously, the sea buffeted us, kelp streamed along in the ocean currents. All was utter confusion. Three times on the next three days we stuck our noses out as he ordered. Sails trimmed, the helmsman ready to make a run for it but each time Eb judged the risk too great and ordered him to return to the safe anchorage.

"On the fourth day we sailed once again from our haven. As we neared the open sea we heard the screaming of the wind and faced those tumultuous waters yet again. Everyone of us on board was heartsick of the noise, the cold and the tension, and to me it was a wonder a man could still stand there and make a sound judgement.

"'Mr Mate,' Eb shouted above the howling gale. 'What do you see?'

"Truth to tell I'd not looked up at the sky, I could not take my eyes off the fearsome sea.

"Strange, very strange when I looked up I saw a patch of blue sky dead ahead.

"I always remember the little smile playing on Eb's lips

'enough blue sky to make a pair of sailor's trews,' he repeated the old saying half to himself.

"That break in the cloud gave us just what we wanted, the westerly suddenly backed off and in its place came a spanking breeze from the east.

"He shouted his orders to the helm and the vessel leapt forward into the Pacific. The turmoil of the last weeks were left behind us." Ben paused for a moment. "No Sir, I'd rather spend one hour with Eb Bunker than my whole life with some of the yellow bellied captains I've known."

We sat in silence for a while. With the water gently slapping against the sides of the ship, the wind caressing and soft upon our faces and bodies, it was impossible to imagine such wild weather could ever blow up and sweep ships and men away to the bottom of the ocean.

CHAPTER EIGHT

Eternal Father strong to save
Whose arm doth bind the restless wave,
Who bid'st the mighty ocean deep
Its own appointed limits keep;
O hear us when we cry to thee
For those in peril on the sea.

William Whiting 1825-78

The loss of those eight men who left the *Venus* at Port Dalrymple was sorely felt. Once out of the sheltered waters of the great Reef and back in the turbulent ocean every single man on board, saving old Lanky, was working round the clock.

Young Tommy and Billy jumped to it with a will and Kelly never had to repeat a single order, whilst Cook soon proved himself a better seaman than a cook. Fortunately our Dicky was as well versed in the sea as any of them so he worked steadily beside Kelly. Thommo was quite handy though you could tell his heart was not really in the venture – he could never forget he'd gone against his calling.

Nothing would stop Redmonds from getting at the grog so he was more or less left to get on with it.

That spell in the placid waters of the Reef had given us valuable time to become used to each other and familiar with the running of the ship. We were more like a family than the mixed bunch who'd been thrown together only a few weeks before.

Like a family, everyone had their weaknesses and their strengths. Kelly was by now the undisputed leader, he'd proved his steadfastness and good judgement on every occasion and with Kitty by his side they made a fine pair.

Vainly Kelly tried to talk some sense into Redmonds and

keep him away from the bottle for he sorely needed a reliable second to back him up. Kelly was a cautious man and even though he was confident with the charts and the general running of the ship he preferred to have another's opinion as well, but most times he just relied upon himself.

Fortunately on the only occasion when Redmonds was really needed he was not in his cups.

Heading north as we were at that time it became apparent that stretching across the sky as far as the eye could see there was a band of cloud so dark it appeared we were sailing straight into the Day of Judgement.

"Seen that afore," Redmonds muttered to Kelly, "seen one of them off Owhyee three years back."

"Wrong time o' year," Kelly never took his eye off the evil mass of cloud.

"A cyclone's a cylone," Redmonds shook his head.

"That there's a storm – really bad one I grant you. Ain't no cyclone though."

As we were well within sight of land he ordered the helm put over and we made out to the open sea with all possible haste.

"Batten down the hatches. Close the ports!"

Every single thing that could be lashed down was secured on deck. Any barrels which could be put below were shoved into the hold. Our fire in the galley was quickly doused and Kelly ordered Kitty and me and the baby below deck.

"I want to stay up here with you," Kitty begged, because the thought of being in the bowels of the ship terrified her. But he would not allow it.

"When this storm strikes you'll be grateful. And watch out for the wee one too – you'll be thrown about like beans in a bottle."

"We'll be safe though, won't we?" She searched his face for reassurance.

"We'll always be safe together," putting his arms around her he held her tight.

Not for the first time did I feel a twinge of that desolate feeling which can creep up on you. You couldn't call it envy, for I never grudged Kitty a single pleasure. She was one of the best and she deserved all that was good in life. But just for once it would have been a comfort to feel that I also was loved like that, that someone cared whether I lived or died.

Perhaps one day I'd know what it felt like to be the most important person in another's life. Until then there was just one other human who loved me as deeply as I loved her, my little Anny. When I looked into those blue black eyes and tickled her till her whole face creased up into agonised enjoyment I knew what love was. That was the kind of love I'd settle for till any other came along.

Down in our cabin Kitty and I clambered into one of the lower bunks with Anny sandwiched between us. We waited for the worst.

And did not have to wait for very long.

First of all there was a deceptively gentle movement as the *Venus* appeared to gather speed then wallow in the waves for a few moments. With a creak and a groan she rose and fell reluctantly as if in anticipation of what lay ahead. The storm appeared to be playing with her.

Next moment the movement became sharper and more confused.

All hell broke loose.

No time to feel sick, no time to feel frightened. This was just a time to hang on. We had to trust in luck and the judgement of Kelly as he shouted his orders to the man at the wheel.

Fleetingly I thought of that legendary Captain Bunker. In weather like this he'd be standing beside the helmsman, eyes narrowed and a faint smile lingering about his lips. As we bucketed on our beam ends he'd scarce turn a hair.

Kitty and I clung together in that thundering, spinning, bucking, roaring hell for several hours. Holding on to each other with little Anny tucked between us we made sure she never suffered one knock or bump during the whole time.

We'd even become used to the turmoil and I was starting to feel drowsy.

It was then we heard a groan from outside.

"Holy Mother of God! Someone's dyin' out there."

It took the two of us to push the door open, for whoever it was out there had slumped against it.

"Lanky!" Squeezing by, I managed to get round the edge of the door and out into the passage. "Lanky ... what's up?"

Not a sensible question. The poor old fellow was on his last legs. Together Kitty and I dragged him into the cabin and laid him on the other bottom bunk. I covered him up and smoothed his brow while Kitty disappeared, coming back with a tot of something in a mug.

"This'll help ... this'll bring the roses back."

But truthfully we both thought we were tending a dying man.

The liquor certainly warmed him for he ran his tongue along his lips and even managed a faint smile. "Where's the bairn? Is she safe?"

Anny was always his first thought. His face would light up when I placed her in his arms, for with him being so sick he was always sitting somewhere quiet and could nurse the child while I got on with whatever was to hand.

"Don't you fret. She's been fast asleep. Now she's stirring for the first time. Reckon the ship'd rocked her off."

Another fit of coughing racked his thin body.

"Take a sup o'this," there was still some sugary water in the bottle I kept for Anny.

When the coughing stopped he just sat there, reminding me for all the world of the old grey mare who pulled the cart up our lane come haymaking time.

Patient and stolid she'd drawn her load and waited between the shafts with never a twitch or a fidget. Out in the sun or the rain she just took life as it came.

Lanky must once have been a fine figure of a man for he was tall and large framed. Putting an arm around his shoulder just to cheer him up I could feel the breadth of him. Now he was just skin and bone.

"Thankee … thankee …" and I knew he wasn't thinking of the syrupy draught, it was instead the comfort of another human's touch.

"Come on, this'll be more comfortable," I pulled the bedding off the top bunk and tucked him in nice and cosy. At least he wouldn't come to harm down there and we could keep an eye on him.

Several times I thought our last hour had come. The vessel twitched and juddered with a crack of timbers that made you think she'd come apart, but worst of all was the noise. The howling of the wind combined with the creaking of the planks and the crashing of a hundred and one cases and boxes sliding across cabin floors throughout the vessel kept up such a level of confusion that our eardrums felt quite bruised.

"'Tis like all the banshees in Cork!" Kitty kept crying over and over again as her fingers clutched in vain for that lost rosary.

"We'll be alright," to admit fear at that time would have been too overwhelming.

"'Tis a marvel yer milk ain't curdled," she eyed me as I fed the baby and we both laughed in that exhausted way that is all you have left when you are at the end of your tether with fear.

By the finish of those few, yet agonisingly long, hours we were both wrung out as dishcloths.

"'Tis over …" Kitty whispered, "the storm's gone. God be praised … we're still alive … 'tis over!"

The companionway was awash and somehow two barrels had wedged themselves across the bottom of the steps. One of the hatches had broken free but we managed to struggle up on deck.

The scene up above was a real mess. They'd obviously not had time to take down the last sail for it flapped in shreds above us. Where there had been four large crates lashed on deck, too awkward to be stowed below, there was nothing remaining except the broken rail of the ship where they had cannoned out into the deep.

Weed draped from some of the rails and a huge fish trapped in one corner of the deck slithered about helplessly. It was as if we'd been down to the bottom of the sea and come back up again.

"Get back below!" Kelly roared at us from above. "Get back!"

"But 'tis over," Kitty protested, "'tis over and done with thank the Lord."

"Over be buggered," Redmonds was at Kelly's side, his dark face even darker with fear. "We're in the eye of the storm, that's where we are. Get below and stop there."

We didn't pause to argue. We had no idea what he meant but it was obvious we could be at peril once more so we sloshed our way back along the passage. After having seen the confusion on deck I had the most uncomfortable feeling I was shutting the lid on my own coffin when I shut that door, but there was no choice in the matter.

Lanky was lying on his side when we got back in the cabin.

"If Ben says that, then that's gospel's as far as I'm concerned," he grinned as we told him how matters stood. He was trying to be cheerful but when he split his face with a smile it was more like a death's head grinning at us from the gloom.

I sat on the end of the bunk and offered him another sip.

"No. Ain't no drinkin' man, Charlotte. What's our Kitty up to?"

Kitty was kneeling in the opposite corner of the cabin praying. Even if she'd turned her back on the Holy Mother before, now we were in such dire straits she needed to make her peace.

"Confessin' her sins I'd say."

"Sins! What sins have the likes of us to confess!" For a

sick man his voice rang out loud and clear. "'Tis the sins of them as put us here as needs be shriven. Scarce any of us 'as done more'n steal and who wouldn't steal if they saw their little nippers starvin' to death?"

"Tell me," I said for his eyes were shining with the light of recollection. If Kitty was preparing to face her God perhaps he felt the same.

Lanky was a quiet man. He'd never put himself forward like Dicky Evans and yet, sick as he was, he'd never been one to backslide. He'd done his best to help and we'd all come to rely on his steadiness.

"Paintin's always been me trade," he pulled himself up and tried to take a deep breath but only choked the more. There was nothing left to give him so I waited while the spasm eased off.

"I always reckoned 'twas summat in the paint as give me this because me and me brothers was always strong and well set up lads but by the time I'd passed me thirtieth year I was coughin' me heart up each morning.

"Slower and slower I got. Then the gaffer sacked me, said he couldn't keep on a man who was idle with the brush. I ask you? Bin with the bugger since I was twelve, worked me guts out for 'im I had." Lanky shook his head as though he still couldn't believe the turn of events.

"Four little nippers we had … one younger than young Anny here. We'd always managed but not any more. There ain't a man alive as can stand the sound of his little ones hungry and crying out for bread. 'Twas a torture and when a family wakes up in the morning with empty bellies and goes to bed with nought but water and maybe a few crusts to see 'em through the night then 'tis beyond what any father can bear.

"I remembered a house I'd been working at six months before. Bin took on to paint their staircase.

"The larder! I'd been called into the kitchen by the cook to give her a hand with a barrel of vinegar she wanted put up on some bricks so she could run it off easier. That larder was bigger'n our whole kitchen back home! I'll never forget it. Two hams hanging from the ceiling, several loaves of bread on the shelf, a crock of butter, a great slab of yellow cheese, a line of jars with labels on them and a great piece of beef, just a few slices taken out of it, red and oozing with the richness of the blood," even as he remembered his eyes glistened. "And there was my little uns crying for want of a crust of bread."

"You don't need to tell me," I could still see the gleam of the candlelight on old Wright's yellow teeth, I could feel the coldness of that gold.

"Now look at me!" Lanky buried his face in his hands. For a moment there was silence. "But what does that matter. T'ain't me as matters. What o'them? That's what I keep asking meself – what o'them? Where are they? Did the parish take them? Are they on the streets? Are they still in this world? Tell me, tell me."

His eyes must have been swimming as tears spilled through his fingers and spilled down his cheeks.

"If me poor gal had to take to the streets wi' em they'd stand no chance … "

A violent tremor shook the vessel. The tempest had struck again. Lanky buried his face in the blanket and said no more.

Yes, that was nothing but the truth. Them up the top skimmed the cream off life. Us down the bottom was left with nought but the leavings. And it wasn't only the really poor who was robbed either. Those officers on the *Earl* spent seven months on the high seas coming out from the old country but by the time we'd reached Port Jackson they'd not been paid a penny and their shirts were in rags. Many of us women did a bit of washing for those above decks and we knew the facts because we heard the officers grumbling amongst themselves. They had no money to give us so they had paid for the laundering in tobacco.

Life must be very sweet for them up there with a good roof over their heads. 'Twasn't too bad for the rest either ... until things went wrong. Till work was lost or sickness struck or old age crept up on aching joints and useless limbs. Then look out!

Often, when I'd left Anny with Lanky there'd been that warm light in his eye that only a father would have. He'd wrap her little limbs up tight and rub his cheek against her fuzzy head. All the more wonderful now I knew the true despair which would be eating him away inside as surely as the distemper which was consuming his lungs.

I gave him another hug and blessed my good fortune. My life was my own, I had no regrets nibbling at my conscience, whereas never a day would go by when he wouldn't be fretting over that lost little family.

The *Venus* started to corkscrew into the depths of the ocean. My head swam and my stomach cramped up till my whole body ached with a violent retching. Up to that point seasickness had not struck. Since those first few weeks aboard the *Earl* it was a sensation which I'd mercifully been spared.

Now it was back. That full retching, vomiting, spewing agony as your stomach and guts voided themselves and you'd not care if green water flooded in and finished your life off.

Kitty clamped herself tight against the wall. I rolled from side to side vainly trying to save poor Anny from my sickness, but by the time I'd pulled my exhausted body to the edge of the bunk I'd thrown up anyhow and the child was sopping wet.

There is a terrible time in the middle of really bad sea sickness when you truly do not care what happens next. The rocking, battering and thumping do not matter a jot, you could close your eyes and just die.

I'd felt that before when we'd left old England, when we met our first storm in the Bay of Biscay. Not this time. Much as I'd have welcomed death several times over I also knew it must not happen now. That little life clinging to me had to be saved and saved she would be.

When we'd finally weathered the storm I could scarcely open my eyes for a while. Whenever I forced myself to peer out at the world, my head swam around in an even worse fashion than it had at the height of the confusion. I'd hit my forehead against the side of the vessel, and a bruise the size of a pigeon's egg was beginning to raise itself.

"Kitty!" Kelly's voice came from the other side of the door. She was lying, silent and motionless, face against the wall. I could hear him rattling at the handle. "Kitty! It's over … we're safe! The door's locked, why's the door locked?"

Forcing myself to get up off the bunk I stumbled across the cabin. The door was not locked but it was jammed tight shut with the force of the battering the whole ship had received.

"Give it a shove! Real hard! I'll pull on the handle."

The door flew open.

Kelly threw himself across the tiny cabin and gathered Kitty in his arms. Her face was so white I wondered for one dreadful moment whether she was still alive or had been mortally injured in the tremendous battering of the last hours.

Even as I stared at her a little colour came creeping back into her cheeks. She nestled closer to Kelly with a contented sigh.

"You're brave gals." He put out an arm and pulled me and little Anny close.

Standing there for that moment I knew I belonged at last.

But there was work to be done. "Can you tend Anny for me?" I guessed Lanky wasn't asleep. He nodded as I settled her in beside him then made my way up on deck.

White horses galloped all around us. The storm itself had departed leaving lumps of thick cloud torn and twisted by the tempest, scudding across the sky.

The galley was a shambles. Broken shards of crockery lay everywhere and I made my way to the ship's side time and time again clearing up the rubbish.

"Look lively! Tend them lines!" Redmonds shouted at the two young lads.

The sea was evil and dark green, one slip upon the deck and you'd be gone. There was no way the *Venus* could turn back in this weather if anyone went overboard. They'd just be left for the fishes.

The ship had ridden the storm well ... or so we thought at first.

It was our Dicky who first gave the alarm. 'A mite sluggish' were his words for he was never one to panic.

"Sluggish! 'Tis a sight more'n that!" Josh shouted accusingly. He bellowed for Ben to join him in the hold. For once Ben had not noticed anything wrong, maybe he'd been too taken up with Kitty, but when the two mates came back from having a look round both their faces were grim.

"Canvas! Get me some canvas," the lads were soon hopping to carry out his command.

Some planks had sprung during the storm and a slow leak was allowing water to seep in below the waterline.

Nothing ever set him back. I don't doubt any ship he sailed upon had been as shipshape as a naval vessel. He knew everything that was needed to be known and he never hesitated.

In no time at all he had the boys down below with a length of canvas which he stuffed into the gap and across the leaky planks. Against the canvas he ordered them to stow several bags of potatoes which must have once been on their way to Port Dalrymple. Water still seeped in so he ordered them to take spells baling out all they could, but very little was coming through anyhow.

"Gotta get to the Bay quick smart," Ben told us that night when we assembled on the deck. We'd worked all day clearing up the mess. The lads had searched out some spare sails and there were light timbers lashed across the gap where the rails had once been, to prevent anyone sliding overboard.

"These are busy waters ... we're sure to come up against

some other buggers," Redmonds muttered as he sat with a mug of rum. "I'd say we head back for the Reef, can make our repairs in peace, get some speed up then."

No one said a word, Redmonds swigged away and the others just looked to Kelly. Undermanned as the ship was, dangerous as the ocean can be, it was in our mind's eye that if we met one of the navy ships at this moment we'd be fair game. We'd never get away a second time.

"There's no help for us back there. Just a few savages and calm waters. Why there ain't even any decent timber in them parts. The timber in New Holland's sorry stuff. If we get to the Bay there's fine, strong wood. In those forests there's trees so sound you'd never find better in the whole wide world. And there's natives to give a hand. Them Maoris know all there is to know about boats. Plenty of help, plenty of timber." Ben had made up his mind.

The two men tossed the subject around time and again. You couldn't say it was an argument for it was obvious both views had their drawbacks and advantages, but in the end they decided to make for the Bay and take a chance of encountering any ships.

For the sake of us landlubbers Ben explained the direction he'd take in terms we'd understand. "We're a trifle too far north for the usual shipping lanes so we should be safe from interference. We'll head south-east and that'll bring us to the shores of New Zealand. The Bay of Islands is on the east coast so we need to sail north to the top island and round some rocks called the Three Kings. Once past them we head due south and should be there in a day or so."

The storm which had blown us off course took a full three days to finally disappear, the sea remained choppy and gusts of wind came up from time to time to harass the *Venus*.

When it came down to it, the crossing of that stretch of ocean took us nigh on ten days and by the time we sighted land we were heartily sick of the sea for every waking hour was spent down below helping with the baling.

The leak was growing steadily worse.

Ben's repair had saved our lives, no doubt of that. Even so, water gushed in day and night and sometimes we were hard put to it to stay cheerful.

"Me back's breakin'," Thommo was a lanky fellow and he spent hours each day doubled up with the baler. We'd formed a chain ... two chains in fact. When one was working the other rested. Day and night we laboured against that relentless flow and the old *Venus* ploughed through the waves on her merry way, very little the worse for what could have been a fatal blow.

The sea was a relentless enemy as well as our best friend. Each mile we sped towards that new land took us further away from the authority of King George and the merciless end we could expect. But she extracted a hard price and tried us to the very limit of our endurance.

CHAPTER NINE

Joseph Banks writes in his Endeavour Journal.

December 24 1769. Land in sight, an Island or rather several small ones most probably 3 Kings, so that it was conjecturd that we had Passd the Cape which had so long troubled us. Calm most of the Day; myself in a boat shooting in which I had good success, killing cheifly several Gannets or Solan Geese so like European ones that they are hardly distinguishable from them. As it was the humour of the ship to keep Christmas in the old fashiond way it was resolvd of them to make a Goose pye for tomorrows dinner.

25. Christmas day. Our Goose pye was eat with great approbation and in the Evening all hands were as Drunk as our forefathers usd to be upon the like occasion.

"Land hoy!" As usual Dicky Evans gave the first shout.

"'Tis all woods! Look at that. Forest as far as the eye can see."

"But there's a mountain back there ... look at that snow. My oath I've never seen no snow in ten years or more."

"Where? What's up?" The young lads crowded up close. Of course they'd never seen snow in all their lives, being brought up in New South Wales.

That first sight we had of New Zealand was of wooded foreshore and a distant peak. We were off the north island on the western side. The chart was always spread out up in Ben's cabin. I'd often take a look at our position and soon got the idea of where we were heading.

"A likely place!" Ben was scanning the coast with his spyglass.

"Likely? Likely for what? Nothin' to get excited about I'd say." Kitty had been looking forward to arriving in the country he had talked about so much. Ships, people, a bit of life would be a change she reckoned. She was sick and tired of the sea and the occasional glimpse of land.

"Woodin' and waterin' ... a likely place for woodin' and waterin' ... that's what, me girl," he chuckled and snatched at her hand, drawing her close. "You'll have your fill of fine berths by the time we're settled down nice and snug, never you fear."

"Looks a dull sort of spot to me," Kitty always liked the last word.

We'd reached the mouth of a shallow bay. Tall headlands jutted out to sea and the sandy beach within looked a haven of contentment. There would be fresh water and a chance to stretch our legs and maybe even some fresh meat if the men were lucky with their muskets.

"Swing the lead, Cooky!" Ben was full of good cheer at the thought of dry land once more.

As Cook shouted out the fathoms, we slipped past the gaunt rocks and came close into shore.

Places look so different in your mind's eye from what they are when you really get there. Somehow I'd imagined that this country would be just like New South Wales. Silent and empty, giving you the feeling that there was a host of eyes watching from the forests. I'd thought that all the natives in this part of the world would be the same – fierce maybe, but keeping to the woodlands for safety and either scared or uninterested at the thought of the white man.

I could not have been more wrong.

"What's that?" Kitty called out to Ben. She was up on deck with her arms full of a mass of linen, as we were still catching up with the washing after our seasick hours, fitting in as much as we could between stints with the baling.

In the distance there appeared to be a disturbance upon the calm waters near the shore.

Putting the glass to his eye he muttered something to Redmonds who hurried up and took the wheel from Evans.

"What is it?"

"Canoes! War canoes!"

Even as we watched, the movement on the water became clearer. Two long canoes were streaming away from the land in our direction.

"Holy Mother of God!" Certainly the sight of them was enough to strike terror into the boldest heart. Kitty's words echoed all our thoughts.

Each canoe was filled with Maoris. The rowers gleamed with oil, their muscles were taut and all those bodies worked at the oars in perfect accord. Standing up were several of the most fearsome individuals imaginable brandishing weapons and thundering defiance at us.

The canoes were low at the bows and high in the stern. Every piece of wood was carved and decorated. They might as well have come from another world when compared with the simple little craft we'd seen back off the shores of New Holland.

"Look! Look!" Everyone scrambled across the deck at Thommo's shout.

"Craft ahoy!" Dicky Evans bellowed from the crosstrees. "Craft ahoy, she's gainin' on us to starboard!"

Bearing down from the south beyond the two heads came a third canoe. She was twice the size of either of the others and came at us like a devil from hell with her square sail billowing aloft. A horde of chanting, cursing men taunted and shouted abuse at us.

They were rejoicing. By sheer good luck they had us bottled up in that bay. Two canoes paddling towards us from land and this deadly craft outside with the wind in her sail and her boatload of warriors waiting for us.

"Get them muskets up!" Ben shouted at us. I tucked Anny under one arm as I almost slid down the hatchway. Kitty came up with two weapons, Cook had his sword in his hand and I was so put about with fear I twice fumbled and dropped the musket I'd grabbed before I handed it over.

We were in a perilous position, caught on a lee shore with very little room to manoeuvre. But Ben never faltered. Once he saw we all had arms to hand he bellowed orders at the lads as they scrambled up into the shrouds to break out more canvas. Not for the first time did I watch for those sails to fill with my heart in my mouth. Those fateful minutes at Port Dalrymple seemed but yesterday and now we were caught in a doldrums once again.

"We'll be alright," Evans viewed the approaching canoes with a confidence I hoped he truly felt. He'd brought up his musket and Cook's knuckles were bony and white round the handle of his cutlass.

But we weren't alright. Not a breath of wind was to be seen. We were too sheltered by the headlands on either side.

For the first time since we'd left Port Dalrymple real fear took hold of me.

The storm had been bad enough but this was far, far worse for we were in extreme danger. One look at those men in the canoes left no doubt that we'd be done for if we were caught.

My guts turned to water, same as they'd done that day in the courtroom back in Worcester when us prisoners from the gaol waited for the old judge to give his verdict.

His judgement would have been merely a matter of a few words for him … then back to his sirloin and his port. For us miserable wretches t'would be the difference between life and death.

The clerk's voice had risen shrilly as he read out the list of all our names and the details of our crimes. Not one sentence had been pronounced so far, so it appeared whatever the outcome, it would be the same for all of us. One fate awaited us all. 'Charlotte Badger for stealing four guineas and one silk handkerchief 6d. The property of Benjamin Wright.' My name was last.

I was in the worst company possible and feared the judge had lost his patience by now and was just in a hurry for his dinner. Well you never know but seeing that there was a murderer amongst our number who'd dropped some poor soul in a lime pit we could not expect much mercy.

When I heard the words, 'His Majesty hath been graciously pleased', the blood surged through my veins, then came the next words 'transported to the Eastern coast of New South Wales or some one or other of the Islands adjacent and during the several terms following. By order of the Court.'

The fellow next to me gasped with relief. 'Every last one of us for the Colony. There's none for the drop.'

But most of all I remember the stink of piss rising like a benison, for many of us had voided ourselves in our distress.

Once more the sour reek of terror rose in my nostrils, my body shrank from the fate that seemed unavoidable.

Now the situation was just as dire as it had been back in the courtroom. We wallowed like wounded ducks in a marsh. Not a breath of wind came to our aid. The largest canoe with the sail was so close we could see every detail clearly.

There must have been at least sixty shrieking men in that boat. As if the sight of their tattooed faces and great red tongues sticking out in derision was not enough, the spectacle of that vessel was such as to strike fear into the bravest heart.

She'd be every inch of sixty feet long and from her prow a fearsome creature leered at any poor enemy in her path. That figurehead's carved horns and teeth like razors were fast bearing down on us, its wretched prey. Even worse, giving the whole monster a terrible life of its own, were its eyes. Real eyes they appeared to be as they caught the daylight and glinted. They must have been inlaid by something for a gleam such as the inside of an oyster shell had us in its gaze. The sight was so fearsome and struck such terror into all beholders that many a fight would have been won before the natives even joined battle.

But what really filled me with dread were the fringes of black feathers a-fluttering from most of the woodwork of that vessel. For all the world they brought back the funeral plumes of the hearse back in old Bromsgrove.

Sure and certain death surged towards us. For myself I was ready to lay down and give in. There were well over a hundred men in those canoes out there baying for our lives. We were but ten and the *Venus* was at their mercy.

Ben never flinched. He didn't budge an inch as he watched them thoughtfully. Never for a moment did he give a hint of fear.

Looking left and right he summed up our position. The headlands were cutting us off from the sea breezes beyond. Outside the bay there would be safety where the white horses galloped along the coast. He muttered something to Josh Redmonds who hurtled to the stern where the longboat was tied up.

"Get that line! Tie her fast. Make her fast Dicky," he fed out rope as Dicky secured it round one of the seats on the boat.

"Heave ho lads! Heave ho!" Between them, Dicky, Redmonds and Ben pushed her over the side.

"Hold tight! Go easy!" As the boatline played out Ben leapt across to one of the bollards and secured it.

Truly I thought he'd gone mad. What was he doing launching a boat when the chanting and insults of the natives were loud in our ears. This was no time to parley, they'd run down any boat in a trice.

"Fire over their heads!" Ben bellowed at Dicky. "Josh! Look lively. Cook! Over the side quick! Tommy, Billy … over you go."

Dicky was a fine hand with a gun. Maybe he'd be even handier with a cannon but those years in the gunnery had taught him a thing or two.

He took very careful aim. Seemed to me he spent too long getting whatever he was aiming for in his sights but he knew his weapon, he was judging it fine.

At his first burst of fire that monstrous canoe faltered. A hole appeared in the sail and even as we watched the wind tore it down further and further till the cloth just flapped uselessly. Confusion spread amongst the natives. When Dicky fired a second time some of the paddlers lifted their oars and hesitated. The other two canoes had caught up now.

Yelling, shouting and waving their weapons the warriors screeched defiance at us as they tried to regain their previous state of bluster. They'd been set back on their heels but they certainly did not look as though they'd given up the chase.

Like angry bees gathering as their hive is attacked, so the Maoris hovered in the water and watched our next move.

"Pull! Pull lads! Pull for your lives!" Ben bellowed at the lads as the rope tightened and the rowing boat began to make headway.

A roar of rage came from the Maoris now it was obvious that we were not just going to stop there and be attacked. The other two canoes had joined the sailing craft and their leaders shouted at the rowers. Paddles were dipped once more as the three vessels came towards us in a head-on attack.

"Fire lads! Over their heads! Fire!" Ben yelled at Thommo and Dicky. He leapt along the deck and snatched up a musket.

"Sure. 'Tis simple enough," Kitty had grabbed one and handed another to me. "Come on Charlotte, 'tis now or never or we'll nary see the dawn."

I pushed Anny into a corner and knelt beside Kitty.

I'd seen the lads with their muskets often enough to know what had to be done.

But nothing had prepared me for the shock of the firing. I fell backwards and fully expected to see one of those Maoris leap over the side of the ship.

"'Ere ... reload for me ... look slippy!"

Thommo grabbed another weapon and thrust his musket at me. With shaking hands I took Thommo's weapon and pushed in the powder, the ball and then the wadding.

"Good lads! Good lads!" Ben shouted encouragement to the four of them in the boat, rowing for their very lives. The rope was tight as a bowstring and once she was under way the *Venus* fairly flew across the water. It was as if the poor old ship knew exactly what fate had in store for her if she was taken. "Keep going till we clear them heads!"

Once more those war canoes bore down upon us.

Yet again the musket shot flew across the crowded natives. One man, standing near the stern of the largest vessel appeared to be injured as he dropped out of sight and a furious hubbub filled the air.

At that moment a triumphant shout from Ben drew our eyes to the sails. They were filling slowly. Steadily they bellied out and we could feel the lift of the deck. Almost clear of the headlands the *Venus* was picking up the ocean breeze.

"Shorten the line! Prepare to board!"

Soon the ship was moving so fast that the longboat was being dragged through the waves and the lads were hard put to it to shorten the rope and get alongside.

Dicky held the rope ladder steady and willing hands helped them over the side. The longboat had to be left trailing till we were a safe distance and could get her aboard.

Rapidly gaining on the three canoes we headed out to sea. The infuriated screeches of the natives gradually fell out of earshot. All that was left was the distant verdant mountain sides and the brilliant blue sea.

So peaceful and so treacherous.

"Iron. That's what they want ... always iron," Ben muttered as he left Redmonds' side and came down to look at some repairs Lanky'd been making.

"What do they want iron for?" Lanky choked as he straightened himself up.

"Everything – spears, hatchets, nails, just anything. When they get a ship they burn her down to the waterline, let fire consume the whole vessel and when it's over they just pick out the iron for their use."

"And what about the crew? What about the men?" Thommo didn't say much but he listened alright.

"They eat them. That's what!"

"Bloody hell!" Thommo looked as though he wished he had not asked the question.

"I've heard tell of a ship where they took all they could and the poor lads as were left made it up the rigging. Those bastards let them stop up there, left them till they had to come down, one by one, too exhausted to stop up any longer."

"What happened then?"

"Like I said. They ate 'em."

I heartily wished we'd not made this journey. The coasts of New South Wales seemed a veritable haven compared with this wicked island.

Ben grinned at the others, "But don't think that'll happen to you ... no Sir. We'll get to the Bay and you'll be safe."

"Can we be sure?" Thommo piped up.

"They're used to sailors round there. They want our goods, they want our trade. Why, some of those Maoris make the best whaling men I've ever come across. Have no fear. We'll be alright when we get to the Bay."

We were sailing north now and the winds were favourable to us. As the *Venus* ploughed through the waves we watched for any more warring canoes and at night as we caught the occasional glow of a fire I for one blessed the creaking timbers of the old *Venus* for keeping us safe and sound. It was only a couple of days before Dicky, up aloft, shouted to us and we all peered ahead.

"The Three Kings, them's what Ben's bin aiming for, when we clear them we turn east and then head back down south to the Bay." Redmonds was standing staring out at the scene.

"Will there be war canoes there as well?"

"Not on your life. They knows better than that. They make their livin' with the whalers and the sealers round these parts. Mind, you never know what to expect, they're tricky people. One minute you're their friend, the next their worst enemy."

CHAPTER TEN

*Letter from Governor King to Earl Camden, Sydney,
New South Wales 30th April 1805*

... the many vessels that have put in the Bay of Islands
and other parts of that coast have never, as far as I have
learn'd, had any altercation with the natives, but have
received every kind of office and assistance in procuring
their wood and water, etc., at a very cheap rate in barter ...
An anxious wish to promote and secure those advantages
to the whalers has induced me to direct the Commandant
of Norfolk Island to send a number of sows and other
stock occasionally to that island by any master of a whaler
in whom he can confide, to be delivered to the most powerful chief at the Bay of Islands or amongst the different
families or tribes.

"Well! No one ain't comin' out to meet us here," Redmonds
had the glass to his eye and was keenly scanning the scene.

"What's all that smoke?" Thommo shifted nervously
from foot to foot, possibly thinking we were looking at a
cannibal feast.

"Trypots ... that's what. Boilin' down the blubber."

The scene was one of tranquillity. The Bay itself being more
a huge bight into the land rather than a very sheltered bay.
Everywhere you looked there seemed to be islands and little
inlets. It was easy to see where the settlement was, several vessels were moored out in deep water and whaleboats pulled up
on the waterline. Huts and tents were huddled together up
above the beach. Smoke from the trypots shrouded much from
view but even at our distance from the shore we could see
quite a number of people going about their business.

"Why 'tis the *Eliza!*" Redmonds grinned at the sight of
one of the ships and passed the spyglass to Kelly.

"Would they be friendly?" Thommo was standing at his

elbow. "Looks more like a wreck than a decent ship to me. Why's she all black up aloft on those sails?"

"The *Eliza's* a sturdy craft. Out of London like the *Albion* and the *Britannia*. One of the best found vessels in these waters. Sure she's filthy, her sails would be black as night. 'Tis the whale oil does that."

He shouted through a hailer and several seamen came to the rail and waved at us.

"Keep away, they're British ships," growled Kelly. "The news from Port Dalrymple shouldn't have reached here yet but you never know. When it does you'll call no one a friend – they'll all be after the bounty. They'd turn in their own grandmothers for that."

"We're beyond British justice here, remember?"

"Look you here," concern had brought an unusual edge of sarcasm to Kelly's words, "we may be beyond what you call justice – no soldiers and the like around. But there's plenty willing to put you aboard and take you back where King George can give you the drop."

Kelly looked speculatively at the tiny settlement but did not give the order to let the anchor down. "I'm not taking us in while there's British crews ashore. I know one thing, Chief Tip-a-he's a friend of Governor King and for that reason, as good as any other, we keep away from the main settlement and go to one of the outlying villages."

Kelly set a course for the south and the *Venus* was scudding through the waves when a shout brought everyone on to the deck.

Standing at the bows Redmonds pointed ahead.

"Lightning! Holy Mother of God, don't say we're headin' for another storm," Kitty exclaimed pointing ahead. Some fat, black clouds were hovering on the horizon and lightning forked into the sea.

Kelly himself was at the helm. The vessel lurched. The next moment a tremor went through her timbers akin to a shudder of fear. Turning in surprise, I caught the fleeting glimpse of trepidation upon his face. To my best knowledge our leader had never shown any qualms before.

"What's ailing you Ben?" Kitty was tuned to his every change of mood.

"Lightning's a bad sign." The moment he said those words he seemed to regret them for he gave a laugh and shrugged his shoulders. This was not the time to spread speculation or gloom amongst the crew, and seamen are the first to snatch at any superstition.

"But 'tisn't like that. The sky's not black like it was before. 'Tis only a summer storm," Kitty stared at the dark cloud. There was a distant growl of thunder and even as we watched the sky ahead lightened.

"Forget it, it was just a passing fancy after all, just one of the things they believe in hereabouts," but he was still scowling as he steadied the wheel.

"What do you mean 'hereabouts'? Why's lightning any different here than back home?"

"The Maoris believe if you see lightning in your path you should hurry away at once. If you are going on a journey then postpone it, if you are going in any given direction, then change it."

"For goodness sake, how can a thing like lightning bring bad luck?" Kitty scoffed.

"They say it's a warning of trouble to come."

All that silly talk appeared to have been forgotten by the time we finally fetched up in a small bay several leagues to the south of the main settlement.

The shore seemed quite deserted as we dropped anchor.

Kelly surveyed the land and when he put down the glass he nodded his head. "There's an inlet over there, the village is almost hidden in the trees but you can just see a bit of the palisade if you look."

"What do you mean by a 'palisade'?" Kitty was at his side.

"Oft times they protect their people by building a great

134

fort or a *heppah* as they call it. Outside are the huts and the plots of land where food's grown but in times of trouble everyone can retreat into the fort and defend themselves."

We all stood at the rails and peered shorewards as he went on talking.

"This place ain't nothin' like Port Jackson, nor Twofold Bay nor any of the places you might think of. If the Indians of the Colony are backward in coming forward then let me tell you that the Maoris are nothing anything like."

"You're tellin' no lies," muttered Redmonds.

"They're warlike. 'Tis shameful for a man to die of old age, they're expected to end their days in battle. For another thing, they have proper settlements where they grow crops and keep pigs, they're jealous of their possessions and look after them – they aren't forever moving from place to place like the Indians do. And most important of all, have a care, tread carefully – many things are *tapu* … that's forbidden. For instance if I was to go ashore and meet the local chief, which I must certainly do, then I must not on any account hold out my hand and touch him. Remember that."

"Why not?" Thommo always wanted to know the whys and wherefores.

"Because he's *tapu*. You'd be killed on the spot for touching him. A few years back I saw one of their own children – a tiny lad who could scarce toddle – meet his end. He would have understood nothing of what is allowed and what is forbidden. No one was watching in the crowd and he crept forward to grab one of the feathers on the chief's cloak. There and then they swung him by his heels and knocked his brains out against a tree."

I clutched Anny to me. In truth I did not even want to think about living in this savage place. 'Twould be better for us to go on roaming the seven seas for the rest of our lives.

"You listen good, Ben's right," Redmonds nodded his head, for once his breath not reeking of the grog. "They can be as treacherous as a greasy pole one minute, next they'd fight to the death by your side. You never can tell, but like he says, be careful in all your dealings with 'em."

We watched the two lads lower one of the boats, then they went over the side and settled themselves at the oars.

Kelly turned to us before going over the rail. "On no account allow anyone on deck while I'm gone. If any canoes come out then stand to defend yourselves. Don't let a single one of 'em come on board. Thommo, give the women a musket each. Josh, if we don't come back inside three hours don't come lookin' remember … just up and away to the south and wait off shore. We'll find you. If we don't come after that … well you'll know what's happened."

"Don't go!" Kitty flung herself at Kelly, but he gently pushed her to one side.

"I'll be fine. We've got to come to some understanding with them."

"Let me come too!"

"Women are best kept out of these matters. Don't worry, all will work out right."

We watched with our hearts in our mouths as the little boat made its way through the water. Not a soul came down to the shore.

Kitty sat on the half deck with her weapon between her knees, her eyes fixed on the forest. Josh Redmonds had his blunderbuss and a cutlass by his side and Thommo had his musket at the ready. Cook eyed the firearms with positive dread and kept his hand upon his own cutlass with a native spear close by.

Minutes slipped past with agonising slowness and if our thoughts could have been spoken aloud I'd swear they were all the same. Were the three of them even alive still? What would we do if a horde of savages came screaming out of the forest launching their boats and bearing down upon us like those wild creatures we'd seen a few days ago. Could we get away in time? I sorely doubted that. I wondered how long we could keep them at bay. Would we be able to shoot at them as they clambered up the sides, would I manage to aim straight or would I panic and waste my fire?

So many fearsome possibilities crowded through my mind that I did not realise the boat was returning till Redmonds yelled out to them across the water.

"Any luck?"

Kelly was grinning from ear to ear. Relief writ plain on his features.

"Couldn't be better."

Clambering aboard he explained that the chief of this particular area had fallen out with Tip-a-he over a matter of some stolen maize and the village was left in somewhat straitened circumstances by virtue of the fact that apart from the maize being gone several of their pigs had also disappeared. Blame could be laid at various doors on this account but obviously they preferred to accuse Tip-a-he's followers.

"I've explained we have stores a-plenty and they've agreed we can stop ashore where no harm will come to us."

Not long afterwards three canoes paddled out and Kelly allowed some of the tribesmen on board. Even so he made sure Redmonds, Thommo and the boys were on the upper deck with the muskets and Kitty and I watched from one of the doorways.

"Holy Mother of God! Look at them! The size of them! Legs like tree trunks …" Kitty clutched my arm as we shrank into the doorway.

Truly you would never in all your life see such fearsome human beings. The very sight of them was meant to strike terror into the beholder.

Every man jack of them was tall and broad shouldered. There did not appear to be a single runt amongst them. Clad in cloths which reached above their knees and were tied at waist and shoulder they nearly all had short beards whilst their hair was tied back with feathers sticking out of the top-knot. Unlike the Indians of New South Wales who lived so peacefully with next to nothing in clothing or belongings, these people were well clad and adorned and gave the feeling that they expected the universe to bow down before them. Every inch of their great bodies spoke of enormous pride.

Furrows of tattooing swept in great whirls and curlicues across brows, down chins and particularly along every nose. Their brilliant eyes stared out from dark faces made even darker by artifice.

It was as though they challenged the very appearance Mother Nature gave them, for nearly every face was decorated thus and the young men who were not yet so adorned had their lips scarified jet black.

Kelly shouted to the lads to stand at the top of the steps with their weapons. Whether this show of strength convinced the tribesmen that we were quite able to defend ourselves, or whether they were in fact without any intention of attacking I don't know, but several of them brought out greenstone ornaments and paddles which were laid upon the deck.

"Bring up a barrel of that dried pork," Ben yelled to Cook, then he turned to one of the canoes and held out his hands to them. He didn't have much knowledge of their tongue but he seemed to make them understand and when he said the word 'patoo patoo' they searched in the bottom of the craft and brought out a couple of green stone hatchets.

"Nearly everything of value's made from green talc. Fair exchange for that pork."

But he'd not reckoned on them being so shrewd. In the end they had to have a barrel for each canoe and then three hoes, three spades and three bags of nails.

"Greedy bastards," Redmonds hated to see any of our stocks being depleted.

"Reckon it'll pay off. They'll know we've got plenty more but also know we look after ourselves."

Now we were at anchor he'd lashed canvas to the outside of our leaking planks to stem the flow. "We can get on with the work tomorrow. Reckon we're in a snug harbour now."

Even so, all that night the men kept watch upon the deck. Kelly was taking no chances.

He continued to be extremely cautious when next morning he came ashore with us and Redmonds. As he explained, he wanted Redmonds with him, as being a mulatto he was familiar with much of the life of those who lived in the islands of the Pacific.

I tried not to look terrified but truly the faces around me sent my heart into my boots. When one came forward and stopped in front of Ben I felt I'd die on the spot for I surely expected him to raise his club and strike our leader to the ground. His expression was fixed and fierce, his eyes flashing with pride. Instead he put up his hand to Kelly's cheek and rubbed his nose upon the other's.

A greeting as Ben explained later, a sign of friendship which ensured our acceptance by the tribe.

Another sign of acceptance or perhaps it was more approval, was even more strange, for as we approached the village several women pressed in close to me and I swear someone pinched me. Scared stiff, I hugged Anny even closer and looked neither to left nor right. I kept my eyes on the ground and it was only when I heard Redmonds guffawing that I dared look up.

All eyes were on me. I couldn't understand why, for when it came to any female beauty then it was Kitty who had the sparkling eyes and the jaunty step.

We were told to stand beneath the shade of a tree and await the arrival of the chief and it was then that Redmonds explained why everyone was staring at me.

"First off, they ain't never seen no white women before. Men yes, plenty of men, but never a woman yet. And then, and this'll give you a laugh, they don't hold much with skinny sort of females. They wouldn't think much of what we call a comely wench back in old Sydney town. No ... the bigger the woman the better. Shows she is well looked after, comes from noble stock. Why, over in Owhyee, their royal

139

ladies are so fat they have to be carried everywhere, they eat day and night and are expected to do absolutely nothin' but grow fatter'n fatter."

"I'm not that fat!" No ignorant fellow the likes of Josh Redmonds was going to laugh at me.

"Not nearly fat enough by their standards but I'll tell you this girl, you're a sight plumper than the rest of us. You're a big woman, Charlotte. You've got a child too and that golden hair of hers has really got them hooked. You play your cards right and you'll be a favourite wife before long."

Such crude thoughts may have amused that oaf but they did not make me smile. Even the thought of those savages coming near me sent the shivers down my spine, so I pulled myself up straight and gave them all a haughty stare.

There was no doubt the women were generally very well covered, plump and extremely comely. Their faces were often broad and I was continually struck by their beautiful eyes. Their tattoos were not so marked and they did not have the fierce expressions of the men. Many of the women gave me kindly looks whilst several held out their arms for Anny.

It took some doing at first but then I decided I'd best make friends with them so gingerly I laid Anny in one woman's arms. She laughed and everyone gathered round and pinched the baby's fat knees for all the world like the old aunties and grannies might do back in Bromsgrove when they came calling Sunday teatime. Then someone sat down and they took off all her clothes to the last stitch and looked her over in wonder. I swear they thought that maybe her body was black like their own and only her face and hands were white.

After that, all was friendship with the women, though the men held back.

CHAPTER ELEVEN

The New Zealanders, Joseph Banks' Account, March 1770

The women without being at all delicate in their outward appearance are rather smaller than European women, but have a peculiar softness of Voice which never fails to distinguish them from the men tho both are dressd exactly alike. They are like those of the fair sex that I have seen in other countries, more lively, airy and laughter loving than the men and have more volatile spirits, formd by nature to soften the Cares of more serious man who takes upon him the laborious toilsome part of War, tilling the Ground etc. That disposition appears in this uncultivated state of nature, shewing in a high degree that as well in uncivilizd as the most polishd nations Mans ultimate happiness must at last be plac'd in Woman.

Several days passed before Kitty and I felt safe enough to move about the shore but we had to admit that no one had acted towards us with any hostility. It was the strangeness of the place which held us back, the sheer difference from anything we'd ever known before.

Stretching inland as far as the eye could see was endless forest. The sea lapped upon shores as golden as those we'd seen along the coast of New Holland. But there the likeness ceased, for the inhabitants of this new country were truly a foreign race.

Huts, fences, well tilled plots of land marked them as a people who husbanded their crops and guarded them against marauders. Skins were laid out to dry, strange bunches of herbs hung from their rafters, smoke spiralled into the air and the smell of cooking food came to us in tantalizing wafts.

Dominating the whole village was a great wooden fort.

"I don't see how it would save them. Their enemies could hack it down in a trice. Look at those axes the men carry." Kitty always needed to be convinced.

"Ah ... but you'd have to reach it first. Just think, it must be eighteen foot high, they'd have the advantage of any enemy who approached. I tell you, the Maori are ready for anything. There ain't any fighters like them anywhere round these parts."

As usual it was Kitty who ventured away to chat with anyone she could find, admitted 'twas a matter of gestures and giggles and laughter but soon she was sitting gossiping with a Maori lady outside one of the huts and joining in the general hubbub.

"Her name is Mamoe. I've worked out that much."

She'd been taken under the wing of this kind lady and went on to spend the best part of the day exploring the village and the outskirts of the forest.

The women were so gentle compared with the men. Well, anyone could be considered meek and mild compared with those fierce creatures. The ladies were not as heavily tattooed and their broad faces shone with good humour most of the time. But it was in their voices that you really heard the sweetness of them for when they sang you could be forgiven for thinking you were listening to a choir of angels. Beautiful chants and songs which made our old choir back at St John's seem no better than the frogs croaking in the village pond.

"And look what I've brought back!" Kitty's arms were full of lush green plants, "Wild celery, that's what 'tis. We'll have some rare soup tonight, me girl. Dicky bagged three pigeons ... you wait ... we'll have a fine broth."

Mamoe and her friends had helped us gather enough wood for our fire and one of the men brought over a lobster in a neighbourly fashion.

"A meal fit for a king ... who could want for better?" Ben grinned and gave Kitty a squeeze.

142

"You're a fine cook and a bonny wee wife. When we're back in Nantucket you shall have the good wives pushing each other out of the way for a place at your table, I promise you that."

"Captain Benjamin Kelly and Mrs Kitty Kelly! Who'd ever have thought it?" She snuggled up against him and laid her head on his shoulder.

We were preparing for our first night ashore for we had been given a hut. To be sure the door was barely high or wide enough for a man to crawl through, giving it the appearance of the entrance to an old dog kennel. But the hut itself was large, about eighteen feet long and nearly six feet high with a sloping roof.

Next to the door was a square hole serving as a window which allowed you to see who was approaching. That same window was also the chimney, a fire could be lit in the middle of the floor for warmth and the smoke needs must make its way out there.

Outside the door was a kind of porch where there were crude benches and a fireplace for the main cooking.

"Who's to stop aboard first night eh?" Kitty had gone into the hut and Ben eyed the crew.

Josh straddled the entrance. His chin jutted forward in a defiant manner and his eyes narrowed with scorn. He was taking orders from no man. Nowadays he always kept his musket at his side. He'd taken to wearing a bright red shirt and with his black pigtail and golden earrings was the object of great admiration ... amongst the ladies.

Mamoe's family were gathered outside their hut close by. Three daughters, the eldest no more than sixteen, were sitting with their mother plaiting the fronds of some plant into a basket. From the giggling and sideways glances you'd know they'd already made the second mate's aquaintance.

"No harm'll come to the old tub, she's safe at anchor," Josh snarled, "leave her be. No one'll be comin' down this bit of the coast."

"And what if the locals should take a fancy to her?" Ben snapped.

"There's no mischief in 'em ... we're 'mongst friends ... any dolt can see that."

Pointedly Ben ignored the veiled insult. "And I say we don't take no chances. No less than four sleeps on board her each night. Two on and two off the watch. We'll take it in turns."

Ben was on the alert all the time.

Neither Kitty nor I would credit that any evil could befall us, for everywhere we went in the village we were met with smiles and a welcome. For myself it was a joy as Anny was beginning to feel her feet and my heart had always been in my mouth on the heaving deck of the *Venus*. Now she could crawl upon the ground and soon was gathered into the life of the children. The older girls never tired of running their fingers through her soft fair hair or lugging her around in their arms or giving her a piggyback. All the world over girls are the same, trying out their mothering.

So we began our new life.

"To think I'd be spending my days being thankful to the common bracken!" Kitty could barely credit the myriad uses our new friends had for the green ferns which grew everywhere. They covered the floor when it was damp, they were used for bedding – a heap of dried fern underneath a blanket was a perfect place to lay your head. And apart from those uses their roots were dried and pounded and chewed and eaten with just about any meat or fish that was to be had.

"But one thing I an't touchin' is that dog!"

Dogmeat was quite special for them, a treat you might say. Their dogs were fat, squat creatures, but according to Mamoe they made good eating.

Dogskins were dried with tremendous care and so much prized they were often cut into little strips and sewn upon cloth to make the most of them. A cloak made in this manner was a luxury.

Their food was mainly birds and sea fowl and fish. To bulk out the flesh there were potatoes, sow thistles, maize, palm cabbage, yams and sweet potatoes, and these were often the main meal if the fishing and hunting was unsuccessful. The weaponry we brought was a great help to our hosts for Dicky and Thommo were good hunters and went out into the forest each day with the men. On every occasion they came back with pigeons, parrots and once we even ate a great sea goose.

Kitty wrinkled her nose as she watched me pluck and draw a couple of doves for dinner.

"Well I'd not complain if I were you. Remember that salt pork?"

"And them weevils ..." Kitty had to agree. "But I'd sell me soul for a platter of roast beef!"

"Hush now! Keep them thoughts to yourself," Ben smiled as he leant forward and put some more wood on the fire.

Sitting round the blaze in the evenings as always, made the end of the day a delight. From nearby came the singing of the women and the occasional deeper notes of the men. But as soon as it became really dark our little group dwindled as Josh and the others slipped away in the darkness. Often there were only us two women with Ben and Lanky left.

Ben said little but he became more and more thoughtful.

"Still got to replace them planks." It was time to think of the future after a couple of days settling into our new home, bringing supplies off the *Venus* and hanging much of our goods from the rafters to defeat the rats and the ants. Ben was determined the ship had to be seaworthy. Even if his eventual aim was only to make for the Bay and find an American vessel, he wanted that boat in good order. More than likely they'd find a buyer for the *Venus* amongst the whaling men.

The chief had ordered a party to go with Ben into the forest and select the right timber for repairs, then he gave him several slaves to work on the ship.

"Slaves! 'Tis certain sure they'd not really be slaves?"

"Kitty … you've seen how warlike they are, they spend most of their time fighting. What do you think they do with the prisoners?"

"Sure, and how would I know?"

"Eat 'em or make slaves of them."

"For one thing I'll never believe they eat people. You're not after tellin' me that Mamoe would take a bite of another human being!"

"Believe what you will girl, but always remember, you are not back in Dublin."

So Ben, the two lads and Dicky Evans worked on the ship. Redmonds with Thommo and Cook in tow appeared to be off hunting with the men and what they did in the evenings could only be imagined.

"When are we headin' back to the Bay?" Kitty was curious. 'Seems like we've been here for ever and it kind of gets under your skin, don't it?"

I knew what she meant. Every day we'd been on board the *Venus* we'd been alert and watchful. Approaching ships, storms, coastal drifts to set us off course, latterly the constant baling to keep her afloat. Now all was peaceful and the routine of the village had begun to seep into our very souls.

Each morning we scrambled up to the sound of people making their way to the water for an early splash, dogs barking, children crying and the birds calling out from the forest. It was like a chorus heralding in the work of the day.

Both men and women tilled the vegetable patches. Though often as not the men would be ordered off by the chief to make up some hunting party or even on several occasions to join a raid on a nearby tribe. Then, as in the world all over, it was the women who stayed at their work.

There were fish to catch, birds to snare and fires to build. There was a rough sort of bread to make from the fern roots and shellfish to gather.

And when a spare moment presented itself there were

baskets to weave and skins to scrape and lay out in the sun. And the women were always busy with their sewing. We managed to find some bodkins for them from the stores and they were entranced, for all they had before were clumsy things made of greenstone or black stuff called jasper.

That green talc was their most common material. Its lovely shade was much prized in ornaments but also used for common things such as *patoo patoos* as they called their hatchets and suchlike.

"'Tis a beautiful spot," Ben looked at the huts nestling in the curve of the bay with the setting sun cloaking the forest in deep, deep green. "But give us a couple of weeks I'd say. Don't want to fetch up with the *Eliza* again. She'll be heading off before too long. We'll find what we want pretty soon."

"And you knows what we want, do you?" There was no mistaking the nasty tone of Redmonds' voice.

"We need to get back home."

"Your home? Or ours?" For Josh Redmonds considered himself a native of New South Wales, even if we all knew he came from some hole in the corner place north of the Colony.

"My home!" Ben drew himself up with pride. "The new world! A place where we'll be free. Where you ain't forever touchin' yer cap. A place where there ain't dukes and duchesses and kings and princes."

"A place where there an't dukes and duchesses? What about them up at the manor, what about the lords and the ladies?" I couldn't believe such woolgathering.

"Where I come from Charlotte there's none o' that sort of thing. True a few of them have come over from the old country and some folk'll still kowtow to 'em, but you don't have to abide by 'em. Jack's as good as his master in the new world and I can't wait to get back there."

I was lost for words. Who would make the rules? Who would give the rewards?

"We're all the same where I come from. You'll see when we get back to Nantucket – there's a different life back home," Ben had the bit between his teeth now, "If you've got a grievance you'll be heard – your word's as good as the next man's."

"And what about them blackamoors? Them slaves?" Dicky piped up, "What kind of say does they have?"

"True," Ben considered for a moment, "but they also has a god-fearing life given them. They're well fed and they're taught the ways of our world, which would be better than livin' in a jungle half clad and never knowing where your next meal's comin' from and oftimes being sacrificed to some heathen god."

Dicky wasn't giving an inch. "Didn't look like they had much say in matters in that new world of yours when I seen 'em up aloft one of your ships as been settin' sail. Seemed to me they was doin' all the real chancy jobs. Like great black-birds perched out on the yardarms," he mused to himself, "I'll give you that though Ben, they were certainly black. Coal black. Never seen such black, black men, they make these folk look just sunburnt."

The two of them wrangled on. Slaves, masters, freedom, a war to free people from other people's laws and ways. They spoke of a world which was so different from the world back in Bromsgrove that I began to wonder if I was hearing right.

"Well, whatever that there new world's like I ain't in no hurry to leave this one here," guffawed Josh Redmonds.

"Found yerself an easy berth eh?"

You didn't need to be a gypsy to read what was going through Josh Redmonds' mind.

Likewise 'twas crystal clear that Ben had his own plans for us.

Whilst he'd been working and getting everything ship-shape he'd watched the second mate frittering away his days ... and his nights. You could tell Ben wanted us back on the *Venus*, safe and sound under the relentless rules of the sea. The devil finds work for idle hands.

Very gradually the differences grew into undercurrents which changed the course of our lives. Those that had similar leanings merged together and those that knew not which way to go drifted hither and thither. Without our battle against the sea to keep us united we went our separate ways.

Ben was still the leader but he was more and more bound up with Kitty. Each day brought a foretaste of all the things they yearned for. Their longing for the bliss of family life loomed large for them. Kitty spoke of little ones and her eyes misted over as she watched Anny romping amongst the other toddlers; Ben reckoned up the cash he'd earn from his next voyages and the home they could have. They talked of gardens and furnishings and perhaps a maid and even a horse and carriage one day. They built their castle in the air one day and rebuilt it the next. From their first early morning walk to the fireside reveries after dusk they planned their future and revelled in their closeness.

The roaming seaman and the convicted felon were gone for ever. Instead their blossoming love had brought about a wonderful change in them both. Lean, bronzed and decisive Ben no longer paced to and fro as he had done on the deck of the *Venus*. Instead a peace had taken hold of him and I counted Kitty a fortunate being to have found such a steadfast mate. And she had changed, her skittishness was a thing of the past and she had softened. There was so much to look forward to in their lives.

They curtained off the far end of the hut, and when they retired there each night I felt again that pang of envy. His arms would be enfolding her and her very most innermost thoughts could be whispered, and never again would they lie in the dark and feel alone.

"Seems like you and me'd better make the best of it," Lanky was unable to go out and work on the ship, and he wasn't up to hunting with the men, so more and more we spent our time together.

Poor old fellow. He must have felt the same as me, only

difference was he at least had known a happy life with another human being. I could only dream and so far I'd not found much fabric in those dreams.

You can but feel pity for a fellow who's only skin and bone and won't see another twelve month round and pity is akin to love. Lanky was a good friend, a really kindly companion, and for what it was worth I gave him that kind of love which comforts. I'd lie beside him and hold him as his body shook with the coughing, I'd let him know that his agony was shared and he was not walking down that lonely road alone.

He loved my Anny. She could be a little demon come bedtimes and he'd hold out his arms for her and rock the child to sleep.

"I ain't happy, our Charlotte," he always spoke to me like that. It was comforting to feel part of his world. Must have been the way he spoke to his wife and his sisters and all the womenfolk in his life. "That Redmonds ... he's up to summat."

"Easy to find out. Ask one of the lads. Tommy and Billy can never keep their traps shut."

"And that's the point. Those boys are keeping mum. 'Tis like they're hatching summat up between 'em. He's a powerful persuasive fellow ... they'll pin their ears back and listen to a mongrel like him."

Perhaps if Ben had not been so taken up with Kitty he'd have seen the way the wind was blowing. More and more there were the four of us in the hut and the rest roamed as they pleased from village to forest and out to the *Venus*.

Our chief was a mighty man, full six foot tall in his dogskin cloak he ruled his clan with fists of iron. Slaves scurried, warriors stood aside and women fell back from the crowd when he passed by. He accepted our little group with a lordly grace, though he never deigned to acknowledge us women.

Twice in the first few weeks there were raiding parties sent out in the direction of the Bay and once there was a scare when strange tribesmen were spied lurking in the depths of the forest. Were Tip-a-he's men once more come to pilfer? We were herded into the *pah* along with the women, children and folk and had to sit crammed within its walls. Our lads stood guard alongside the warriors for best part of a day but it turned out to be a false alarm.

Our firearms were a great bonus to them. Muskets were not commonly found amongst the tribes, though doubtless that would soon change as more and more white folk came to their shores. They still depended mainly on their fearsome axes and clubs but gunpowder could achieve so much more. Fortunately for us, Ben and the lads were good marksmen and I fancy were soon regarded with as much respect as their own warriors.

"I've learnt this much," Kitty tumbled into the hut one day brimming with excitement, "the chief's off to the Bay, he's taken most of the men ... that there old feud's on again."

"How do you know it's the Bay?" For we had great difficulty as the language was quite beyond us.

"'Cos it's where there's lots of ships and them trypots ... that's what Mamoe says," and she mimed her friend's description of the smoke rising and the ships swaying at their moorings.

"The raiding party set off through the forest not more than six hours ago."

I shivered. Dark and cavernous beneath the towering branches the evil spirits of the forest seemed to await anyone unlucky enough to wander in. The sea sparkled and the sands gleamed but once beyond the settlement those dark glades were like crouching animals waiting to swallow you up.

"'Tis so fearsome ... so dark, so silent."

"Oh come on, Charlotte. They say there's not one fierce animal to be found. What could harm you?"

"'Tis silent as death ... I can't think how anyone can go into that forest without being terrified."

"Remember Twofold Bay … you didn't find that too frightening."

"Somehow that was different. Back in the Colony there were forests alright but it never looked so gloomy."

"Because those Indians were not like the Maoris, they weren't forever warring and killing each other, eh?"

"Must be that."

"Anyhow, stop fussing. Just remember, Josh and the others have been hunting there for days and no harm's come to them. Come to think of it, where is Josh?"

I couldn't suppress a bit of a laugh. "I'd say 'tis a case of while the cat's away the mice'll play!"

"What do you mean, Charlotte?"

"Now the raiding party's gone have you seen Mamoe's husband?"

He was a giant amongst the warriors and we reckoned most likely a kinsman of the chief for he was always close at hand when that fearsome individual strode out.

He was a seasoned clansman. Several healed gashes showed up as weals upon his limbs. Nearly always he was in the background when the men of the *Venus* were at our hut. He kept a weather eye on the women of the family.

"If what you're hintin' at's right, Josh'd best beware. Don't give much for his chances if her old man catches up with him."

The second mate had become a real will o'the wisp. Ben still kept up the watches on board the *Venus* but whether Josh spent the night there or not was the question.

Ben was a born leader, I reckon he could have been captain of one His Majesty's navy ships and lead whole fleets to victory. It was in his bones and now he was put in a terrible fix. He needed to keep his crew together, maintain the same control he had on them when on land as at sea.

So he suggested they might build a hut from some of the wood left over from the repair and any timber they could bring in from the forest.

"Sure and we've got a perfectly good home!" Kitty couldn't see the sense of it, "What do you want with more labouring when we've got this dear little home of ours?"

"'Twill give the lads work to keep them busy. Besides, it'll be something to leave the village when we've gone. A place built with good timber and nails will be a tidy offering for all the favours we've received. Goodwill never comes amiss." But I knew he was trying to keep those idle hands away from the devil.

"You ain't plannin' to build this hut too large? Not if you want it finished soon." Redmonds eyed the pegs which Ben had told the lads to drive in for the marking out of the four corners. "Because we ain't stoppin'."

"Sure enough we ain't stoppin'. In a few weeks we'll be off to the Bay. Find ourselves some berths," Ben agreed.

"Not on your life Mr Mate. We ain't headin' for no Bay."

"What do you mean? We're all together," Ben demanded.

"Hold yer jaw Mr Mate. Not when it comes to this we ain't. Like I said, I don't want to live 'mongst no savages, good as it may be for a while. And as for looking for a ship ... I ain't thinkin' of spending the rest of me days in the stink of oil. We've got a ship of our own ain't we? We want to keep goin'. There's rich pickin's in these waters and we've a mind to keep goin' till we find a bit of life again. You know ... proper port out in the Islands somewhere. Place where we can all disappear and no one'll be any the wiser. Could sell the old tub and set up in something ourselves."

"Hold on ... who's in this?"

Dicky Evans, Thommo, the two boys and Cook stood there, silent to a man. Admitted the boys shifted a bit, scuffed their feet in the dust, but when Dicky said, "We're with Josh ... reckon that's the way to go," they sidled across.

"You fools!" Ben leapt to his feet. "Don't you see? While we're together there's hope. There's strength. On our own we'll be lost!"

"Well, we ain't on our own, are we? We got Josh!"

"Evans ... where's yer brains? You'll end up on some lee shore else you'll be sunk at sea. Think o'that!" He did not need to put into words his views of the second mate's navigating ability.

Dicky shuffled his feet about and finally spoke up, "Like Josh says, we want to get back to where there's folks and a bit of life an' ..."

"An' where like as not you'll be taken."

"Let the lads make up their own minds Mr Mate," Redmonds had that nasty tinge to his voice again. "They ain't to be swayed."

"If we stay here we can get work aboard plenty of ships that come into the Bay. I'll stake my future on an American ship. No love lost 'twixt the English and the Americans like I said before. We'll soon be away, until that time we're safe here. On the other hand if you take to the high seas again and call in at any port in this part of the world you'll be spotted at once."

He looked at them each in turn, Redmonds standing there so sure of himself, Dicky with his eyes cast down but not budging an inch, the two lads who scarcely had a bit of sense between them all grinning and eager for adventure, Thommo as dithery as ever but I could see he felt he'd have more of a chance with the lads than with Ben and us women, and Cook, well he just wanted to get back to sea and find his way home to his own country. None of them was content to stay amongst the Maoris and bide their time.

"What about you Lanky?" Ben finally turned to the skinny frame of old Lanky. Every day he seemed to wither away a bit more.

"You don't get rid of me that easy Mr Mate ... I'm stoppin'. Any more storms and tempests the like of what we had out there'll see the end of me. Reckon I want to leave my bones on dry land." To make his point quite clear Lanky came and stood right behind Ben.

The two groups were now quite separate. "You're doin'

the wrong thing," Ben repeated, "like I always said the best shot is to stay here and find an American ship ... or maybe even French. If we get settled here we can get over to the Bay from time to time, keep our eyes open. We'll find a berth, believe me."

"An' all the while living off fern roots and sleeping on a bed o'bracken! And watchin' them savages deck themselves up to go murderin' their neighbours and the women diggin' away in them vegetable plots!"

"That's their life. 'Tis a simple life but we're safe while we're with them."

"We want a bit more than that Mr Mate," Josh Redmonds drew himself up tall and the men edged even closer to him.

"What do you want? Do you want to make it across the sea to some place like Feejee? You won't have much chance there."

The lads looked up at Redmonds. He puffed himself up and swaggered up and down for a while, for all the world like a captain addressing his crew.

"Take no heed lads. There's places you've never even dreamed of out there. There's towns we can come ashore and set ourselves up with all we've got to trade. See a bit of life ... why one time I come ashore in Batavia and I can tell you the wharf was lined with gals and ..."

Ben cut in, "And you'll be dead of the fever in a week."

Redmonds ignored him, "There's Otaheite and places like The Navigators. We can sail right across the ocean. Think of Valparaiso, think of all them ports in Chilli. We can sell the old tub and we can set up and trade all that gear down in the hold. Cloth and crocks and ... well you name it."

"You're woolgathering man. Like as not you'll go to the bottom before you get anywhere near them places. Next thing you'll be telling me you'll make easting round the Horn!"

"Mock us if you care to, Mr Mate," Josh Redmonds snarled, "but time's runnin' out. If you ain't with me then you're against me. What's it to be, me hearties?"

There was no question. The lads all stayed with him. Us two women and Lanky remained at Ben's side.

After that there was nothing more to be said, except that over the next few days the split became more bitter with the wrangling over stores. Argument over who should have what took up most waking hours.

There were enough goods on board the *Venus* to keep the settlements of Van Diemen's Land going for several months so there should have been well and enough for us ten souls to divide between us, but human nature's very greedy when there's any serious reckoning afoot.

Everything of any real value was eyed by Redmonds with a view to being taken off and traded at some distant place. "What do you think these savages want wi' all this 'ere?" He picked out boxes of linen, clothing, pots and pans and lengths of cloth as well as taking more than his share of all the every-day articles such as hoes, hatchets, balls of twine and suchlike.

"True, but I say share and share alike," Ben muttered as he stood at Redmonds side.

"Aye, aye, Mr Mate," the second mate replied promptly with mock servility, "well seein' as how there's six of us 'gainst only four of you then you'll agree we takes the share we're due? We'll leave the longboat and that'll serve for get-ting you up to the Bay."

Those workaday items would of course be of more use to us living amongst the natives, but it was obvious the other man was just taking everything which had any worth amongst white people, and it was my guess Ben had been planning to keep some of the luxuries aside to barter his way on board any ship for us.

Now that Redmonds had the majority of the men on his side the balance had shifted and it would have done little good to have caused ill feeling by any disputation. Ben was on the horns of a dilemma, unable to enforce his will but needing to provide for two women and a baby with only a sick man for a backup.

When it came to portioning out the liquor there was no stopping Redmonds. He fully intended taking the lot until Dicky Evans spoke up for us and a couple of barrels of porter and a cask of brandy were off loaded into the boat.

Ben had not particularly asked for the spirits. I fancy he did not care for the thought that the natives might develop a taste for heavy liquor and trouble could ensue, but he accepted it and stowed it away in our hut.

Already there was a distance between us. The lads were never to hand, Thommo avoided us and sometimes I caught a sheepish look on Dicky's face for he had been a good comrade, no one better.

Ben watched his erstwhile crew hob-nobbing with all the young lads and lasses of the village. Horseplay's the same whatever end of the world you live in.

"That there hut's got to be finished!" That was the only order he gave them but he was hard put to keep them at their labours. "We'll aim to have it finished by the time the chief's back. That'll be a token of goodwill and we're going to need as much of that as we can get if we have to hang on here much longer."

By the time the raiding party returned the main frame was put together but he spent more time rounding them up as they drifted off amongst the huts than he spent with them on the actual work.

"'T'will be good riddance to bad rubbish when they slip the hook. Good riddance, I say."

CHAPTER TWELVE

The thing that numbs the heart is this;
That man cannot devise
Some scheme of life to banish fear
That lurks in most men's eyes.

Fear of the lack of shelter, food,
And fire for winter's cold;
Fear of their children's lacking these,
This in a world so old.

A Starry Night at Arue, James Norman Hall.

"She's gone!" Kelly stood outside the entrance staring at the empty inlet. Not a sign of the *Venus.*

"Look!" Kitty leapt up from her bed of bracken. With a blanket wrapped about her she was staring through the little window. Turning back she snatched up one of the muskets.

A number of Maori men were roaring along the beach. Bellowing with rage and hurling curses out to sea they shook their weapons and stamped their feet. Then they swerved away from the waterline and came thundering towards our hut.

"Heavens save us!"

"Put that down!" Kelly shouted at her. "We'd not stand a chance if they saw that! Think!"

Hands on his hips, mustering all the nerve he could command, he faced those angry men. All the while others came running from the surrounding huts and the groundswell of shouts and chanting grew louder and louder. The deep grunts from those tattooed men chilled me to the very marrow. Eyes flashed and tongues were red and hungry looking. I dared not look at Lanky or Kitty, somehow to have seen fear on any face would have been too much. Gathering up Anny I watched from the window.

Above the shouts of the men came the continued wailing from the village women. Kelly raised his hands to the heavens. Whatever language you could or could not speak his actions spoke for him. He was showing sober consideration and making it plain that whatever was infuriating them was being given careful thought. He made it plain he was listening to their voices and understood their distress.

One furious warrior pushed his way to the front. Every inch of him spoke of impotent rage.

He shouted at us. He shook his fists then spat such hatred that I found myself flinching into the shadows of the hut. Every inch of him spoke of a thirst for revenge.

"They'd no right to make off with the *Venus* like that!" Kitty shook her head, "Why sneak off at night?"

"And what's upsetting that big fellow? He's the one who seems to have really got it in for us."

"That's Mamoe's husband," Kitty said grabbing Ben's arm.

"Reckon our Josh has taken her with him," Lanky was behind me at the window.

It took a few moments for the enormity of that to sink in. Easygoing in their family life as the Maoris might be there was no doubt that their ties were the very basis of their strength. Marriage was the cornerstone of the families grouped around the village.

To defile a wife and mother would be an evil of the very worst kind.

More and more villagers raced towards our hut. Ben had backed up against the wall. He was next to the window.

"It's that wife of his. Redmonds has taken Mamoe. The bloody fool! He's left us to face 'em."

The crowd grew larger and soon we were surrounded on all sides. A chanting had begun and, as if moved by one single spirit, the tribesmen started to shift and sway in that dangerous unison brought about by a common grievance.

Piercing cries and wails came from the back of the crowd.

The menfolk moved aside as a bunch of women pushed their way to the fore.

Their usually placid faces were inflamed with hate. They screeched and yelled at us. Shoving her way to the forefront of the crowd came a distraught woman.

"Holy Mother of God. 'Tis Mamoe herself!"

So Josh Redmonds hadn't taken her after all. We all stared in amazement at the nigh demented woman.

Kitty's erstwhile friend writhed with rage and grief. Clutching a daughter on each side she screamed for revenge.

"He's taken the eldest ... he's taken Tarore." It wasn't the mother that crafty devil had been courting. He'll have had the old one alright but all the time he really had his eye on that pretty young thing.

"A virgin too, I'll be bound."

The crowd milled around our hut. More women came howling to the fore.

"We're done for!" For once Ben was facing true disaster. Such trials as beset us on the sea he could handle with ease but this was outside his usual run of things. He stood firm but he yelled at us to get the muskets.

"No!" I could scarce believe my own ears ... I just spoke up. "We'd never get the better of them now ... look at them! They're that wound up they'd wear a few deaths for the sake of vengeance."

"What's to do then?" Lanky was already raising one of the muskets and Kitty had pushed a weapon through the window to Kelly.

"Wait! Wait!" I was clothed in a robe from Chinee which we'd found in one of the trunks bound for Van Diemen's Land. Being light and soft 'twas a simple thing to cover me when I rose in the morning. Moving about first thing seeing to Anny I found it a comfort to be decently clad. "Get that cask Kitty."

The silk was brilliant yellow with red dragons embroidered upon it and the huge sleeves were lined with purple.

A regal looking garment and it must have been intended for someone of good stature as it hung in folds and trailed on the ground and certainly added even more to my girth and height.

Pushing Lanky aside I grabbed Anny and crawled through that opening with as much dignity as possible and stood up in front of the crowd.

A sigh went up from the great mob of Maoris, a kind of universal sucking in of breath when no one quite knows what to do. Perhaps they'd expected us to grovel in front of them?

All eyes were upon me. I kept a very high and mighty expression on my face. I laid Anny on the ground at my feet and lifted up my arms as though in supplication to some being up in the heavens above. Kitty squeezed out right behind me. In her arms was the cask of brandy. She laid it in front of the man, taking care not to approach too close to him.

Half of me feared in case this could be the ultimate insult. Perhaps they'd consider us beneath contempt to balance a girl's life against a barrel of grog. Luckily for me such was not the case. They were not in the habit of having spirituous liquors. But they knew about them from the shinnanikins of Redmonds and his crew and they knew there was much pleasure to be had from a few swigs.

I said nothing. This seemed to be a time for silence and not supplication.

With a snarl Tarore's father snatched up the barrel. He planted his legs fair and square and fixed Ben with a piercing stare. Obviously women were below him but even so, he had acknowledged our presence by accepting the barrel.

The grunts of the men ceased.

The women were not so easily appeased. They continued to shriek for vengeance but the men held back. Clutching the barrel the wronged father turned on his heels and marched away. Immediately there was a lessening of tension. First one followed, then another, then a small group. The women wavered for a moment then some of the men shouted at them to come away and they followed turning back all the while to shake their fists and yell final insults at us.

"Not a good move," Kelly's face was creased with worry, "grog ain't for the likes of them."

"Holy Mother of God, it saved us that time didn't it?" Kitty snapped, "that's as near as I'd like to get to the end of a club I'm telling you."

"It gives us time," I backed her up, "we just need time, every day they get more used to us being here. Maybe the girl'll be sent back ... who knows."

Time was certainly needed. Time for their rage to cool down, time for that much desired American craft to call in at the Bay, even a bit of time to get over the deception that had been practised upon us by those we had almost considered our brothers.

For I'd always felt a fellowship with the lads, excepting for Josh. The comradeship of the ten of us had been a revelation to me and I fancied others felt the same.

Until we all boarded the *Venus* in Port Jackson we'd been leading our separate lives. For us prisoners we'd been taken from the closeness of our families many years ago and even the seamen had put their ties aside and were roving men of the sea. Those nights on the deck had brought us together, we had needed each other and found pleasure in that companionship. The whipping had struck such a spark that we'd acted as we did. The weeks and weeks with shared hazards upon the sea had caused us to depend upon each other absolutely.

I'd come to feel I was part of a family. We needed each other and depended on each other. The core had been that wonderful love that had grown up between Kelly and Kitty but something of its strength had appeared to affect us all. We had been bonded together by events and now, to be left thus, was very painful.

How had they been so foolish to have just gone off like that? How could they have listened to the bragging of Josh Redmonds instead of the wisdom of Ben Kelly?

Very little was said over the next few days about the departure of the *Venus*. Fortunately the women of the village had quietened down. "Things'll ease up soon. Reckon them ladies is trying to forget the whole thing," Lanky gave a rare chuckle as we sat together round our fire.

"Must be a terrible thing to have your daughter taken from you," I couldn't think of anything worse.

"Aye ... and worse still if you've been tricked into the bargain. Reckon our poor Mrs Mamoe's bin sold short."

"You think he'd been making up to her?"

"A sight more'n makin' up if I know Josh, and I reckon she wasn't the only one by a long chalk ... half the ladies in the village'll be missing our Josh. Reckon he's been warming a few beds alright. So, like I said, things'll go real quiet now."

"He's really left us stranded, hasn't he?"

Ben shook his head. "Wouldn't matter too much except he didn't even leave us the longboat."

Yes, it had not occurred to me before. How were we going to reach the Bay?

Lanky shook his head. "Selfish bastard. Still, reckon there'll be someone in the village who'll let you use one of their canoes?"

"Only if we leave the girls here. They'll never just let us up and away like that. We're next best to their property now. With our guns and stores we're not going to be allowed to make off. Besides which they'll be reckoning on the *Venus* coming back to fetch us one fine day. They've got a score or two to settle there. They'll never let us go at this rate."

"Don't you think the lads'll come back, Ben?" Kitty asked.

"Not on your life. That sot'll have them at the bottom of the sea in no time. Can you see him sailing the *Venus* into any safe harbour?"

163

Glumly we had to agree with him.

For the moment we were safe. Somehow Kitty had got it across to the women that we were equally in the dark over the kidnapping of Tarore as they were themselves. With much shaking of her head, tearing of her hair and clapping her palms to her forehead in distress Kitty even got herself back into the good books of Mamoe.

"Poor soul! Young Tarore was promised to one of the chief's sons. Fat chance he'll want her now even if she ever gets back."

But in our hearts we knew she would never come back.

"I'd keep clear of that woman," Kelly told Kitty several times.

"Poor soul. She's eating her heart out. How can you be so cruel?"

"She's come round too quick for me ... acting more like a fairweather friend than a Maori mamma."

"You wouldn't trust your own grandmother Ben," Kitty laughed off his suspicions.

"All I'm trying to say my love is that hell hath no fury like a woman scorned. Remember, it's like the good book says 'an eye for an eye, a tooth for a tooth' and these people live for revenge. She's got no cause to forgive us folk ... any of us. I'd steer clear."

But of course Kitty never listened and soon she and Mamoe were back, thick as thieves.

As the days went by and then the weeks started to pass we slipped once more into the routine of the village.

Slowly we were accepted again into the life around us, Anny was the main reason for she just toddled across to each and every hut she wanted to visit and sat playing in the dirt.

"Take heed," Lanky shook his head whenever we saw a warrior nearby, "I know she ain't likely to, but have a care in case she took a fancy to them feathery cloaks or dogskin covers and such," for we all were conscious of the dangers of breaking a *tapu*. There was one poor old fellow who'd transgressed in some manner and he had to sit in his hut and be fed for a whole year. Not once was he to touch food. And of course we'd never forgotten Ben's tale about the chieftain and the little lad who touched the cloak.

I'll say this for my Anny. Maybe she was a mite demanding at times but I reckon she had a good head on her little shoulders. Perhaps she'd picked up the need to follow all that was told her, after all our lives had depended on doing the right thing at the right time and no questions asked. Anyhow if I shook my finger and said 'No' then 'twas certain sure she'd obey. Every time a Maori fellow came by I made sure she never touched him … for all I knew some of the other men were as sacred as the chief. Anyhow she shrank when they approached and I didn't try and stop that.

"She's a good girl, our Anny," Lanky chuckled as he watched her making mud pies in the dirt. "There ain't nothin' like havin' yer own flesh and blood. You're a lucky woman, Charlotte."

There was no trace of envy in his voice, yet he must often have thought of those four little ones left behind.

"In the end it's all the likes of us can count on in life, ain't it?"

"What do you mean, Lanky?" Kitty asked.

"Well, we'll never have anythin' in our pockets will we? We'll never have a roof over our heads as belongs to us, most likely we'll never have a name over our graves. We'll come and go from the earth and not leave a trace. 'Cept our young 'uns," he sighed deeply, "blood's thicker'n water and that's a fact."

"Maybe our blood a'nt as good as them up the top either?" Kitty laughed.

"But we feel the same don't we? We hurt like they do, we suffer like they do. The pox'll catch up with them same as us. And there's our little nippers … never seein' their …"

"Just sometimes things go differently." I knew the way

his thoughts were heading, nothing would come of going over that again, best to think of something a bit more uplifting. "I heard of a young fellow who turned it all round for himself."

"How? Come on, me dear Charlotte. Time for you to tell us a tale!" Kitty's eyes sparkled; she liked nothing better than a good story.

"His name was John Jauncey, a convict lad. He's ended up a landowner who could buy or sell some of the richest squatters in the land."

"Don't believe that ... come on ... tell us!"

"His father had been a god-fearing man, did his duty and served his country. Well, he was wounded fighting for King George and came back unable to work."

"Like me, thrown on the scrap heap!" Lanky muttered.

"Well, this poor fellow had a family to feed and in desperation he stole. Not being a thief he wasn't that handy and was caught out first time. And no mercy was shown. 'A felon' he was said to be, 'a thief and a rogue'. That poor father was sentenced to be transported and sent to gaol.

"Well he had a son of thirteen. This lad was certain sure his old man would be pardoned. He could not believe his brave father who had fought the French across the seas would be kept in a prison with murderers and cut throats.

So what did he do? He decided then and there he'd go with his pa and went out and stole some money, certain he'd be sentenced. He did not run away when the watch came looking for him.

But his plan had not worked. Instead he was flogged. Poor boy when his body would have been as soft as a young calf still."

"Go on, our Charlotte ... t'ain't like you to spin a yarn," Lanky hadn't taken his eyes off my face.

"'Tis no yarn," I snapped. "Well this young John went out the very next day, while his wounds were still open and bleeding and went straight back and stole once more. Can you believe it? This time he was put in prison and when the trial came up he got his deepest desire – he was sentenced to be transported to New South Wales."

"Lucky he didn't get his neck stretched," Lanky muttered, "young lad Dorchester way was caught out with some men rick burning. He was that light, being only fourteen, they had to put bricks on his feet for the drop."

I shivered. Suddenly the world was so wicked I wondered how I'd go on surviving. Only the glow around the fire was cheerful. The huts had some sort of safety around them but beyond, the sea roared and ground upon the sand, and all around us that black forest waited to swallow us up.

"Go on … go on …" Kitty pushed some more wood on the fire.

"Well by then his pa was long gone to the hulks and the lad himself spent a year or so in gaol. Whatever happened I don't know but those two were separated by years and space for a very long while. Still, when young John reached New South Wales his luck changed. He was assigned to a good place, a family of decent folk who immediately saw his worth. They realised he was a boy of honesty and purpose and young enough to be like a brother to their own son. So he worked out his seven years upon their property and then, having proved himself such a treasure in those hard times, they gave him a place of his own to manage.

"His time being up and before he took over his new job he asked for leave and went looking for his father. He searched and he searched and being of such a steadfast and determined nature finally found the old man. By this time the cruel hard work had taken its toll of old Father Jauncey. The years had finished what good King George started. He was bent and racked with the screws and could just about make a living chopping wood. He scraped a living chopping firewood with his axe.

"Can you imagine young John's delight! He took his father with him back to his own place and looked after him till the end of his days and from what I was told he inherited much property and wealth from his kind masters … but most important he'd found his old pa and done what he intended to do."

Nothing was said for several minutes. The flames that flickered on our faces showed up more than just our features. Tears had gathered in Kitty's eyes and she brushed them away quietly, Lanky smiled to himself as he thought of that wonderful chance in a million reunion but Ben frowned.

"What's up Ben?"

"Well Charlotte, seems to me that young lad took a chance. 'Tis only by sticking yer neck out you get anywhere in this life. What are we doing, sitting round like this, it's time we made a move."

"But you said … you said we'd wait a while and go to the Bay?" Kitty looked worried.

"The *Venus* ain't never coming back … the folk here'll never give us a boat … reckon I should get to the Bay and see what's happening."

"How?" we asked together.

"Through the forest."

"Oh no Ben." Kitty cried out and shook her head fiercely. "What if you met up with one of them raiders or anything. We don't know anything about what lurks in that forest! And when you get there … what will happen then? What if you get taken, what if …"

"Hush," he laid a hand on her arm. "See here."

He pulled from his jacket a leather pouch. "Look at that!"

A pile of golden coins shone in the firelight.

I felt sick. I shut my eyes for a moment and took a deep breath. Coins laid out in all their abundance had done their evil before.

"My, where did they come from?" Kitty could not take her eyes from them.

"Chace's cabin. Doubtless for the purchase of stores, harbour dues and the like … well I suppose that's what they

were for … anyhow they'll see us aboard any ship we want …
and I can always work my passage and that'll get us all
a berth."

I looked at those deceptively warm and glowing coins
and I shivered.

Kitty nudged me. "What's up Charlotte, someone walking over your grave?"

Having said that, it was a while before the subject came up
again. We had another alarm and were herded into the *pah*
once more. Kelly stood on guard with the Maoris and several
times joined raiding parties when they went skirmishing in
the forest.

"Won't hurt to get the lie of the land," always a cautious
man he knew too well how all our lives were in the palm of
his hand.

Luckily the alarm didn't last many days, because not long
after we got back from the *pah* poor old Lanky began to
cough up blood.

Always trying to do his share he'd spent too long chopping wood for the fire when the first spasm seized him. Up
till then he'd coughed and choked most times, but this
was different.

I found some cloth and wiped his mouth as he could
scarce move with the violence of the attack. Then he settled
himself in one corner and I sat beside him with an arm
round his shoulders. Words were no help, there was nothing
to give him for the sickness, all anyone could do was keep
him warm and offer him a bit of comfort.

Several of the men had been slightly wounded in the
fight, the women worked swiftly covering their open places
with cobwebs.

"Sure 'tis enough to make sure they're dead in a week!
'Tis filth they're putting on the poor souls' open places."
Kitty couldn't believe her eyes.

"Every Maori warrior goes to war with cobwebs at the

ready. 'Tis their way of healing a wound," Kelly told her. "Something in the spider's silk has more healing power than pitch."

All was furious activity in the village. The women getting their huts in order, some of the men still coming in from the forest.

"I'm goin' tonight."

"No! No ... don't leave us Ben."

"Like I said. I've got to get on the move again."

"Not tonight," Kitty clung to him fiercely.

"Every man jack of them's that busy, no one'll bother about me slipping away."

"But what'll we say afterwards when they see you have gone?" I didn't fancy facing any more angry Maoris.

"Tell 'em it's for Lanky. Tell 'em I've got to get to the Bay to our own folk for some potions ... tell 'em something like that. You'll be safe. They'll not harm you. We've been here over three months now. They've seen us all together and they'll know we're sticking together. When I find a ship I'll be back for you. We've plenty of stores to give the chief and some gold, and there's the hut we built. They'll let us go alright."

I was doubtful. "Seems they could get nasty."

"Give 'em a few of these," he tossed down the bag of gold. "They know what gold is ... admitted they don't use it in the village but the word's out about the gold that comes into the Bay ... about the nails and tomahawks and suchlike it can buy."

"Aren't you taking money with you? You said it would help get us our passages."

"Look Charlotte," and he gave a laugh, "I'll use one of those old sayings you're such a one for digging up all the time. Never put all your eggs in one basket! I've plenty with me, the rest stays here. Remember that, girl! This way we're safe. I'll stake my life on that."

A full moon shone that night. Sitting beside Lanky I felt his body quivering with the effort of taking in breath.

Kitty and Kelly lay in each other's arms as though this farewell must last them for ever, even though both had sworn that in a few days or a week at the most Kelly would come rowing back into the bay with a boatload of our own folk and they vowed our future had never looked brighter.

Before he left, Ben foraged amongst the stores for sweet wine to keep Lanky's spirits up and ease his throat. He found the poor soul a quilt too and even the luxury of some boxes of almond sweetmeats which had been bound for Van Diemen's Land.

"You'll be alright, Charlotte." After leaving Kitty with her face turned to the wall as she sobbed to herself he came over and sat with us. "Look after my gal for me ... she's a touch too headstrong, but she listens to you. I'll be back soon, we'll be away across the ocean in no time at all. Why we could all be watching ol' Nantucket looming up out of the mist within a few months. The sea air'll make all the difference to old Lanky and that little 'un'll never be any the worse for all these goings on."

"I'm sure you're right Ben, but have a care."

"How can you doubt me! All this to look forward to," and he gestured to Kitty, "and the best friends in the world to share the future with. Do you really think I'd risk all this if I wasn't sure we'd be alright?"

Before I could answer he was gone.

He slipped out and the black night swallowed him. All was silence.

But next morning when it was seen that the white warrior had left, there was a hubbub from the direction of the chief's hut.

This time I did not act on impulse. Instead I pushed some of the golden coins into Lanky's hand and told him to go to the chief whilst urging him and Kitty to explain to Mamoe about our need for white man's medicine. I was not as clever with my tongue as Kitty and between them I knew they'd get across more than I could manage.

Whatever was finally explained, the outcome was in our favour. The money was taken and by the middle of the next day we were no more the centre of any attention.

At least a day, maybe even two, I reckoned it would take Ben to reach the Bay. Possibly only one full day if he'd been able to just walk without a care in the world but he'd need to watch his step. He'd have to move cautiously and keep his eyes skinned for any who could cause him harm in the forest. Added to that, when dusk fell he would most likely find a safe retreat and wait for first light before continuing.

Kitty busied herself with the women at their weaving and Anny played with the children all day long. I spent most of my time indoors with Lanky.

That night Kitty brought some baked eels from one of the women's huts and we treated ourselves to a few sips of wine. We chattered and Lanky tried to keep up our spirits with talk of the ships that might be waiting at the Bay, but all the while a desperate fear plucked at our hearts and each of us thought of Ben out there in the forest and what he might find the next day.

Late on the next afternoon I was fetching water when I saw the terrible omen.

To the north, flashes of lightning lit up the sky. Dark and angry as the sky had become it was the growls of thunder which sent shivers down my spine. About now would be the time when Ben reached the Bay and the foul weather would be right across his path.

Keeping silent I hugged my fears to me and told myself how stupid I was. Anny and I had survived this life so far and what was there to be scared of in a bit of lightning? Lightning might frighten a Maori but coming from the other ends of the world there were different superstitions for us white people. Their dark gods could not touch our fate – that's what I kept telling myself.

Two more days passed and two more nights went by when we sat increasingly silent by the fire.

By the time a fourth night passed Kitty was beside herself with worry. We were hard put to it persuading her not to follow Kelly's path into the forest.

"He's been taken ... I know it ... I can feel it in me bones." She burst out as we stood together and stared out at the dark wall of forest in vain.

"He could have been caught by one of the other tribes, they might just be holding him prisoner. There's no cause to think the worst."

The next night we had what Lanky called a council of war. We sat round and tried to work out what we should do next.

Kitty was all for following him to the Bay but Lanky pointed out that Kelly would not want us to court disaster. "Anyhow," the sensible fellow said, "for all we know he's making arrangements this very moment for us ... thing's can't be done just at the drop of a hat you know. If we go rushing in on him we may undo all his good work. No, he expects us to wait here for him and wait for him we must do."

Poor Lanky, he did not have to wait much longer.

The morning after we'd come to this agreement we were woken from our sleep by musket shots out at the inlet.

Leaping from the hut I was out first and rushing down to the strand glimpsed the dark shape of a rowing boat approaching.

"He's here!" Kitty cried out as she dashed to the water's edge only to stop suddenly and hold up her hands in horror.

Sand spurted from near her feet as two musket balls ploughed into the beach.

Even before the boat thudded into the sand five seamen leapt out and strode through the water with their muskets at the ready.

"Got yer mate!" one of them yelled.

"He's bein' took back to London!"

"Come and join the party!" A great lout who was still in the boat stood up and squeezed both hands round his neck and made his eyes to pop out in a dreadful imitation of a hanging man.

"Run for it girls!" Lanky half cried and half croaked at us as Kitty turned to run back up to the hut. "To the village ... to the village."

I shoved the baby in Kitty's arms and grabbed him by the shoulder. "Come on ... come on ... best foot forward."

I dragged at him for I was twice his size. His skinny frame faltered as he tried to run and I got my hands under his armpits and pulled.

But he just sank to the ground. "Leave ... leave me ... and ..." he choked as he struggled to speak.

Poor old Lanky! He just had time to give me a helpless sort of grin ... he was so scant of breath the words were barely above a whisper. "Go ... go you silly wench," and he hit me with the last of his strength to make me let go of his hand.

CHAPTER THIRTEEN

1807 Port Jackson

Captain Bunker arrived at Sydney in *The Elizabeth* from the Bay of Islands bringing news got from Captain Turnbull of the *Indispensible* and what he had himself learned at the Bay in December of the previous year.

Captain Bunker stated that, in addition to Kelly and Lancashire, two women and a child were put on shore from the *Venus,* and that the charge of the vessel had fallen into the hands of a black man, who had stated his intention of returning to Port Jackson but unfortunately, he was incapable of piloting the vessel.

One of the women had died on shore, and the other, with her child, had refused the offer of accompanying Captain Bunker.

Tasman to Marsden, History of Northern New Zealand from 1642 – 1818, Robert McNab

That night I cradled two people in my arms. Anny fast asleep on one side, and Kitty sobbing the hours away on the other.

Lanky had been right in his swift decision. We'd fled up to the village just as the Maoris had stormed out with their clubs and axes to face the seamen. Anyone coming near their stronghold with such aggressive intent would have been faced in that fashion.

First of all the leader of the seamen's party had tried to talk to our chief but the great man would not even deign to listen. He ordered the boatload of men from his shore. They attempted to linger but to no effect so they satisfied their pride by setting fire to a patch of ground and firing a few musket shots in the air before they departed, dragging poor Lanky with them.

As I sat in the darkness of the little hut I could find no tears – what use are tears when disaster has truly come?

Far worse than my plight was Ben's terrible fate. All I could think of was our Ben, our brave and true Ben, imprisoned on that ship. Vividly I recalled the tale of Mary Bryant and her agonising journey aboard the *Gorgon*. Chained and manacled he would have to suffer those thousands of sea miles only to end up in a gaol with the gallows waiting.

And Lanky. Lanky who'd done no one any harm, just gone along as best he could with events as they unfolded. Would he even survive their rough treatment long enough to reach dry land again?

Life had indeed offered up a bitter draught.

I held Anny closer. If the authorities got their hands on us she'd be snatched from my arms in a trice. Kitty and I would be whipped through the streets of Sydney at a cart's tail or put in the pillory with our ears nailed back and we'd be hanged for certain.

Now that everyone knew of our existence it would be no time at all before they came looking for us. Maybe not at once, but give them time to muster up a number of boats and a real force of seamen and we would have no chance. For the first time desperation crept into my heart.

Truly I felt like finishing it all there and then.

That night was the blackest of my whole life. Sitting half propped up with the others on my breast I truly wished to die, to turn my back on this dreadful suffering which was all I saw before me.

There was no way out. A British warship would call in sooner or later and send the soldiers after us. The Government back in Sydney could never allow two women and a baby to stay free and thumb their noses at authority. If the navy didn't get here first then the whalers would do their dirty work for them. Bringing back two runaway convicts was a valuable prize. Convicts who had taken part in mutiny and piracy were prisoners any master could be proud to hand in.

Clutching the two of them closer I bowed my head in the face of the dreadful images I could not shut from my mind. The only vestige of hope was to stay with the tribe and trust that one day the *Venus* would come back, but that was a very faint chance as now her whereabouts were known she'd be hunted up and down the coast and pursued across the high seas till she was captured.

I truly think that Kitty's loss unhinged her mind. When her sobbing ceased and she fell into a fitful sleep her fingers gripped and tightened on my arm all the time. Her heels drummed upon the hard earth of the floor. From her occasional shrill cries it was as though she were being pursued through a nightmare land by all the devils from hell.

"Charlotte!" she screamed. She woke with the first light creeping across the floor of the hut. "I must go to him ... I must go."

My fingers dug into her shoulder, "You forget about that. What good will it do?"

I clutched at the hem of her gown as she struggled to her feet. Now she was completely deranged, her hair like mouldy hay, eyes red-rimmed and face white with the bitterness of distress.

"You're heartless! How can you sit there when at this very moment my Ben's facing death?"

Before I could stop her she raced from the hut.

She could not go far. The palisade and Maori dwellings hemmed us in on all sides. She screamed for me to follow her, shouted that if we hurried we could make our way through the forest and reach Tip-a-he's village before the day was out.

"We can save him! We must go, come Charlotte, come!"

Anny woke up and began to cry. The strangeness of the surroundings, the screaming woman and the dark faces that began to gather outside the hut to stare at us had the combined effect of terrifying the child. She too began to scream and in all the confusion the women muttered amongst themselves as Kitty frantically threw herself against the palisade.

"Coward! False friend!" Kitty screamed at me. Now her face was contorted by such hatred that I shrank against the side of the hut. Trying to comfort the child was fruitless and her cries only seemed to increase Kitty's frenzy.

Finally she sank to the ground exhausted from the extreme of distress gripping her. I tried to disentangle Anny's arms from around my neck but they were gripping my hair as though her very life depended on me, and at that time I'm sure it did.

I dared not move. The eyes regarding me were not friendly. The women stared at the crumpled woman lying half senseless in the dirt.

Fleetingly I wondered if a Maori woman was ever allowed to display such emotion. Had she transgressed a code which we did not know of? Their silence was more terrifying to me than any enraged shouts would have been.

It was then I heard a faint muttering and realised they were all pulling back, moving away. Their chief was coming towards us.

He must have been disturbed by Kitty's screams. As he approached, the group of women scurried off to join the men who were watching from a distance. The great man paused and looked at us as though curious to know what the commotion was all about.

He was not dressed in his fine cloak, instead quite simply garbed, and I would say possibly woken from his sleep. Flanked by his kinsmen and the warriors who were nearly always at his side, he stared with disdain at the crumpled form of my friend.

Whether her grief had subsided for a moment, whether the terrible transport of misery was passing, I don't know, but she stirred and sat up staring around the group with eyes half unseeing, a demented look on her face.

"Coward!" she screeched, catching sight of me, "Craven coward." Then she saw the men. Relief spread across her features immediately as she recognised the chief.

I could read her thoughts like an open book. He was the man who had given us shelter, he was strong and powerful – he must be able to save Kelly.

She staggered to her feet and steadied herself with one hand against the palisade.

He was not even looking at her. Women's matters were of little import to him.

He looked up at the sky as though glancing to see what weather the day had in store, he'd found out why this terrible screaming had filled the air and he muttered something in passing to one of his men, in fact he'd half turned to walk back to his group of huts when the disaster happened.

"Don't go!" Kitty screeched at him for all the world like one of those banshees she spoke of so often. "Don't go!"

Of course he merely went on walking. Then she made the fatal move.

Kitty threw herself forward and grabbed at his hand in a transport of grief.

A terrible sigh went through the crowd.

Even I sighed just as the Maoris gasped for we all knew. what she had done.

Kitty had broken the *tapu*.

She'd not have had time to realise properly what was happening when the chief spun round shouting to his men.

Thankfully she was grovelling at his feet with her eyes in the dust as the club was raised.

I did not scream. Something told me that her fate could be mine in a trice and so, drawing myself up, I buried my Anny's face in my bosom.

My eyes were shut. Oh God if only my ears could have been closed too. That sickening thud which shook the ground might just as well have been upon my own skull.

Me next?

Would they toss Anny from man to man and then smash her against the palisade?

Eyes tight shut I just stood there. Not a sound came from the assembled crowd.

I had to open them in the end. Perhaps by some miracle I'd imagined that thud, that the club had not been raised. There had not been a single sound from Kitty. She had not screamed out, she'd not cried for help.

Her eyes met mine as she went. In spite of that terrible blow she'd half lifted herself up as she was dying. One eye was closed but the other flickered upon my face while the blood streamed down her cheeks.

And her last word to me had been 'coward'.

How much closer would I get to death before it claimed me?

The Maoris walked away leaving her body in the dust. My time had not come yet.

No one came near us for the rest of the morning. I swear that children can sense when a situation is serious, for Anny did not cry for her food, she dozed fitfully in the shade by the great fence whilst for a while I nursed Kitty in my arms. Blood had gushed all over her face and I wiped it off as best I could. I must have lost my mind for a while because my thoughts would not come together, instead snatches of this and that from the past kept flashing through my mind and I truly felt myself besieged by all the evil possibilities of this world.

That shrilling filled my ears, just as it had done years ago in the dock at Worcester. That terrible noise in my head which shut out the world and any sensible thought. The sight of Kitty receiving that death blow was too horrible for the mind to absorb.

What should I do now? Where to turn to?

Neither Maori man nor woman came nigh us and I told myself that now the *tapu* had been broken anything could happen.

Round and round the memories went, each one snatching at the heels of the other. That single yellow tooth of old

Benjamin Wright gleaming in the candlelight, the stink of piss as we clung together in the dock at Worcester Assizes. The vomit and the crowded bodies on the *Earl*, then the cut of the whip, and the slow filling of the sails as we waited with our hearts in our mouths outside Port Dalrymple.

And then I remembered Lanky. His stolid good sense and his tireless good cheer. Thinking back thus, some of the good times came back ... the good times we'd had sitting out under the stars on the deck of the *Venus*, the chatter and the laughter. I thought of Kitty and all her talk of finding a handsome officer and then the happiness she'd found with Ben Kelly.

As these memories came crowding into my mind I became calmer and that terrible high pitching whining in my head slowly went away. So much had happened. The bad times could not be allowed to swamp the good because there was that other human being, right at the beginning of her life, lying not more than a few yards away, kicking out in her sleep and snuffling to herself in the contented fashion babies have.

I remember going over to the women's huts, so I must have pulled myself together somewhat. Blood streaked my dress and filth from the dust on the ground caked onto the stickiness. I held out my hands and made a scooping move-ment. They'd soon have understood that help was needed to dig Kitty's grave.

Mamoe stared at me as though she had never seen my face before and several of them turned their backs on me.

No one would help me but when I picked up Anny and held her out to them a couple of the older women took her and disappeared into one of the huts.

I found a spade at the back of the hut then had to drag Kitty's body a long way past the dwellings where the remains of the burnt patch still smouldered in the midday sun.

"Sorry. Sorry dear," I heard myself saying as her shoul-ders snagged against a rock. Truly I must be going mad!

Well, if this was madness then at least Anny was safe, for surely the women would care for her.

I rolled Kitty down the slope behind the huts and began to dig. Luckily the ground was soft and never having lost the knack for labouring with a spade the work was not difficult. Before too long her grave was waiting for her. My arms were aching now and I was reaching the end of my tether but in a way that workaday contact with the earth had done something towards calming my grief and forcing me to think far more clearly.

Scooping out the last handfuls of earth I tore some of the harsh grass from nearby clumps making a soft lining for her. It did not seem right that anyone as pretty and dainty as Kitty should have her body pressed into the mud.

Then I rolled her over and over across the ground into her grave.

As I settled her dress and smoothed it round the waist I felt something hard beneath the fabric. It seemed indecent to be burrowing in a dead person's undergarments, but decency was a thing of the past. Tied around her waist was a calico bag – the money from the *Venus*. Of course, Ben would have made sure she kept it in a safe place.

This was to be my last gift from my friend. I did not open the bag, the sight of those coins would have sent shivers through me. But there was no doubt about it, the cash might be needed if Anny and I were ever to escape.

There, commonsense was returning again. For the first time that morning it seemed life must go on for Anny and me even if the others had lost theirs.

Kissing Kitty's cheeks I covered her face with grass and scraped the earth over her.

Poor, ever hopeful, gallant Kitty; ready to take on anything the world could throw at her. At least she'd had those few months of love with Kelly, at least she'd known the delight of being in another's arms and letting the world go by. If our lives were to be short then at least they had their joyful moments.

Standing over the grave I did not know what to say. Not one single prayer came to mind. How strange that all those words the parson had said from the pulpit meant so little now.

Screwing my eyes tight shut, I tried to cut out everything around me. The smoking stalks of grass, the brilliant blue sea and the strange birds wheeling overhead. I made myself remember St John's back in Bromsgrove, the neat pews and everyone in their Sunday best with their heads bowed.

Still not one word of comfort presented itself. Then into my head came a couple of lines, not of a prayer, but of a saying written on one of the church bells.

Each bell had a different inscription and Father spoke proudly of the ninth bell which was cast in 1790. Everyone was taken up by this shining new bell and the words engraved around it still rang faintly in my memory:

I to the church the living call,
And to the grave do summon all.

I stood there staring out at the foreign sea in a foreign land and said those words to a god who was mostly foreign to me but I hoped would remember Kitty even if she did that dreadful thing with the rosary.

Having barely repeated the sentence a second time there came the sound of musket shots from the corner of the bay. The thick trees hid my view so I raced down to the strand to see who might be coming. Was the *Venus* sailing in?

No. A rowing boat was approaching with about half a dozen men. Four were at the oars, one sat in the bow and another at the stern with a musket in his arms.

My blood froze at the sight of them. This truly could be the end. Even yesterday there'd been a faint hope that the Maoris would allow us to stop with them but they were not stupid people. Now they realised every hand was against us they'd certainly not risk continued conflict with our kind by harbouring those who were obviously being hunted down.

The arrival of that boatload of sailors and the capture of Ben and Lanky would have had a profound effect on the way they thought about Anny and me.

I couldn't hide, for they'd seen me run down to the water still holding the spade in my hand. There was nowhere to go.

"Charlotte Badger?" A very tall man stood up as the boat grated onto the sand. Leaping over the side he waded ashore. When he was about ten feet away he stopped and faced me.

Even compared with the Maori warriors he was a big man, broad shouldered and barrel chested.

His grey eyes flickered with amazement as he stared at me. I must have been a terrible apparition upon that lonely shore. Mud streaked my skirts, my bodice was sticky with Kitty's blood and my hair hung down beyond my shoulders like a furze bush.

Standing my ground I raised the spade. What could be done with just a spade against a man of such stature? But I was not going to let him get any closer.

"Charlotte Badger, Ma'am?" he asked again. His voice was not harsh, the words were reasonably spoken and his square face had concern writ large upon it. "Where's the child? Where's Hagerty?"

No point lying. "Anny's with the women in the village and I've just buried Kitty." Those stark words tore at my heart. Tears threatened to spill out. My voice wavered but with a tremendous effort I held back the flood and stood my ground.

He came no closer. He too stood his ground. He stared at me with wonder in his eyes as we faced each other in silence.

"Eb Bunker of the *Elizabeth*, Ma'am."

The famed Eb Bunker! The man who'd doubled the Horn so many times, who'd made the fastest journey out of London, who'd taken the first real shipload of whale oil back to London. The man Kelly respected above all others.

"I know the name," my knuckles were white upon the spade. "What's happened to Ben Kelly?"

He shook his head, "On the *Britannia*. They've already upped anchor and they're making easting back to London."

"Traitor!" I heard myself screaming. "He went to find you! You let them take him! You let him ..."

Bunker held up his hand and his face was creased with despair, "Wait, listen to me Charlotte, listen to me!"

"Why should I listen to a traitor? Ben Kelly admired you above all others. He said 'I'd rather spend one hour with Ed Bunker than my whole life with some of the yellow-bellied captains I've known.' He came to find you ... and you've let them take him."

"I never saw him," Bunker bellowed back at me as if in pain. "He was taken the moment he got to the Bay."

"Then how do you know about me, and Kitty and Anny?"

"Common knowledge. Talk of the coast and the islands. Everyone's after you. They've taken that other man, Lancashire, onto the *Brothers*, taken him back to Port Jackson. I could do nothing."

Men! Useless men. I spat on the ground. Such a thing as spitting I'd not done in my whole life but words were not enough to express my disdain.

"Ben was one of my oldest shipmates," his grey eyes were clouded. "For Heaven's sake girl, put down that spade!"

Gripping it even harder for good measure I took a step closer to him; tall he might be but I was nearly up to his shoulder and would not give him an inch.

"I've come for you both ... and the baby. You say that Irish girl's dead ... how did it happen?"

In a few words I explained.

"So there's only you and the little un?"

"And the boys'll likely to be back with the *Venus*."

"Never," he looked grim.

"Why do you say that?"

"Every tribe along the coast's up in arms against them. That mulatto boasts he's taking the ship back to Port Jackson, says he was forced into the mutiny against his will.

But he'll never be allowed to leave these shores alive, believe me. Down the coast he made the mistake of taking a chief's daughter. When he finally put her ashore it was amongst a hostile tribe, she was killed and eaten. One of the young chaps has drowned, that soldier they had on board's had his throat cut. When the Maoris finally get to the *Venus* she'll be burnt to the waterline, mark my words, and any who's left alive will be eaten!"

"You're lying," I screamed.

"Charlotte! They've been marked men from the beginning! Listen to me. They have no chance. Everyone is out looking for them ... white men, Maoris, the lot. This is no place to leave a woman on her own! I've come to offer you a chance."

"What chance can you offer me," I stared at him. How wonderful it would be to have trusted him, he was so solid and he looked you straight in the eye. You could tell he was an honourable person. But at the same time the ways of the world are such that you might deal with a man like Captain Bunker one moment and the next be passed on to someone with the mind of a ferret who only wanted to hunt you down till you were cornered and at their mercy.

"You can come back with me to Sydney ... I'll take you back and speak up for you. You women were persuaded to follow the others I'll tell them. I can do no good for Kelly and Lancashire, they are lost men, but I could still save your life."

"No you couldn't. Nothing would save my life. Look what's happened to Ben and Lanky."

"Then at least let me take the child. Give her a chance amongst her own kind. I'll find some kind soul who'll care for her."

"No."

"Trust me. This is probably the last chance to save your lives."

"No thank you."

I did not even have to think about it. Save my life! Give

him his dues, he'd try alright. But honest decent men who spent their days fighting those straightforward elements of sea, sun and wind would have no idea of the devious lying ways of some of their brothers ashore. Doubtless he truly thought he could speak to an officer or even a magistrate and put me back into the life of New South Wales.

Even if it could happen and the noose was spared, what would my existence be? Back to gaol and servitude and I'm certain of one thing … they'd take Anny away. I'd go back to the Female Factory in Parramatta and she'd be sent to the Orphan Asylum.

"No thank you," I repeated.

Consternation clouded his face, "Have you thought? You've just buried your friend and now you're quite alone here. Have you thought what is going to happen to you?"

"Sir," I said, "Mr Bunker, I understand you to be an honest man and truly thank you for your efforts on my behalf as you've rowed a long way to find me, but 'tis safer here amongst these people than back in that miserable hole of Port Jackson."

He shook his head in disbelief. It was clear any seagoing man used to order and cleanliness, routine and profits could not understand such as me.

"Think of the child … think of the child. You'll die here, die amongst these savages. Come with me."

"No thank you, I'm not going to Sydney like poor Lanky nor on any British ship to anywhere in the world, if I go on any ship it'll be American."

He shook his head again and the faintest of smiles touched his features.

"You poor girl. You don't even know where America is and you're pinning all your hopes on it."

"And that's where you're wrong Sir," determination was beginning to flow back into my veins, I even put the spade down and took a step towards him. "I do know where America is, and I even know where I'm bound for."

"Where are you planning to go?"

"Nantucket."

"Not a hope in hell."

"We'll see about that, Sir."

"Come back with us to Sydney. Have some sense Charlotte."

"Thank you kindly, Sir but the answer's still 'no'. I'm in no hurry to get my neck stretched."

CHAPTER FOURTEEN

"... the natives told us that the "Venus" from Port Jackson, had anchored there a long time ago, and further that she had put in at the North Cape also and had taken two native women, one from the Bay of Islands and one from Bream Cove; that she went from thence to the River Thames, where her people got Houpa and one of his daughters on board with an intention to take them also away; but when the "Venus" sailed from the River Thames Houpa's canoe followed her, and he waited his opportunity to leap overboard, which he effected, and was taken up by his own canoe, but none of the women have ever since returned. The "Venus" brig belonged to Messieurs Campbell & Co., of Calcutta. She was taken by some convicts, who were on board of her, at Port Dalrymple and carried off the coast. Such are the horrid crimes which Europeans, who bear the Christian name, commit upon the savage nations!

Rev. S. Marsden's Account of his First Visit to New Zealand. December 1814.
Historical records of New Zealand. Vol 1, Robert McNab

I hurt so much I ached inside. My head ached, my chest ached, every bone in my body ached.

The worst ache of all was in the heart. My heart ached for those dear friends I'd see no more.

The miseries of loss, remorse, fear and guilt at myself being the only one of us four left free were all rolled into one agonising torture.

Daytimes were fearful, when I was not peering across the inlet for the approach of a boat in case more whalers came in pursuit, I was forever glancing into the forest to see if anyone was lurking in the shadows. Nightimes were even worse. Every sound was magnified in the darkness and sleep was just a series of catnapping nightmares crammed full of uncertainty and terror. So instead I struggled with the pain.

The last time I'd suffered such grief and distress Kitty had been there. She'd sat and listened to me at the Factory as my anguish spilled out. Now there was no one.

I hurt so long and hard I feared never again being able to face the world, becoming unable to defend that which still mattered most to me, my Anny.

The loneliness of our situation bit into me so much that on occasions all I could do was sit in the gloom of the hut shuddering at the emptiness of life. They had all gone.

Kitty's blood-streaked face haunted my dreams. The horror of Ben and Lanky in irons and awaiting execution never left me for a moment day or night. That those on board the *Venus* were in such strife took away the last thought of any aid which might come my way.

Day after day the empty waters mocked me.

Night after night my grim memories taunted me.

In the midst of the busy life of that village I was utterly alone and worst of all could see no way ahead.

Fear consumed me that I might offend the Maoris, break some *tapu* and endanger Anny's life. My own seemed to be of no import except that it was needed to guard hers. I kept strictly to our hut and only left it to work alongside the women in the fields.

There was always doubt and uncertainty. How did they view us?

The Maoris had seen that we alone had survived the disaster and death that had visited our small band. Perhaps we were *tapu*? I made sure I drew myself up and pulled myself away when any man approached; I never allowed myself to touch another's hand, never permitted myself to meet a man's eyes and kept Anny away from the chief's hut and those of his wives.

There was no way of finding out how we were considered. Talking to them was difficult, words almost impossible to find. Kitty had always done the chatting. The few phrases I knew had only to do with food and the planting of crops but all my senses were so alert I felt sure I'd detect any changes in their attitude towards us.

For several weeks after Captain Bunker's visit I maintained my fearful vigil upon the waters and the forest. If marauding whalers came with their guns as they'd done before then there'd most likely be safety with the villagers. But if a naval ship should call at the Bay, if soldiers should be sent after us, then there'd be no chance for us.

The village life continued as it had always done, only mine was shattered beyond anything that could be imagined. Sheer drudgery became my lot.

Watching every single event that happened in that village, I remained forever vigilant for fear of giving offence, painfully aware all the while that I was quite ignorant of the natures and many customs of those around me and even more lacking in any knowledge about the ships and activities at the Bay.

Soon our chief took many of his warriors away on a raiding expedition to the south to settle the feud which had caused the last couple of alarms. I understood he might be away for a week or more.

Life in the village returned to its normal routine.

Perhaps my presence in this isolated place was of little interest. Possibly it did not cause the speculation and gossip Captain Bunker had maintained? Had he been wrong? The powers that be might have forgotten about me. I'd reassure myself with this thought time and time again as I laboured beside the women.

From sunup till dusk I worked and took it that this was the way in which I had to pay for our keep as there were always fern roots and taro and occasionally some fish laid at the entrance of the hut.

The nature of the work was extremely hard. Obviously they intended that I did more than my share. My condition was scarcely above that of a slave.

Each day they took Anny from me and I was set to work digging out stones, chopping up wood, levelling the ground for sowing and, most tedious of all, collecting yellow mud from the river and rolling it into balls to make the ochre for decorating their bodies.

How lucky I had always been so sturdy. Many white women would have crumpled under the burden which was now laid upon me. I'm not one to puff myself up but I'm very strong ... certainly not beautiful, but what good would that have done me?

Even so, the years were beginning to take a toll. I was no longer the girl who'd been taken off to Worcester Gaol in my prime, and nightfall always found me quite exhausted.

Was my life to be nothing now but endless toil? Sitting in my solitude each night with Anny snuffling in her sleep, Captain Bunker's words kept coming back to me. "You haven't a chance. Come back with me."

Had I done the right thing refusing him? Alright, perhaps my fate was already sealed but Anny would have her life before her. Even if it was as an orphan she'd be alive. The way things were I could be taken anytime by a mob of sea-men and she might die in a hail of bullets or be left uncared for amongst the rag tag and bobtail of the Bay.

Then one day, there was unusual activity in the forest, a friendly band of hunters, most likely kinsmen of our clan had come out from that dense belt of trees. They'd been hunting deep in its heart and brought pigeons and a number of par-rots to share. Several of the men went down to the water's edge to clean their weapons and a few of our villagers gath-ered round to exchange gossip.

Next morning the women did not come to the hut for Anny, neither did they wait for me as they made their way to work; instead they walked off with never a look in our direction.

A small sign but not a welcome one, they were distancing themselves from us.

I'd been torturing myself so continually with so many doubts and fears that my keen sense of being in touch with the Maoris must have become blunted. Now it was obvious that their attitude towards me had changed.

I held my breath as Anny broke away from me and ran down to join them but they completely ignored her. Never had such a thing happened before. Anny had always been picked up and played with and taken off to join in the fun of the other children.

All backs were turned to us.

Taking a gourd we used for fetching water from the stream I went to the water but found my way barred by three women.

With stern faces they made it clear I had to return and stay in the hut. As they stood there Mamoe came stumbling up to us and stood in front of me.

In stony silence she stood pointing at me for a full minute, then she let out a torrent of words. Like a witch she screeched and swore and I could only guess the terrible curses that were heaped on us. She pointed at Anny and bared her teeth in fury then threw herself upon the ground and, pulling out some sharp shell from her clothing, cut herself and slashed at her arms and legs till the blood ran.

Mourning! Once before we'd seen an old woman who was mourning her son in just this way. She'd sat outside her hut and screamed and moaned for days on end, all the while gashing herself. Tears had streamed down the poor soul's cheeks and she was covered with blood as some of the cuts were really deep. We were told the deeper the cut, the deeper the mourning for the departed.

So that was it. The men had brought back bad news of Tarore.

The women joined in. Wailing and screeching at me they pushed me back into the hut and stood outside shouting to the whole village. Finally the storm of rage appeared to have blown itself out and they left to return to their homes but our hut was left completely isolated and no one came near us.

By the time the sun had gone down I was desperate for water. We had some yams and dried fish in the hut but without water I'd become thirstier and thirstier on eating the fish. To my relief, when darkness fell, one of the slaves came sidling over with a gourd of water. He would have put it down and retreated at once but I hissed to him from the window. He may not have followed my words very well but he certainly knew the reason for my concern.

I held my hands out in supplication – a universal gesture that he'd surely understand.

Glancing fearfully from left to right he swiftly sliced across his throat with one hand and rolled his eyes to the heavens in a travesty of death. "Tarore," he muttered and was gone.

Whatever had happened, it was clear this was the last straw for these people. We were considered unfit for them to mix with any more.

Why had no harm befallen us so far? Why were we being kept like this?

She'd spat her venom at me. She'd cursed me with every vile oath she knew.

Ben's words came back, 'Hell hath no fury like a woman scorned'. She had been twice injured ... spurned by her handsome lover and doubtless been the butt of some nasty remarks when her daughter ran into his arms.

She'd had to hide the full extent of her resentment and sorrow. Now that her daughter had been done to death she could give full vent to her thirst for revenge.

Without respite I worried and worried about what could possibly be done to save my Anny ... and me. Why had we been shut away like this? The violence of that woman was enough for half the village to have fallen upon us there and then and clubbed us to death.

Half the village! That was it. A goodly number of the men were away with the chief and he was due back any day.

They were waiting for his blessing, then the aggrieved mother would seek her revenge in full.

When the chief returned our fate would be sealed.

Sheer terror now gripped me. What shocking end was awaiting us?

Panic kept sweeping through me, great waves of trembling fear sending me hot and cold in turns till my clothes stuck to my body and my hair hung in ratstails about my face. Again and again I beat my fists against my temples and mouthed useless pleas for some kind of guidance. No Ben, no Kitty, no Lanky ... I was truly alone and always would be. I battled with the terrible premonition of death till my mind was so numbed that exhaustion took over.

Slumped against the side of the hut I lay for what seemed hours, paralysed with dread. Anny tugged at my skirts and whimpered but I hadn't the heart even to give her a cuddle.

Still, nothing lasts for ever. Even that agony had to come to an end.

As my mind cleared and thoughts became orderly once more the first nigglings of more sober consideration brought guilt. Guilt that I lay there like a great pudding while my daughter had grizzled herself to sleep.

Then came the questions I must ask myself. Should I plead with the women? Should I plead with the chief? Should I just stay out of the way and hope all would turn out for the best?

Or should I escape?

Silence engulfed the village and even the dogs ceased barking. Anny now slumbered deeply on her bed of bracken. In my state of heightened awareness each hut seemed to contain a huddle of whispering men and women. Our fate was being mulled over. The loss of Tarore would be on everyone's lips and retribution eagerly awaited.

What could I do?

My mind began to clear. There were so few hours left to take any action whatsoever and as the panic receded more sensible reasoning began to take over.

I'd noticed before that whenever I stopped worrying about matters which could not be altered and switched my thoughts to solid facts I always felt better.

What should be my next step? What ought I to do next?

Slowly that paralysing thing which is fear began to retreat.

Get away we must. They would demand an eye for an eye and a tooth for a tooth. Perhaps a daughter's blood would be considered the rightful sacrifice to pay for another daughter's blood?

I would end my days as a slave.

I'd die first.

If I could get to the Bay I might find Captain Bunker again. There could be no salvation for myself but I'd beg him to take Anny. He would do that for me I knew, after all he'd put the very thought into my head in the first place. He was a man to be trusted. He'd take her away with him, he'd find a decent home for her, he was a man of honour.

The trouble with making my escape was that our hut was in that part of the village where the palisade protected it from any sudden attack. When darkness fell the entrance was closed for the night.

On many a sleepless vigil I'd tussled with my doubts while standing at the entrance of my hut and staring up at the night sky. I'd always felt safe with the fence between the sleeping village and the dark forest outside. Now it seemed more like the walls of a prison. As morning approached several early risers regularly went down to the water's edge, whether looking for fish or perhaps for a swim I did not know, but the palisade would be opened and they'd be off in the half light of dawn. My only hope was to wait for that moment.

Impatience seethed inside me at the tedium of that last night with the Maoris. Anny slept soundly as usual but I did not manage one wink while waiting for the dawn. What if on this occasion they did not arise early? What if they slept till the sun was high and the village busy and all eyes watching whatever was going on? What if …

Again doubts swirled round sending eddies of fear through me.

By the time the first fingers of light touched the eastern sky I was half consumed with terror at the thought of going off into that forest and half taken over with excitement at the thought of getting away. Fortunately I had enough sense left to dig up the little bag of gold coins and tie it round my waist.

I need not have worried. The sky could not really have been said to lighten, it just became less densely black and some birds stirred in the bushes outside the palisade. Grumbling in that half waking, half sleeping manner folk have when they quit a warm bed, several men plodded to the wooden fence and pushed some of the uprights to one side.

My chance! I shook Anny; she barely moved. She was never a light sleeper and could dream her way through a thunderstorm. Wrapping her in her blanket I hoisted her out of bed and tucked her head under my chin. Gone were the days when she was tiny enough to fold in a shawl around my shoulders but she was still sufficiently small to bundle up like this and carry in my arms. I took a long draught of water and tucked a few fern roots and a couple of pigeon legs inside the shawl.

I crawled out of the hut and crouched listening. Not a sound. Clutching Anny tightly to me I slipped round the back of the hut.

Not a soul moved.

The distance across open ground to the palisade seemed enormous. Surely someone would see me?

Now or never.

I flew across to the deep shadow of the palisade in a trice.

Hugging its side I made my way to the gap and paused for just a moment in case the men were still outside. Not a sound. There was the faintest grinding of shells and sand as they made their way down to the water's edge.

Slipping out of the palisade I raced for the cover of the forest.

I half expected to hear shouts and yells but there wasn't a sound. The village was asleep and would be for another hour at least. Give them perhaps another hour after that before it was discovered that my hut was empty. We had a good headstart.

CHAPTER FIFTEEN

Like one that on a lonesome road
Doth walk in fear and dread,
And having once turned round, walks on,
And turns no more his head;
Because he knows a fearful fiend
Doth close behind him tread.

The Ancient Mariner
Samuel Taylor Coleridge, 1797-98

I plunged into the dark forest. Like a swimmer diving into the sea I floundered through bushes and between tree trunks in that first desperate bid for freedom.

Over the many weeks we'd lived with the tribe we'd seen the villagers making their way into the forest times a-plenty. Likewise there'd been many days when travelling groups of Maoris came out of its depths to visit their kinsfolk. Hence I knew roughly where to find the path.

That path was all important, for without it I'd have to fight my way through bushes and thorns and clinging vines.

Even in the half light of dawn its well trod outline was easy to make out. To the south meandering off to other villages, to the north leading to the Bay. Quite often we'd watched men returning from thence, often carrying casks or kegs or blankets which they'd traded for baskets and green talc and jasper. Obviously they used this route to visit the whaling men at the settlement.

I had not realised it would be so narrow and dark from the encroaching trees nor so tortuous in all its twistings and turnings. Roots snagged at my feet many a time, trailing vines caught my hair and my toes were constantly stubbing against rocks. Encumbered with a sleeping child, progress was much hampered by all that undergrowth.

But fear lends wings to your feet. I pressed on, not daring to look back once over my shoulder.

How heavy Anny had become. Her weight had not mattered when I'd carried her about the village on occasions, but to try and hurry for long periods on end with a child that size was burdensome and by the end of the first half hour my lungs were bursting with the effort.

Fortunately it was about this time she woke up. Her first little cry became a frightened yell and I stopped abruptly to sit down and cradle her in my arms.

"Ssh ... ssh ... not a sound." The poor child was scared out of her wits. She'd been comfortably asleep in our familiar hut and now she was out in a dark gloomy forest, it would be enough to frighten anyone. I cuddled her and stroked her hair, poor little mite, lucky she did not know what peril we were in. "Would you like a piggyback?"

She nodded, that was a great treat for Anny, it was also a life saver for me. Far easier to carry a weight on your back than in your arms.

With Anny firmly perched behind me, her hands holding on to my hair and my fingers grasping her plump little legs, we set off again along the path feeling far more comfortable.

Even so I did not pause. Would the villagers pursue me? Unencumbered as they would be they'd soon catch up with us. From that vengeful gleam in Mamoe's eyes it was difficult to imagine she'd forsake her quarry so easily.

By midday the sweat was pouring down my face and I badly needed a drink but nothing was to hand. To get some rest I moved off the path into the undergrowth and pulled the grass to one side to make a place where Anny and I could stop for a while.

My mouth was parched and this was not helped by Anny having a good drink, for she still took plenty from the breast. Even though she was a well grown little girl I'd kept up with the feeding, safer by far considering the outlandish life we'd lived ever since she was born. The milk she took from me was the only constant thing in her life. Poor wee thing, she drank her fill and then turned on her side and promptly fell asleep. Taking the opportunity for a doze I lay down beside her in the thick scrub.

That short period of rest may well have saved our lives.

The barking of a dog woke me up. The noise it made was followed by a yelp and a whimper, then silence.

My first reaction was to look up and see what was happening back at the path but good sense prevailed and I did not move one finger. I lay and listened and hoped with all my might that whoever had come this way was passing by. But I needed to know in which direction they went so finally I lifted my head just enough to get a sight of the path.

About a dozen Maori warriors were loping along in single file. They were moving in the direction of the village. From the stealth of their movements and the clubs and axes gripped in their hands there was no mistaking that they were a marauding party.

Silently I rejoiced. That would keep our warriors occupied. But just as suddenly I realised my own peril. Was the whole forest alive with these tribesmen?

I did not shift one half an inch, I did not lower my head either for the slightest movement would have caught the eye. If Anny had stirred we'd be finished.

Silent as shadows, fifteen men slipped along that path. Even when the last one was out of sight something bade me stay still. Some instinct cautioned against even the blink of an eyelid.

A minute or two went by. Anny was deeply asleep and that uncanny instinct for danger a mother has, kept me rigid as a statue. A minute can seem like an hour when you are straining every muscle to remain in one position.

My eyes never left the path. My ears strained for the slightest sound.

Surely they'd all passed by now?

Then I saw him. Another warrior who must have been

posted at the end of the party to watch – he was their rear-guard. Black eyes flashing from side to side, he advanced along the path. When he drew level with where we were hidden, he paused.

Did he catch some whiff of us fugitives?

My heart stood still. Every muscle froze as that wily war-rior raised his club. His flaring nostrils sampled the air. Such an expert hunter would surely detect the slightest pulse of any living creature.

He was suspicious. Infinitely slowly and with great cau-tion he stretched himself up to his greatest height and peered into the undergrowth. Tattoos covered his face and continued along his arms, both his great limbs were scrolled and decorated with the ebony markings. His rippling mus-cles shone with ochre and oil and, as he drew his jet black tattooed lips back from his teeth, he sniffed the air. His fin-gers tightened around the club in readiness.

Truly I was facing a devil from hell.

The world stood still as I held my breath.

Suddenly he lowered his club and stood stock still for half a minute listening intently. Then he sped off after the rest of the party.

At that I sank back beside Anny. My heart thumped as it made up for those minutes when I swear it stopped. Sweat poured down my face.

Quite some time passed before I could persuade myself to wake the poor little mite and go back to the path. If they were intent on attacking our village then they'd be returning this way in a few hours and right now might be the safest time to make my way to the Bay. Every minute was precious.

Once the heat of day was over I moved more comfort-ably. Again Anny was perched on my back enabling me to maintain an easy pace which helped to keep up my strength. Every so often I paused and moved off into the bush listening with all senses acute to the sounds around me. Though the likelihood of being able to hear anyone approaching was quite remote, at least there was comfort in taking precautions.

All through that long afternoon I never faltered though every bone in my body was complaining and occasionally a strange light-headedness made my head swim. Perhaps it was due to hunger, or was it thirst?

Finally the thinning of the forest warned me that my journey was coming to an end. First of all there were just a few stumps of trees in amongst the standing timber. Broken branches, tangled boughs and piles of twigs littering the ground showed where the axe had been wielded and trees had been felled.

The forest which had surrounded and protected us, now receded on all sides. Soon we would be quite exposed.

The settlement had to be close by. Wood chips were scattered everywhere and as the space between standing timber became greater it was vital to watch carefully for cover. Quite a distance from the path some large stands of trees remained so I decided to risk it and move across the open space to seek concealment and see what might lie in that direction.

Just as well, for when I'd slipped in amongst the trees there came the sound of voices, shouting and yelling from dead ahead.

Putting Anny down I touched her lips with my fingers and shook my head vigorously, frowning all the time in that eternal gesture demanding silence. At all times the urgency of the situation must have been felt by the child, perhaps some current of fear had swept from my body into hers as she'd hung on to my back clutching at my hair. Her eyes were round with wonder and her little face had a bewildered look but she never uttered one sound. I took her hand and she walked, albeit a bit unsteadily, beside me. We did not need to keep up our mad dash. The relief to my arms and my back was enormous.

We came upon the ashes of a fire, still warm, and then passed by several felled giants of the forest. But there was not a soul in sight, obviously the woodcutters had finished for the day since the light was beginning to fade from the sky.

Voices were louder now. The trees thinned out to such an extent that I had to run from one sheltering trunk to another. Almost immediately a couple of roofs came into view and I found myself looking out on the settlement itself.

When we'd seen the tiny port from the deck of the *Venus* it had looked a thriving place, with ships moored in the bay and smoke rising from little huts scattered along the shore.

On closer scrutiny it was a ramshackle collection of dwellings surrounded by piles of cut timber, great vats of whale oil, crude huts and Maori women with half caste children scrabbling in the dust.

Several groups of men lounged in the dusky light engulfing the bay, sitting smoking outside the huts or idling amongst the boats drawn up above the waterline. Only two vessels were moored offshore, one a grubby little trading ship much smaller than the *Venus* and the other a whaling craft with a foreign name on her bows; even as I screwed up my eyes to read the words she swung on her anchor and I had difficulty reading the letters … *Santa* – something or other.

Certainly not the name of any vessel Captain Bunker might command.

A pretty fix. I did not fancy walking down amongst that crowd of rough looking fellows. Yet to stay in the forest much longer would soon be impossible, for Anny was beginning to grizzle with hunger and we both badly needed water.

The crowd lounging by the huts certainly made up a motley bunch. Poor Ben, had he approached them only to be met with deception and betrayal? They did not look the kind of people I'd willingly ask for help.

It was then I noticed a third boat close in by the shore. One of those large native craft, the like of which we'd seen on occasions once we'd come into New Zealand waters.

Compared with the shipshape lines of the other two vessels she was an untidy sort of craft. Like a double canoe in fact, both canoes joined together with beams and a bare mast towering up from the centre. She was pulled up against the shore and no one moved on board.

Sitting there, back propped against a tree with Anny grousing away at my empty breast, I was quite secure in the knowledge that no one could see us, for what little light there was left in the sky came from behind me. The sun was setting apace.

That dizziness returned. I was so hot! A fear began to niggle at me that perhaps this was no ordinary feeling of warmth. Every time I wiped the sweat from my brow more came back and once or twice the forest trees blurred before my eyes.

I lapsed into a dreamy state and several times had to drag myself back to consider our present predicament when all I really wanted to do was fall asleep.

My mind was awash with all the possibilities – or rather the lack of them – that were open to me. Increasingly all decisions were too hard to make and it was impossible to face any of them as I kept drifting off into a doze.

Should I ask for shelter down at the huts? There was still that gold. But once they knew what was concealed upon my person, then I might very well be taken prisoner. Given another few days there might be other arrivals at the bay ... possibly an American ship?

Perhaps I could creep down under cover of darkness and steal enough food to keep us going up here? But that had many drawbacks – even if the men and women did not look particularly alert, their dogs would be. Hounds and curs sniffed their way round the mean looking dwellings all the time. And where would I find the food we needed? And what of water?

Round and round the choices went – but they were no choices really. I could expect little aid from those who lived here. I'd be turned in as soon as a British ship arrived.

Caught between the whalers and the Maoris, there was

little chance of surviving. In fact the only chance at all was to escape from this place.

Once again I looked at the strangely built native craft. Where had she come from?

Something told me she was not Maori; she did not have the workmanship of any Maori canoes I'd seen. There was a slap-happy look about the vessel. If she did not come from hereabouts then possibly she'd sailed from some distant part of the ocean where there was a host of islands. Those islands with names like Feejee or maybe even Owhyee ... I had no idea how distant they were except I'd listened to Ben's tales of the whalers calling in at Otaheite and the warm welcome they all received. He'd dwelt lovingly on his voyages in that part of the ocean.

Staring at that strange vessel I noticed from time to time natives came back from the settlement carrying bundles, stowing them and hurrying back again. No one was left aboard as watchman.

Fighting back the waves of drowsiness and sweatiness, I kept my eyes fixed on the scene until gradually daylight faded away and the fires on shore took over.

Wild raucous shouts and screams from the women filled the air and twice I nearly jumped out of my skin as a musket went off. Men yelled at each other and in the distant flickering of the firelight folk were shifting about all over the place. More than once I'm sure there was some scuffling going on. But even as I tried to focus on the huts and the cavorting figures around the fires the burning heat of my body set my head swimming.

Fever! There was no mistaking the giddiness which made my eyes water and my body shake.

I was in for a bout of something serious. Before my senses left me I had to make a move. That boat was our only chance of escape. There was a fair stretch of sand to get across. Perhaps we could make a dash for it under the cloak of darkness.

Picking up Anny once more and tucking her in her blanket

I stumbled through broken stumps of wood and over a mass of forest rubbish to the very edge of the sand. From my left came the noise and confusion of the settlement. As I stared at the carousing men and women it seemed all the demons in creation were clustered around those fires.

Ahead was the faintest shimmer of the rising moon upon the water and away to the right, outlined against the night sky, loomed the bulk of that unwieldy looking craft.

For a few minutes I crouched on the beach.

What else could I do? Now or never.

Gripping Anny tightly to my breast I raced across to the boat.

Panting for breath I stumbled against the side of the vessel, it was rough and splintery, nothing like the painted wood of the *Venus*.

With arms like lead I heaved Anny aboard. Then I clambered over after her.

I was right, no one had been left to watch over the vessel.

Fortunately the lashing and ropes holding it together gave far easier handholds than a smooth, planked craft. I picked Anny up and made my way down to what I presumed would be the stern.

What a strange smell! Spicy, fishy and different from anything I'd ever caught in my nostrils before. Gourds, bundles of leaves and piles of mats were stacked up along the side. Oars, wide and flat as paddles, lay ready for use. Coils of plaited fibres, making a crude but strong rope, were tucked behind the paddles. After a fashion it could be said that all was quite shipshape. The boat was in readiness for setting out to sea. The question was … how soon was she going? If I was right in my guess then the men had been loading her up for departure, but then I could be wrong.

In the darkness I pulled out several of the mats and slipped Anny beneath them.

Then I heard louder shouting than before from the settlement. The commotion swelled to become curses and shrieks of rage. A musket was fired and some women screamed.

General pandemonium started up. Suddenly the shouts were closer.

Snatching up more mats I buried myself beneath them.

Rage and fury scorched the night air.

Quite nearby somebody screeched in derision. Men's voices from the settlement answered with a chorus of bellowing. Suddenly the whole craft was rocking and jumping about as bodies flew over the side.

Whoever was the leader of those men yelled his commands as though his very life depended on it. The craft was pushed further into the water by frantic hands. Then more bodies leapt on board and oars smacked upon the water.

For a few minutes all was snorting and puffing as the men strained at their task. Even beneath my covering I could hear folk hurling insults from the beach. There were great gusts of laughter from our crew as more curses were exchanged and catcalls followed. Obviously they'd got the better of those men on the shore.

Anny and I were not the only ones who were escaping with their lives.

CHAPTER SIXTEEN

Extract from *Tongans*, William Mariner, 1817

The natives of Feejee, Hamoa, and the Sandwich Islands who were resident in Tonga, used to say that they did not think it was good practice of the people of the latter place to let their women lead such easy lives; The men, they said, had enough to do in matters of war and the women therefore ought to be made to work and till the ground: no, say the Tongan men, it is 'gnale fafi'ma (not consistent with the female character) to let them do hard work; women ought only to do what is feminine: who wants a masculine woman? Men are stronger, and therefore it is but proper that they should do the hard labour. It seems to be a peculiar trait in the character of the Tonga people, when compared with that of other natives of the South Seas. The exception to this is the natives of Otaheite where the men are effeminate and the women are languorous.

What great luck! How truly fortunate I was in finding that craft!

Of course there had never been a choice. Just that wild dash and an even wilder hope that all would not be lost for us.

Even so I could not have done any better.

Fever was sweeping through me. From hot to cold my body swung. My sight so blurred I could scarce make out the faces which surrounded us.

Once out at sea I'd struggled from beneath my covering of mats. Swaying and wobbling I'd tried to stand upright against the side of the vessel.

For a moment that boat faltered. The oars poised mid-air wavered, as well over thirty pairs of eyes stared.

Then great brown hands reached out and steadied me.

Strong hands with palms like sandpaper, hands that toiled and worked from sunup to dusk caught me and held me upright.

I stood there for a moment with the world swimming around me then bent down and pulled Anny out from beneath the covers.

Gasps of amazement changed to guffaws of laughter as she held out her arms and kicked with her fat little legs.

Eagerly she was taken from me by kindly hands. Hands that tousled her hair and gave reassuring pats. Fruit was thrust at her and someone tipped a gourd up and showed us there was water a-plenty.

Anny clung to her saviours and stared up at the black faces and fuzzy heads with delight.

Obviously the novelty of having us stowaways on board was an added bonus to their escape. The goods they'd filched from the settlement lay about in heaps. A pile of iron hatchets, several bags of nails, whalebone and a fancy looking lady's straw hat were just part of their booty. Boxes and bundles were tucked in every bit of space. Now they had two white females aboard and the whole thing amused them vastly.

From man to man the jokes and laughter rippled round the boat. I groped for the bag around my waist and dropped several gold coins upon the floor.

Immediately an order came from the darkness, someone who stood at the bows was keeping a close watch. The gold was gathered up and from that darkness the voice issued a command, short and sharp.

All levity ceased. They bent to the oars with a vengeance.

Backs strained, muscles knotted and great dark feet dug into the boards. The last sight I recalled was of bodies working in unison at the oars, lines of leathery toes and battered nails with a rime of salt coating each one.

Then all went blank. Whatever the fever was, it consumed me for days on end. Time passed in one long blur. Kind hands brought water to my lips and a mat was thrown over my shivering body. It was obvious that all on board were needed to maintain the course of the vessel and anyone who could not keep up would be left to survive or die with that lordly lack of fuss that is common amongst the natives of this part of the world.

As ever, it was up to me. And I survived. We endured a severe storm with Anny huddled close while the men struggled to keep the craft from being swamped.

I remember them calling in at an island but being too weak to follow them ashore. They took Anny off with them and she came back sucking some sugar cane.

By the time my strength returned we must have been very far across the ocean from the Bay of Islands. Twice British ships passed close by; the first time it was a whaler, on the second occasion I swear my heart stood still for it was a navy boat which crossed our bows. But then I smiled at my own foolishness. What interest would those lordly British mariners have in one of the native craft which plied the seas in this part of the world?

There was a certain amount of argument amongst the crew and obviously a difference of opinion. I am not sure what the leader of the men wanted to do. He remained remote and his word was law. Perhaps he wanted to take us two back to their land but several of the others kept muttering amongst themselves and when we reached a group of islands several weeks journey away from the Bay they wanted me and Anny put ashore.

As we sailed through the scattered isles we came across some quite large masses of land and many smaller ones. Twice native canoes came out to look at us and each time our craft sped on its way. Not until a sizeable island loomed upon the horizon did the men in the boat appear to reach some agreement.

I remembered Ben's words as the craft neared land – the islands of the Pacific were a heaven on earth. So much had happened since those nights when we'd gathered on the deck of the *Venus* and the hateful Captain Chace had lurked in his cabin. It might just as well have been a lifetime ago but the memory of his stories was as vivid as yesterday.

If only the clock could have been turned back. If only we could all have started off again from that point in time. No flogging, no mutiny, no wild flight across the ocean. If only we had gone on in a law abiding fashion to our destination in Van Diemen's Land, Kitty would still be alive and the others would not be facing certain death.

What was the use of daydreaming? Here we were, Anny and me, sailing into strange waters with not the faintest notion of what lay ahead.

Ben had mentioned several times that the islanders of the Pacific were a noble race, often warlike but with a society where everyone knew his place in life. One thing which had stuck in my mind was that in many tribes women were respected, not called upon to do all the menial tasks, and their position was such that if they came from the upper levels of the society, they were fed before the men. Well that didn't even happen in Bromsgrove.

Perhaps life might be easier than amongst the Maoris. For one thing I would be a stranger to their shores with no past to contend with, not the survivor of a ship which had raped and pillaged its way along the coast and deeply offended everyone.

An excited group of people was watching the boat pull in – tall, well-formed men carrying spears and magnificent women wearing intricately woven draperies. A host of children ran about in chattering groups. But most of all I was amazed to see an old white man in their midst and by my reckoning he was equally amazed to see me.

The crew leapt ashore as soon as the vessel ground upon the sand.

Eager hands from the waiting crowd were held out to me and then, from some shouts amongst them, something must have been said because there appeared to be a general hum of indecision and they all dropped back.

"Have no fear," the white man called, "they are not sure if you are taboo."

Looking at those curious faces I was not too sure myself at that moment. Clutching Anny to me I waited.

He walked down to the water's edge and shouted something to the crowd in their own language. Gesturing towards me he shook his head at them and pointed to Anny.

Then he turned to me, his rheumy old eyes bright with the obvious novelty of the situation. "I have explained that you are a visitor from over the sea and are of noble rank. I've told them your countrymen are the same as mine and we do not share the taboos of their world. If a Tongan breaks the taboo he cannot feed himself for a year ..."

Tonga! So that was the name of this island.

"... if he does not have anyone to feed him he must crawl about on his knees and eat off the ground."

Better than having your brains smashed I suppose. Perhaps the Tongans were a shade gentler than the Maoris.

Too amazed by all this to mutter a sound for a while, I finally managed to thank him. My gratitude was sincere because the friendliness of the place was overwhelming. The village did not appear to be fenced as those of the Maoris and there was a more casual air to the natives as they squatted beneath the palm trees or waded along the sea's edge searching for shells. There was little sign of cultivation, no fields or tended gardens.

"Name o' Bill Burney," he bobbed his white head and wiped a scrawny hand across his long beard. "Where you from Missus?"

"Can you help me ashore first ... I'll tell you all later."

My erstwhile saviours from the boat had disappeared up to the village and the old man watched them go quizzically. "Not always welcome them Feejee folk ... terrible fierce they be."

So we'd come on a Feejee boat. We'd been saved by the feared Feejees.

Wading into the shallow water, he took Anny from me. I didn't like giving her up but the woman he handed her to laughed and smiled at the child in the way of all women with a little one. Then he held out his hands to me and I slipped over the side into water which came up to my knees.

How wonderful it was to feel the gritty sand between my toes and be on firm ground again.

The whole crowd of us moved off up amongst the palm trees above the beach. Buzzing like bees everyone talked and chattered at once as they made their way to the village built beneath the giant fronds. Bill Burney kept close to my side. I never took my eyes off Anny and the woman who carried her for one second, but there was no need to worry because the whole crowd was bursting with good humour.

That good humour became even more apparent when we were sat down outside one of the huts and several women brought over water for us to drink. Bill talked to them in their language and they laughed and pointed at Anny's fair hair and one of them even touched my arms and pointed to my cheeks.

"They've never seen a white woman before ... not once," he told me. "They're wondering if you've not been in the sun before, being so white."

I didn't think I was very white. My cheeks were burned red and my arms brown and leathery from the elements.

"I never expected to find one of my own race here." Caution was foremost in my mind. Not being quite sure what to say, I was playing for time to answer his question. What should I say?

"Your name ... what's your name, lass?"

"Charlotte Badger, and this is Anny."

"Where you from?"

"The Bay of Islands."

He screwed up his eyes as though forcing his memory back into the past.

"Never bin there, came from Valparaiso in '88."

That was all he was prepared to say at the time and I guessed he might be as much a fugitive as I myself. Anyhow nothing more was said as Anny had toddled off with that woman and now was playing with some other children. A very strange experience for her suddenly to be amongst others of her own age, but she appeared to take everything in her stride.

They brought cooked yams, some pork, fern roots and more water so we just sat and ate in companionable silence while I waited for the old man to start talking, as it's my experience with old men that sooner or later they get the wind in their sails and then you can't get a word in edgewise.

Once we'd eaten he wiped the bits off his beard and smacked his lips in appreciation and the questions started again.

"So, Mistress Badger, how came you to these foreign parts?"

I hesitated for a few moments. Best not dither too long though, the quicker the answers came the less suspicious it sounded. "I was aboard the *Commerce*," I quickly lied. If he did not even know the Bay of Islands then he'd have little knowledge of the local shipping. "My husband was second mate, he took sick after we left Port Jackson and sadly I lost him when we called in at the Bay." I paused for a while and sighed deeply but I noticed he had not taken his eyes from me. "Trouble arose … jealousy amongst the crew and I did not want to be part of it."

To my relief he nodded. "'Tis always the same. Women bring trouble aboard."

"And there was young Anny to think of too. They were a rough lot at the Bay and I'd no stomach for the disputes aboard the *Commerce*, so I did the best I could. Seeing as that boat was about to leave I took a chance. What else could I do?"

He listened attentively but I'm not sure he believed me. "We get some strange visitors in this part of the world," he finally said. "Shipwrecked sailors, folks as been marooned … and of course escaped convicts from the Colony." He looked me straight in the eyes when he said that. I looked straight back and decided I'd steer this exchange into safer waters.

"Never expected to see another white person here."

"There's a few, not many. Bin here nigh on twenty years meself and in all there's possibly about sixty white folk in the islands. Scattered about, that is."

"Sixty, that's a goodly number."

"In over a hundred islands. Mind you, some are very small, no more than a few rocks. Yes, we get a few folk come off the ships. We even had a boat call in once with a child on board … a prisoner from Port Jackson had smuggled his lit-tle'un back to the old country by a sailor."

With a jolt my heart went out to whoever that unknown prisoner might have been. What love for a child to take such a risk. To bid goodbye for ever to one you'd held in your arms since its birth. To send that innocent out into the world amongst unknown people rather than let it endure the dreadful life of a prisoner.

"Folk here's very proud if they have a white person in their circle. We had a shipwreck here a number of years ago and only one man was left alive …"

"What happened to the rest?"

"Don't worry yourself girl … they have their ways and not always the kindest by our reckoning. Suffice to say there was only one man left alive. Well he became the chief's spe-cial possession and when the chance came for him to get aboard a passing ship they tried to stop him from leaving. He managed in the end but only by killing his bodyguard and stealing away at night."

I didn't like the sound of that. "Can't make them very happy with us white folk … murdering one of their kin."

"Means little, life's fairly cheap. Mind you they're a decent people, nowhere's as near fierce as the Feejee people. Now those are warriors alright! 'Tis said there were no cannibals in these islands till the Tongans learnt the habit from the Feejee folk. Anyhow as I was saying they like to feel they have a white person in their midst. They'll probably find you a woman to look after you. Men and women here often have an older woman, like a foster mother. They'll see you're alright."

By the time Bill Burney left with his friends I'd learnt enough of the customs of the Tongans to realise that if I was watchful and minded my ways at all times, no offence need be caused and we could probably exist amongst them with more harmony than in New Zealand.

Ben Kelly had been right; it was a heaven on earth. The kindness of the women was past all believing. And old Bill had been right about the way I would be treated, so when a woman was brought to me, name of Mahine Fekite, I realised at once that she was the lady who had been appointed to watch over us. A tall, handsome woman whose only disfigurement was a deformed little finger.

Soon it was explained that this was not in fact a deformity but the joint had been cut off in a very painful ceremony when a section of the finger is sacrificed to save the life of a sick relative. The finger is laid on a block of wood and a mark is made with charcoal; a knife or sharp stone is placed at the mark and one blow severs the member. The cut stump is put into steam and then smoked and the wound is treated with grated sweet potato and the juice of sugar cane. In two or three weeks it's completely healed.

Such a rite seemed very cruel to me, but not nearly as barbaric as the ceremony of *Nawgia*, the ceremonial strangling of children. That was a far more powerful remedy for the sickness of a relation. One poor woman of the village was quite mad from having been forced to submit to this. She wandered around the village chanting to herself, mourning her dead baby and picking up shells and upsetting everyone to such an extent that Mahine Fekite told me the chief wanted someone to kill her as she was such a nuisance, spoiling the peace of the village and irritating them all.

She was strangled soon afterwards. Put out of her misery, the villagers said. They could go on enjoying life again without all the wailing.

At first such cruelty was quite revolting but then I considered the whole matter in a more distant fashion and thought of all I'd seen of the world since being dragged, weeping, along the lane by the parish watchman.

Even if those in power in our part of the world did not expect such sacrifices as mutilation and death from folk, they had no scruples about subjecting poor wrongdoers to lengthy punishments and cruel deprivations which would have been quite unheard of in Tonga. To be locked away as I had been for four years was beyond anything which could happen here. The filthy stink of the *Earl* would have been unknown on this sunny shore and the dropping of poor nameless bodies overboard considered a blot on human behaviour. Those wicked punishments, the triangle and the gallows, belonged to the white man alone.

No, there was a different set of values amongst the simple natives, certainly barbaric at times but not with that lingering quality of evil. Not with the savouring of suffering which became an appetite for cruelty. I could still feel the ridges left upon my back from Captain Chace's vicious punishment. Flogging women would have been quite outside their ways hereabouts.

I had never managed to converse very well with the Maori women but I soon began to pick up the language of this island. Of course having a companion at my side at all times made it much easier. Also from the free manner in which Anny played with the children I soon learnt many of the most important words.

Certainly the island of Foa was an orderly society. Priests did not have as much power as chieftains. At the very head came the chief, or *How*, beneath him were the nobles, the *Egi*. Next to them came the *Matabooles* and below them the *Mooas* who were the descendants and relatives of the *Matabooles*.

Old people were held in much reverence, women were treated very well. Mahine Fekite was herself a *Mataboole* so it was into this level that I was introduced, though I moved freely amongst all.

For the first year or so, I learnt everything possible and kept away from their gatherings for it seemed presumptuous to make too much of myself. Anny of course had none of those feelings and she romped and played with anyone who came her way. She was as welcome in the chief's *marly* as she was in the humblest hut. So in a way she became an ambassador for me to follow where her innocent feet led.

Always at the back of my mind was that passing remark about them being cannibals but I saw no evidence of that practice, that is until war erupted between our chief Finnow and the chief of another island.

I'd not connected these people with fighting and bloodshed but it seems human nature never varies and such an idllyic life as we led had to be shattered every so often by violent conflict. They were not forever skirmishing and settling old debts like the Maoris but when they had a falling out, it was a full scale battle.

Fortunately our island was fairly remote from the wars which we heard were being waged amongst the other islands but on one occasion our warriors were called to help a neighbouring chieftain and there followed a feast of giant proportions, probably because there were so many prisoners to be disposed of.

Mahine Fekite and the women were fully occupied preparing yams, collecting breadfruit and plantain leaves, looking over the pigs that had been slaughtered and preparing food to go with the great kava drinking ceremony.

Kava is made from the root of a plant belonging to the pepper family. Unlike our old dandelion wine back in Bromsgrove it is an infused drink made and drunk on the same day. It is drunk frequently at any time and especially when an important ceremony is about to take place, the preparations are elaborate and must begin in the morning. The chiefs and important people sit in one circle; no son may sit in the same circle as his father. Lesser people sit in an inferior circle. The cook brings in the kava and it's given to a man in the lesser group to split with an axe then scraped with mussel shells and chewed by those in that circle. They keep it quite dry, the chewing's mainly done by young persons with good teeth, clean mouths and no colds. Sometimes also women take part in this.

After about two minutes they take it from their mouth and wrap it in a plantain leaf. A great bowl is brought in, sometimes it can be as much as three feet in diameter and the chewed kava put in distinct pieces over the bottom and sides. Two men take over, one brushes off the flies, the other pours water from cocoanut shells over the kava; he rinses his hands and kneads the mixture.

Now the *fow* is put in. *Fow* is the bark of a tree stripped into fibres. In the bowl it covers the whole surface of the infusion and floats up. The next part is performed by an expert – this man runs his hands down the sides and along the bottom carrying the edge of the *fow* till his fingers nearly touch. He makes a roll about two feet long. The edges are rolled over and overlapped, the ends doubled and the whole process repeated. It is a wonderful sight to see the variety of curves and graceful movements of this man when he lifts the roll out and squeezes it and the liquid runs back into the bowl. When the last of the kava is squeezed out he gives it to the person on his left and receives fresh *fow* from the person on his right and repeats the process. This may be done three times till no dregs of the root are left. What is left of the kava root in the roll of *fow* is taken by the inferior circle for chewing. The liquid left in the bowl is now clear and strong. Only a small cupful is drunk by each person.

It's a strange thing that a people who are so clean living have this strange practice but they consider that us

Papalangis are very dirty, for they'd heard we drink the milk of beasts and give it to our children.

I helped the women but kept in the background, not being sure what I would see at that feast.

I learnt this much, that there are two ways of preparing the human body for the table. Firstly it can be cut into small pieces, washed in sea water, wrapped in plantain leaves and roasted under hot stones. Secondly it can be disembowelled and baked whole as you would a pig. The women accepted that I wished to remain separate from the proceedings but they took it all as a huge joke.

"You hear 'bout Langhi's aunty?"

"She who is gone?"

The woman were chattering together as they worked.

"Those four sons of her sister. What they did!"

"To their own aunty?"

"Yes, yes," the speaker was becoming impatient but family ties were very important and had to be quite plain.

"They ask their aunty over for a meal. Say they have a great big yam and want her to share. Never tell her she's the main dish!"

Everyone rocked with laughter.

No sooner was that tale told than it was topped by another about the daughters of two chiefs who agreed to play the game of *Lafo* with two young chiefs. If the girls won they were to divide a yam and give half to the men. If the men won they were still to have half the yam but must go out and kill a man and give half his body to the girls. Well the two young fellows won and early in the morning they stalked a man who had come out of his hut to fetch some salt water in a cocoanut shell. Very soon they caught up with him and knocked him over the head. The woman who told the story considered they had been very brave to follow a man like that – to snare someone unawares and dispatch him so neatly was considered much more clever than to kill a victim in the heat of battle.

So the catching and eating of humans was rather a joke but one which obviously I could not share. When faced with the possibility of attending the banquet at which there were two hundred pigs as well as two hundred human bodies I had to plead the necessity of retiring, as my gods would not allow me to witness such a thing. Horrible as it might sound the smell was very good and if I had not known from whence it emanated I might have thought the feast was solely of pigs. Anyhow I hurried off to my hut and threw myself down on my knees to pray for those poor souls, even if I was not usually one for prayers.

It was hard to credit that I was inhabiting the same earth as that where people dressed in their Sunday best and followed the tolling of the bells into church, where old ladies like Grandmother Badger sat at their tatting and servants polished the silver for folks up at the manor.

But in that other world, little children worked at the spinning till they dropped, they were forced up chimneys to sweep the soot, poor women were put on treadmills and set walking for hours and hours on end till the blood flowed from their wombs and many a baby was lost that way.

To each his own I finally decided and it was not for me to stand in judgement on these kindly people who cared for Anny and me so well.

Fate, chance, the hand of God, whatever you chose to call it had always seemed to be against me up to this point in my life. The theft, the imprisonment, the mutiny and life amongst the Maoris had all been difficult times and sometimes I'd only survived by the skin of my teeth.

Fate had truly played into my hands now I'd arrived in Tonga and instead of battling against the adverse currents of a life where women were often treated little better than slaves, I was bowling along in the mainstream of a culture where there was leisure and comradeship for my own sex.

I've never been a beautiful woman, in fact some have said

I'm exceeding plain. Certainly my stature has always gone against me, but amongst those tall, broad Tongans, this was an advantage. Like them I was strong, my teeth were good and my eyesight and hearing had never failed. Unlike so many poor women from the streets who'd ended up in the Colony, I was a country girl and the life I'd come to amongst the huts and palm trees suited me very well.

And as I said, Fate was on my side for once.

Very soon after we arrived, a ship called in for water. Not many came to our island but when they did it was a great event. I never hurried down to the beach as the others did for I was careful not to be seen. No hint of my presence must get back to Port Jackson. I watched from my hut as the sailors came ashore.

From what Mahine Fekite said, the ship had a cargo of mother of pearl from the Society Islands and was on its way to collect sandalwood from Feejee, then was sailing to Chinee where there was always a ready market. The sea and the islands were a vast trading place for the great lands bordering the ocean.

I'd heard that after the old *Earl* had left us in Port Jackson she'd taken coal from the Coal River up to Calcutta. Crisscrossing the seas, a myriad ships ferried their cargoes to out of the way places.

And cargoes were not all they took. Sickness, the illnesses from our overcrowded cities and dirty towns now left the old countries and came out to these lovely places.

First I heard of a contagion which lurked aboard a ship was when one of the women who'd been aboard a French vessel became ill. Whores were not common in Tonga and most women kept themselves at a respectful distance but any slaves were sent aboard for the money they could earn. This woman must have caught the venereal for she came back, and according to Mahine Fekite, she 'became on fire' and died. When they used those words it meant she sweated and sweated and often as not broke out in sores. All they did for such fevers was to dig a hole down near the water and put the sufferer in its cooling depths.

So when I first noticed several of the women huddled together pouring cold water over one of the babies I hurried over to look. The poor little mite had a rash upon his chest and even as I looked it seemed to be spreading to his limbs.

With much weeping they pointed to the water's edge where others were crouched beside a small pit in the wet sand, several of the women sat bowed and dejected and two had the most terrible cough which racked their bodies. Even as I sat there with them an old woman came over and picked up the tiny boy, starting to walk down to the sea's edge with him.

"What are they doing?" How could they put him in that sandy, watery grave?

The women shook their heads and clasped their arms around their breasts in lamentation.

You didn't need to follow the exact words to understand a mother's fears only too well.

"Stop … 'tis only the measles … they don't have to die for measles." Rushing after the old woman I held out my arms for the little boy. His mother had followed me but it was obvious she did not feel anyone should argue with an elder.

Knowing myself to be safe from the contagion I threw myself on the ground in supplication. Measles had been a frequent visitor to our little town and I did not even fear for Anny, as she'd only lately left off taking milk from my breast and I'd always heard that if you'd had the complaint then you were free for life and any child at the breast was free of it too, for several years.

The two women argued. It was the sort of discourse which always arises between the old and the young. The old woman would be following the only way she knew, the young would be begging for another chance to save the poor mite. And with a mother's desperate pleas she won, the child was handed to me and the old one stalked off.

Hurrying to the mother's hut I wrapped the little boy in a cloth. He was shivering with an ague as his temperature was dropping. I rubbed his feet and blew warm air upon his hands and let him moan and cry all the while cradling him in my arms. He was at the height of the malaise, at that time when fevers snap at the heels of chills and you need to watch over the sufferer every minute of the day and night.

For two days I scarcely put the child down. I peeled away the clothes when his temperature peaked and he cried out with the fever; then wrapped him up as the chill descended and his poor little frame shook with the cold. I moistened his lips with water as he coughed and choked and hugged his quivering little body to me to give him some of my warmth and strength.

The Tongans had no treatment for fevers; their ideas on any cures were very hit or miss. If you recovered from a wound you were lucky. It was only their extremely strong bodies which brought them through their trials. Mahine Fekite told me that the Feejee people are considered the best surgeons. Due to their warlike nature, wounds were more commonplace in that country and ways of healing better understood. Their favourite physic is the application of grated sweet potatoes moistened with the juice of sugar cane, and ulcers are scarified with powdered turmeric and sprinkled with bitter vegetable juice.

Some of their remedies are very harsh and the women spoke of them behind their hands. One affliction of the men who live in those islands was particularly terrible as, on occasions, their male parts could swell up. I was told of one poor fellow in the extremity of pain who actually cut out one of the offending members himself.

A few survived their treatments but mostly, once sick they died. Particularly the children perished if illness came, so when my little boy fell eventually into a long sleep and awoke to laugh and smile at all those around him, it was considered little short of a miracle.

Certainly his survival was a blessing for me and Anny. After that I was treated with even more respect than before and was at peace for the first time in many years, now I'd found a place amongst these noble people.

The months passed so quickly they soon got lost amongst the years. I'd have been hard pressed to say how long I had been amongst them but time was marked out for me by the changes in my Anny.

Her first words. Her first tantrum when she lay in the sand and scuffed it in my face. That change that comes in a little one when instead of stamping on the ants and pulling the tails off the lizards they start to care a bit about those less strong than themselves.

They say as you get older your mind wanders back ever more frequently to your youth. Well I wasn't very young any more, being nearly thirty when we arrived in Tonga. But my mind kept returning to the past and as I watched the women sitting at their basket weaving and their plaiting, I could once again see Grandmother Badger's old grey head as she bent over her handwork and muttered to herself between lips pursed with concentration.

More and more my life relapsed into that compelling routine which anyone born close to the land knows and understands. The sun, the moon, the winds and the rain rule the lives of those of us who live by the passing seasons and whether you come from Bromsgrove or a tiny dot of an island in that great Pacific Ocean you live by the same rules.

I thrived upon the daily round of our village. Anny grew tall and strong. She had the square shoulders and strong build of the Badgers. She also had their blue eyes and straight fair hair. But above all, she was a thoughtful girl and many a time she'd come to me with something that puzzled her.

"Why ... why Ma, why does she have to die?"

What a question for an eight year old to ask. One of the

neighbouring chiefs had died and his wife was insisting that she be strangled. A terrible fate for a young woman. She was a Feejee woman and in those islands that was the tradition. The Tongans did not do things such as that and begged her not to demand the dreadful fate. But the woman was determined and eventually found two Feejee men who agreed to do the deed for her. She kissed the corpse of her dead husband and was laid on the ground with a band of *gnatoo* around her neck and they both pulled till she was dead, then her body was rubbed with turmeric. She and the chief were buried in an upright sitting position as was done in Feejee.

I tried to explain to Anny that the woman had sworn her life would be an endless torment unless she followed her husband in the correct manner, but Anny and the young Tongan girls could not believe it was right.

There were so many contradictions in our lives that I was hard put to it, to explain to Anny that there was another world beyond the coral reef and the brilliant blue sea and another set of values that we, as people from the old world, must live by.

But should we? That was the rub. My thoughts would churn about my head and my vision was sometimes clouded by the press of new images which had become part of our daily life ... the feasts, the singing of the women, the noble bearing of the men. Their generosity never ceased to amaze me. After the first few weeks of my arrival when I left the hut of my kind friend and was given a dwelling of my own I'd sometimes felt quite hungry, for if Mahine Fekite was away and did not come to visit us I had no food. She was amazed when I said this. "Why be hungry? Go into any hut and be fed." She was quite amazed to hear that in my own country people kept their food for themselves.

I could not find the words to explain to my daughter that there was a place called home where people were kept shuffling along with shackles between their ankles. I could not find the words in this happy haven to even describe the filth of a bucket under your nose or the cut of a lash around your shoulders.

CHAPTER SEVENTEEN

A ship which had visited Tonga reported that an English woman with a girl of about eight years had landed there 10 years previously. The woman had said she was escaping from the Maori of New Zealand. Her description, 'a very big stout woman,' fitted Charlotte Badger. A proclamation at the time of the mutiny had stated that she was 'very corpulent'. One account of her life claims that she finally escaped to America, and the ship may have called at Tonga on the journey.

Mary Louise Ormsby. *Dictionary of New Zealand Biography Vol 1 1769-1869.* Published 1990

Only very seldom did I see a white face. Occasionally Bill Burney came to the island but the old fellow was not as spry as he was that first time and sometimes his mind seemed to be wandering. He liked to sit and reminisce and piece by piece go back over the past as old folk do. I unravelled a bit of what he said, separated fact from fiction, and it soon became clear he no more came from Valparaiso, or whatever the place was called than from the moon.

Far more likely was it that he was a deserter from a naval vessel and in the nature of things, as much a fugitive as myself. Whatever he was he had no intention of going back to the outside world.

"But you'd be alright Charlotte … you could get yerself aboard a ship any time you liked," there was a mischievous glint in the old man's eyes and I fancy he was trying to draw me out.

But I was not falling for that. Keep your secrets to yourself I say, remembering poor Mary Bryant and the loose tongue which led to her disaster.

"Mind you, 'tain't always so easy … leaving."

"What do you mean?"

"Like I told you once before. If they take a liking to you they won't ever let you go."

"But they'd do us no harm. They are so kind, surely they'd understand if you wanted to leave to be with your own kind?"

"Maybe. But their ways is different. Take that girl of yours. She'll grow up, do you want her to wed one of them?"

"Seems to me there's worse in the world than the men of these islands," but my heart was not truly behind my words because a part of me longed for Anny to live amongst her own kith and kin ... well maybe not kin but at least amongst those of her own race. All mothers want their daughters to share in the same pleasures of growing up as they themselves had.

Sometimes I daydreamed about how she'd look in a straw bonnet with a daisy chain around her neck, thought of her crashing through the icy puddles and rolling up snowballs in her hands. That life was very far away, but it was our background and at times I yearned for it. How would it feel to see my daughter wed and possibly become one of several wives then spend the rest of her life amongst the palm trees and the huts of the Pacific?

The months slipped away and, by the time of his next visit, my Anny was half a head taller. "She'll be spoke for before the year's out, mark my words," he muttered as he settled himself outside my hut and smacked his lips. He liked my cooking.

"'T'aint a bad life for a woman." Soon he was drinking cocoanut juice and eating little cakes made from the mahoa root, mixed with scraped cocoanut and baked.

"'Tis reckoned the women of Tonga have a good life. The natives of Feejee, Hamoa and the Sandwich Islands say our women have it too easy. Mind you, some have it even easier, in Otaheite neither women nor men work hard, but that makes 'em all soft ... not to mention their lustful habits," he sniffed and took another sip, "Tonga's different; the men are noble and the women keep to themselves, that's as it should be. We can only hope it'll go on that way."

"Why shouldn't it?"

"There's another war comin', that's why. There's a great fight goin' on between the chiefs ... not hereabouts, on one of the bigger islands I grant you, but it'll spread ... it'll spread like wildfire."

Immediately I was alert.

All the possibilities came crowding into my mind. The fighting, the taking of prisoners, the dreadful feasts and the devastated villages ... I'd heard too often the heroic tales of the villagers. This part of their life was not really for us.

Mind you, when I saw my Anny at the wedding of Mahine Fekite's eldest granddaughter, it was clear that she would slip into their ways as naturally as a duck takes to water.

Ofa was to be married to Tootonga, a forty-year old chief who had been betrothed to her for many years. Now she was eighteen and he considered the nuptuals should take place.

As with weddings all the world over the ritual was paramount and conducted with the same mixture of solemnity and joyousness as if they'd all been clad in muslin and lace and making their way along the aisle of St John the Baptist.

Ofa was annointed with cocoanut oil scented with sandalwood and dressed in the choicest of mats from the Navigator Islands where they were wonderful weavers. Soft as silk, it was forty yards in length and wrapped round and round the poor soul till her arms stuck out from her sides and she had to lean against her attendants to even stay upright.

Everyone gathered at the *marly* of Tootonga. He was waiting there with the other chiefs and, at our arrival, we all sat down together on the green outside.

A complicated service followed which I did not really understand. A woman entered the circle with her face covered up, she went into the house of the chief to another woman who gave her a wooden pillow and a basket containing bottles of oil. The veiled woman wrapped herself up and put her head on the pillow and pretended to sleep. No sooner was this done than Tootonga took Ofa by the hand and led her to his house where she sat on his left hand.

A huge feast was waiting with twenty baked pigs and men to carve them in a truly expert fashion. There were yams and kava and even the delicacy of raw fish. Then there was music for dancing whilst many of the men sat in a circle with seven or eight bamboos and flambeaus, held aloft above baskets carefully placed for the fallen ashes. After that followed a moral discourse advising young men to respect the wives of neighbours and not to take liberties with unmarried women without their consent.

Finally Tootonga sent for his bride. The moment they retired, the lights were doused. For a short while we all stood there in the darkness. What were we waiting for?

Poised in the dense blackness of the night the entire party of wedding guests stood silent and expectant. The village was waiting, waiting for something to finish off the ceremony that had taken all day and left us tired but elated.

Three hideous yells split the night air. A man outside the door of their hut screeched in triumph. His cries were harsh and cruel as a war cry. This was followed by all the men making loud and repeated calls on their conch shells.

The entire village shouted and rejoiced at the poor girl's loss of maidenhood.

My blood ran cold. It was all tradition as much as the ribbons and the throwing of the bouquet back in Bromsgrove. But it was not our tradition.

Those cries echoed through my head and seared my heart.

Anny was watching me. Excited and tired she came across and took my hand. "What ails you Ma? You look so sad."

Smiles wreathed my face as I looked at her. Whenever I looked into those soft blue eyes I could see Lizzy. Some of us Badgers are sturdy and strong but not much to look at, like me. Others are fair and dainty looking. Anny was one of the comely ones; she'd grow up just as lovely as our Lizzy.

"I'm not sad." Truly I was not miserable at all but sometimes, just sometimes, I thought of the joys which marriage could bring and which now would never be mine. To be held in the arms of another human being was one of life's great gifts and I would never know that.

What was really saddening was the cry of triumph. Did I want that for my daughter?

The months which followed the wedding left me unsettled and increasingly aware that Mahine Fekite had plans for Anny. The marriage of Ola had whetted her appetite for alliances in the family. She made no secret of the fact she considered us part of her clan. She made it clear that we were near enough her property.

Who could argue with such a kindly tyrant? I owed everything to her good offices, yet could not feel happy when she told me of the chief who had spoken for my daughter.

"She is too young for marriage."

Mahine Fekite gave a gentle snort, "Tooboo Toa is patient. The marriage need not take place for several years. Annike is a fine girl."

"But he is so much older."

"All the better for a young girl. He is noble, he is strong and his wives will make sure she does not have to toil. She will be his joy and his plaything. You should be honoured."

She was disappointed in me. Many girls in Tonga could choose whom they took as lovers and married but the more noble families had their mates chosen for them. We were counted amongst the upper caste.

"She might prefer a younger husband."

"Younger! What does that matter when he is powerful and handsome?"

"Handsome!" Anny's shriek filled the hut and I rushed to the entrance to shield us from the ears of those outside.

"Handsome! Tooboo Toa's like those fat fish that swim in the lagoon. He's got wrinkles and he's only got one ear!"

I had to bite my lips to keep from laughing. It was so true. "He's a brave man, he has been in many battles," I sounded a real milksop as I put my case so lamely.

"No, no, no! How horrible. I'll never do it." She cried and carried on so alarmingly that I grabbed her and buried her face in my shoulder to deafen the cries.

My heart exulted, in spite of our predicament.

Here was a true Badger ... in spite of her base birth out of wedlock, our roaming existence and our years in this beautiful, simple paradise, I still held in my arms a true daughter of old England.

She was tall and strong, her golden hair thick and her skin fair and soft. She was my best friend as well as a good daughter. Some way must be found to return her to her own kind.

To say that these thoughts took over my thinking would not be an exaggeration. They completely overwhelmed me.

My nights were sleepless from tossing and turning just as years before when I'd worried myself into a state of agitation before quitting the village of that Maori chieftain.

Any marriage was still distant but even so it was also a certainty at some time or another.

Village life returned to its normal routine after the excitement of the wedding but the seeds of worry grew furiously and I agonized over what to do next.

In the immediate future I need not have concerned myself for the civil war which was raging upon the larger islands between Finnow and some rebellious chiefs came to our shore and there was no time to bother about weddings.

We lived in a constant state of unrest. Several times marauders had pounced but on every occasion the watchful Toobo Toa and his warriors chased them away.

So concerned were we, watching out for attack from the forest, that no one noticed the ship which anchored outside the lagoon.

"Lookee there Ma!" Anny clutched at my arm as she pointed out to sea.

The tall ship was swaying gently at its anchor. Sails were already down and men upon the deck were shading their eyes peering across to our village.

Ships of such size were rare visitors to our island. Native craft a-plenty came to our lagoon but only about half a dozen times in the last ten years had a large sailing craft anchored outside.

On each occasion when a vessel had arrived I'd made haste into the forest with Anny at my side.

Capture was always foremost in my mind. The sight of a white woman and child would certainly excite interest. How easily they had taken Kelly and poor old Lanky back at the Bay of Islands. The arm of the law is as long as its heart is unforgiving.

This time I could not run.

Who knew where our enemy's men might be lurking?

Mahine Fekite, Anny and I stood and watched the sailors lowering their boat. She was a fine looking vessel. Her crew appeared orderly, did not seem to be the drunken rabble we often encountered. Usually the men who came off the ships were oblivious to all decency, full of zest for some time ashore and full of rum to cheer them on their way.

This appeared to be a decent ship.

I gathered up some mats I'd been weaving. It would not be safe for me to show my white face. I could not approach the sailors so I chose one of the men, the uncle of Ofa who lived in a nearby hut.

"I have no one to trade for me, Langhi," I said to him, "as you know I cannot approach any man from the ship, he might be one of my enemies." I glanced at the dark forest behind to make it clearer that we all have people whom we fear.

He nodded. "What do you wish me to do?" Already he had filled up his basket with yams and cocoanuts, and a couple of piglets with their legs lashed together were slung over his shoulder.

"You have no mats … please take mine, see if you can sell them for me."

"What do you want for them?"

"She wants whale's teeth," Mahine Fekite butted in before I could reply, "so she may give them to Toobo Toa when he marries Annike." Sperm whale's teeth are much prized by the nobility of Tonga.

We watched from a distance as the bargaining began.

The ship's boat was drawn up on the shore and the sailors were now squatting in a circle with some of the villagers. Our people had laid out a selection to tempt the visitors.

Breadfruit, yams, taro, bananas and livestock were spread before them.

Their leader, most likely the captain, stood up and walked slowly up and down surveying the offerings. Then he gestured back to the boat where there was a collection of barrels. Obviously they had come wooding and watering.

Being too far away the words were impossible to catch. I strained my ears to hear him. Did he have that lilt of Kelly and Eb Bunker? Or were his words those of London Town and the hulks?

Was he a man of the old world or the new?

"They need little," Langhi looked downcast when he returned. "They have already taken in much at one of the other islands but they want water and wood. Tomorrow we will take them into the forest."

"My mats?"

"There you have been fortunate, see, these are what you need." He handed me a piece of cloth and, unwrapping it, laid half a dozen whale's teeth upon the ground.

"Ah …" sighed Mahine Fekite in admiration. "A fine wedding gift for Tooboo Toa, he will be much pleased. "Here!" she grabbed several more mats from the corner. "Take these when you go tomorrow. Bring back more."

My thoughts sped round and round like a ferret chasing a rabbit. In and out of all the possibilities my thoughts pursued each other.

Anny would never agree to marry fat, old Tooboo Toa. She would run off with one of the handsome village lads and they'd have a life of trial and tribulation and maybe even early death.

Outside the reef lay that vessel. She might be our only means of escape but on the other hand, she might carry us away to a cruel fate.

Tossing and turning the night melted into dawn and no solution had presented itself. At first light I ventured down to the water's edge and peered across the lagoon.

What did I expect? That someone would shout 'Ahoy there Charlotte Badger. We've come to save you'?

Foolish the thoughts which rush through your head when you are in a turmoil.

When the sun had risen, the boat once more came ashore. Villagers joined the men on the strand, the barrels were rolled along to our little creek and the bargaining commenced once again.

"She'll be going tomorrow," Anny told me. Not a word had been said but I knew from the wistful look in her eyes she was envying those men, taking off into that other world. Over the years Anny had accepted that we had no place to return to, but she still knew it was partly her world out there.

"They've not taken much." We were standing with Mahine Fekite watching the activity on the lagoon.

"Nor caused much grief. Not any." This was a compliment, for the few ships which had called in had left a trail of misery. Broken heads for the men, blandishments for the women. With drink and gifts many a family had been ruined by the casual visits of seamen.

"'Tis human nature I suppose," and that was the sad truth of it.

"Langhi says that captain's a wise man. He don't let his

lads just have the run of the place. He's a strict man."
Mahine Fekite nodded approvingly.

Again a deep longing took hold of me. A strict man. That
was how Eb Bunker would have been. Strict but fair. Honest
and law abiding. A man to use his own judgement.

How wonderful to be part of that world again. To know
the rules and stick to them.

Even so, it was not worth risking our lives. Better stay
here and take our chance with the villagers, just hope something might transpire to stop the marriage. There could be a
battle, there could be sickness and death. So much could
happen in the next few months.

"Langhi's sold your mats," Mahine Fekite smiled as he
walked up to the hut, but her smiles turned to scorn as he laid
some coins at my feet. "What are these, where are the teeth?"

"All was not as before. The teeth are all gone. He had no
more to give. He sent these for you instead."

"Coins! What use have we for these?" Everyone knew
about the white man's coins but no one bothered with them.
What value had they beside tortoise shell and sandalwood
and yams?

Disappointed she kicked them to one side and stalked
back to her hut.

I snatched them up.

They were not pennies, nor halfpence, nor farthings nor
anything I'd ever seen before.

I hurried along to the nearest clump of palms where the
boat was drawn up and peered out at the visitors. My heart
thumped with excitement as I stared at the men. They were
white and a mixture of sizes and shapes, some hair was fair,
some was chestnut and one was a wild carroty colour.
Amongst them was one who was coal black, not the glossy
bronze of the Maori nor with the softer brown of the Tongans.
He was a real black man. Black as old squire's riding boots
back in Bromsgrove. Was he one of the blackamoors that Dicky
had spoken about?

Was I right? Was it just wishful thinking? Could these be the crew of an American ship? For full on half an hour I stood in the shade and watched them.

But I was not the only one who watched.

Anny tugged at my shoulder. "Come on Ma, Mahine Fekite is waiting. We are to eat with her tonight, remember?"

My friend was looking at me curiously. "You wonder when the ship might sail?"

"Ma's really wondering where she came from," Anny spilled it out before I could stop her. "She's wondering if they're friends or foes"

Mahine Fekite stiffened. She was on the alert. The whole village knew I was concerned when a ship was sighted but never before had a thought been given to a ship which might be friendly towards us – one which I could approach.

All evening as we sat around and ate our meal she scarcely took her eyes off me and I suspect she would not breathe an easy breath till that ship had left our shore.

I seethed with impatience. A plan was forming in my mind. We must get to that ship. This might be my only chance. The evening dragged on and I listened to the chatter and all the while I wanted to be back in our hut so I could talk openly to Anny about the plan.

The company was jovial. Other women ate with us and the chatter was shrill and excited. The ship, the fears of a battle, the latest birth in the village, the disappearance of someone's stock of taro – there was plenty to talk about.

Laughing all the while I joined in and tried to appear at ease.

Unbearable impatience gnawed inside.

Another little cake?

Another sip of juice?

Another morsel of gossip tossed into the conversation to be mulled over and considered.

The fretting inside me became nigh unbearable.

Finally, the elder guests having left and politeness observed,

I rose and motioned for Anny to follow. "Time we left you, dear friend. Time we found our beds."

Mahine Fekite put out her hand and took my daughter's in hers. She gave me a long, considered look and a half smile, "Annike shall spend the night with me I think. So long since she slept under my roof and it's company for an old woman like me."

Stunned and completely at a loss I stumbled home.

CHAPTER EIGHTEEN

I am the daughter of Earth and Water,
And the nursling of the Sky;
I pass through the pores of the ocean and shores,
I change, but I cannot die.

Percy Bysshe Shelley, 1792-1822

What could I do?

By the light of the full moon the ship rode at anchor a full quarter mile from shore. Lumbering into the hut I sank to the floor.

Mahine Fekite was like a sister to me. My friend, my companion, the closest person to me next to Anny. Here I was planning to deceive her.

Kitty's furious words rang in my ears, 'Coward! False friend!' I was truly proving her right.

There was no way in the world for me to explain to my kind friend why I wanted to leave the island.

Did I, in fact, have to leave the island?

What was the point of quitting this paradise and moving out again into that conniving, cruel place beyond the blue sea?

Could I not happily spend my days gossiping with my friends and watching my grandchildren grow up around me?

There was the rub. Family and grandchildren.

Anny would become just another Tongan wife and mother. She would be treated kindly for they were gentle with their women. But she would have no life beyond marriage and motherhood.

Foolish woman! My thoughts spun round again. What had my life been but motherhood and strife?

What had I gained from that outside world?

"My God," I could hear myself speaking out loud. "What should I do, what has it all been about?"

Yet I knew, deep inside, it was not about what had happened in my life. It was about the possibilities that might await my daughter.

Mayhap she'd find a place where everything really made sense. Not just sit enjoying the sunshine and waiting on the pleasure of men.

A universe of ships, cities, carriages, fine houses, hovels, rich and poor ... the whole baggage of our world awaited her.

I had to take the chance.

All I could think of was Bill Burney's tale. The shipwrecked man who was determined to get aboard that sailing ship.

There was no way I'd wish harm upon Mahine Fekite but she had to be put out of the way for a few hours. In a short while the tide would turn and the ship would be leaving.

Just as surely as the pull of the deep would drag the ocean away in its never ending cycle of tides, so my whole being was consumed with the need to take this chance.

My gaze flitted round the hut. What was there which could help? I had some ropes, there was the tomahawk and some heavy stones but she was a strong woman. Even if I could terrify her and overpower her it was uncertain I'd be able to bind her and her cries would soon bring help.

It was then that I noticed the clutter of calabashes in the corner. Some small, some large and many half-filled with the dregs of kava which had been left over from celebrations.

I shook one of them. Still more than a quarter full. Was it still drinkable? Sipping at the liquid made my senses reel. Like the old saying that 'the sweetest meat is next the bone' so the strongest kava was that which was left at the bottom.

When I returned to Mahine Fekite's hut she was drowsy and lay with her head propped up and a satisfied smile on her face.

"You are back ... what is the matter?"

"A last drink, my friend. Let's have a last drink," and as I smiled I cursed my two faced nature. But this would do her no lasting harm.

No Tongan can resist kava. She took the gourd and drained it off in one great gulp.

I could not tear my eyes from her, large and happily spreading upon her mat she was the soul of kindness. I loved her for her beautiful nature. She had been like a mother to me for years. Everything she had done for us had been out of the best of intentions.

But we had to leave.

"Tell me how you make the wonderful wine of the ..." her voice was very slow and slurred, "the wonderful dandy ..."

She had always loved a good story. Many a time she'd sat and listened to the tales of Bromsgrove and clicked her tongue in disgust when I told of Worcester, the workhouse and the gaol. She could not comprehend such cruelty.

But when I spoke of the trees in the orchard blooming and the gathering of the dandelions she understood that.

"Well, each summer we'd go down the lane to the watermeadow searching for the very best flowers." She was smiling to herself as she listened. What kind of pictures would this be conjuring up in her mind? "We'd pick only the very best flowers ... not the ones where the dust from the carts had dirtied them."

"Ma and Lizzy and me would fill the basket right to the top and like as not Ma would look up at the sky and tell us to hurry, we had to be home before the sun was too high, the dandelions were best when the dew was still upon them and we would ..."

A very gentle snore came from my friend.

I went on talking for fully a couple of minutes but she did not stir. She was sound asleep.

Moving carefully in the gloom of the hut I was soon beside Anny. The girl was deeply slumbering so I gently tickled her ribs. Silence was vital.

Her eyes blinked and stared as she focussed on my face.

"Come. Come. Not one sound!"

Catlike we left the hut. Nothing but snores could be heard behind us.

"We must go! No time to spare!"

Anny knew what I meant. She was grinning from ear to ear and she hugged me tight. She never was one to argue or back-slide. She'd know just as I knew we had to take this chance.

The village was deathly silent as we made our way down to the shore. Every step had to be carefully watched as a cracking shell or a snapping piece of driftwood would have given us away. In some ways I blessed the light of the moon for we could see where to put our feet, but on the other hand it left us woefully exposed.

Anny moved towards our hut but I pulled on her arm.

"But Ma … I need my cloak, I need my …"

I shushed her. "No time to spare, we go just as we are."

Without another word she followed me to the far side of the village.

Pulled up under the palms were several canoes used by those who went out fishing on the lagoon.

"Here, take this!" Handing her a paddle I heaved one of the craft to the water's edge. Not for the first time did I bless my strong frame.

"In! Hurry!"

With Anny safely settled I pulled up my skirt and pushed her out into deeper water.

The beach shelved very gradually and we were quite a way from the huts before I deemed it wise to get myself aboard.

"Give me the paddle," I tried to take it from Anny.

"Leave me be Ma, I'm better'n you."

In spite of the bother and the fear I found myself smiling. Yes, she was a real Badger alright. Of course she'd be better than me. She'd been brought up half on the water and half in it.

"Don't splash. Keep it quiet. We don't want them back there hearing us. Remember, sounds travel that clearly across water nightimes!" Ben's words came back to me as though they were spoken yesterday.

Without a sound Anny paddled across the lagoon.

If anyone had been watching we'd have been painfully obvious but the villagers slept soundly.

My eyes were fixed on that ship. There was a lantern at her prow and very occasionally I saw the flutter of figures up on deck.

"Hurry, hurry!" What was the state of the tide? As we reached the gap in the reef I was horrified to see nearly a foot of coral above the waterline.

The tide had turned.

"Hurry, hurry!" A full quarter of a mile of dark ocean separated us from the ship. Her outline was stark against the night sky.

Were my eyes playing tricks? The lantern suddenly bobbed about as though some one was moving it along the deck.

I strained my eyes as Anny puffed and panted at the single paddle, dipping it in first one side then the other.

Oh why hadn't I brought a second one? What was I thinking of?

Then I heard it. The shout of a man as he called to his mate, the yells of several others and a cheery 'Heave ho!'

They were preparing to sail and here were we moving towards them at a snail's pace. Soon there would be the rattle of the anchor the thumping of the sails and so much happening aboard they'd never see our little craft.

Taking our lives in my hand I half stood up and yelled across that stretch of water.

No one heard me.

I grabbed the paddle from Anny and beat it on the water.

"Ahoy! Ahoy! Look to the island. Look! Look here."

Tears poured down my face. I was certain no one had heard. But that sound did indeed travel across the water clear as a bell.

More lights appeared on deck and someone called out to us. "We want nothin' more. Lay off pesterin' us!"

"Help! Help!" My voice was hoarse but strong, "We're comin' with you ... wait for us."

'Twas not till afterwards that they told me how the captain had wondered whether they were being attacked. Though they'd been received so kindly by the islanders they were not to know if treachery might not be afoot. It was only hearing his own tongue that made him pause and think again.

When I finally stood before him with Anny by my side he shook his head in bewilderment. Then the questions poured out. Where were we from, how came we to that island, were we alone?

His questions went on and on.

But I had only one. "Where are you heading, Sir?"

"Making easting round the Horn, Ma'am, homeward bound for Nantucket."